Praise for Kerry Greenwood

The Corinna Chapman series

"What a delightful character the unflappable baker and reluctant investigator Corinna Chapman is…Greenwood is a long-established and prolific winner of many crime-writing awards, already a fixture in the history of Australian crime writing… This is a charming, funny, and affectionate portrait of Melbourne."
—*Sydney Morning Herald*

"The endearing Corinna retains her love of food, cats, gin, and her tall, dark, and handsome boyfriend, Daniel… The clever, whimsical crime writing [is] precisely the charm of Greenwood's offbeat series."
—*Courier Mail*

"Gentle, funny, and filled with eccentric characters. This mystery is a thoroughly entertaining read."
—*Woman's Day*

"There's plenty to sink your teeth into."
—*Saturday Age*

"Cheerful, enjoyable, and absolutely incredible."
—*Good Reading*

The Phryne Fisher series

"Miss Fisher is quicker, kinder, racier, and more democratic than any character from Dame Agatha...if you haven't fallen for her yet, prepare to be seduced."

—Australian Women's Weekly

"Kerry Greenwood captures the 1920s style perfectly as she weaves crime and intrigue in the dark streets of Melbourne Town, together with the glamorous high life of the one and only Phryne Fisher... Step aside, Miss Marple. Kerry Greenwood has given us the most elegant and irrepressible sleuth ever."

—Toowoomba Chronicle

"It's *Underbelly* meets Miss Marple."

—Emporium

"Always elegant, always sophisticated, always clever, and damn it always right, Phryne is the finest detective to be found in the 1920s."

—Ballarat Courier

"Miss Fisher as usual powers through this newest case with grace, poise, and unerring confidence. The sense of underlying tension is palpable."

—The Age

"Kerry Greenwood's writing is always a joy."

—Stiletto

"Together with Greenwood's witty and fluid, elegant prose, Phryne Fisher is a sheer delight."

—Toowoomba Chronicle

Also by Kerry Greenwood

The Spotted Dog

A Corinna Chapman Mystery

WYS GREENWOOD

Kerry Greenwood

Poisoned Pen
PRESS

Published by Poisoned Pen Press, an imprint of Sourcebooks
P.O. Box 4410, Naperville, Illinois 60567-4410
(630) 961-3900
sourcebooks.com

Originally published in 2018 in Australia by Allen & Unwin.

Library of Congress Cataloging-in-Publication Data is on file with the publisher.

Printed and bound in the United States of America.
SB 10 9 8 7 6 5 4 3 2 1

Dedicated to David Greagg, the Stout and Helpful Bear;
also with thanks to Anwyn Davies, Alex Lewis,
Eloise Willman, Mark Deasey, Harjono, Kendall Crocker,
Elizabeth Ann Scarborough, Alice Rood, Mari Eleanor,
the Kingdoms and Baronies of the Society
for Creative Anachronisms

Chapter One

Cry Havoc! And let slip the dogs of war!
—William Shakespeare, *Julius Caesar,* Act 3, Scene 1

There should be a law against four a.m.

Unfortunately, there isn't, which meant that I had to get up. I left my beautiful Daniel asleep in my new big bed (what with the two of us and one very sprawly cat, there wasn't room in my old one) and found my sheepskin slippers. I shoved one sleepy foot down and felt something moist and furry and heard a crunch.

Horatio raised his stripy head, ears pricked. I suddenly understood. I had complained about the last mouse because he had left it on the kitchen table. So he had found another place to store it. Somewhere safe. Somewhere hidden.

I disposed of the corpse and left my slipper on the balcony to be dealt with later. Perhaps Daniel could cope with it. He was an ex-soldier, after all. The Israeli army's loss was my gain. I put on the coffee then had a shower, scrubbing my feet with a lot of soap and a nailbrush. A size-twenty woman does really unpleasant things to a dead mouse in her slipper.

I hate four a.m.

Insula, where I live and work, is as quiet as an Egyptian pyramid at this hour. I am the only one awake, save for my faithful apprentice Jason, whose proud duty it is to open the bakery and get everything fired up for my arrival. Therese Webb, a craftsperson extraordinaire with a medieval bent, would be dreaming of ladies and unicorns, while Professor Dion Monk, retired professor of classics, murmurs Juvenal's satires in his sleep. Mrs Dawson would be quietly smiling at reminiscences of a life well-lived in society. Trudi would be dreaming of tulips and *speculaas*. Meroe would be slumbering virtuously in pagan bliss, and Mrs Pemberthy and her revolting little dog Traddles—the only flies in Insula's otherwise harmonious ointment—would be tossing and turning, if there was any justice in the world. Mistress Dread might be still out and about, of course; I couldn't say. Hers is an exciting world of Bondage, Discipline, and Leather, which I am content to admire from a distance. In other words, all was calm, quiet, and serene.

As was I, so long as I had coffee. No one bakes bread without drinking coffee. I paired my second cup with a slightly failed croissant. I still can't get them right. They are perfectly canonical croissants, I suppose, but not anything like those of the proper *artisan boulanger* in Montparnasse, where I used to live. My theory is that croissants are like wine. Terroir—the environment in which the grapes are grown—is critically important in winemaking. No doubt croissants needed flour milled from wheat grown in French earth and butter made from the milk of French-speaking cows. And I probably needed to bake them in a French oven. In France.

Still, toasted and eaten in conjunction with some of Therese Webb's raspberry jam, they tasted fine. Horatio got plain ordinary cat food. Putting that mouse into my slipper had been mischievous. He did, however, get his dab of butter. I am mere putty in the paws of my felines.

Into the stout overall and cap and the stouter shoes. Down the stairs to the bakery—aptly named Earthly Delights—where the big air conditioners have already come on, along with the ovens.

Jason was there, reading a comic while waiting for his first rising to mature.

'Cap'n on deck!' he said, jumping to his feet and saluting.

Jason is an ex-heroin addict who was saved by patisseries and now lives in Insula in a grace-and-favour apartment. He is thin, growing all the time, with curly blond hair like Harpo Marx. I bless the day he discovered *Hornblower* and then Patrick O'Brian. Barely literate, he was nevertheless sufficiently spellbound to persevere with *Master and Commander* and decided he wanted to be a midshipman. I love having a midshipman. Also, he is going to be a very good baker. Happily, his ardour for bread has not been cooled by falling in love with a lot of unsuitable girls. He has a weakness for tall, aloof blondes. So far, they don't have a weakness for him.

Colliding with my ankles in a furry scrum were Heckle and Jekyll, aka the Mouse Police, a rough-and-ready pair of pied old comrades. They are the first, last, and best defence against rodents in my bakery. I viewed the place of slaughter. Two rats, seven mice, and a spider. Quite a big spider. I approved and doled out cat food with a liberal hand. The Mouse Police, at least, knew how to present their prey. Out in the open, for a start.

'Steady as she goes, Midshipman,' I ordered, and began pulling out the tins for my sourdough, a staple of the business. My sourdough had originally come from Italy, nestled in my old master's wife's bosom, or so he claimed. Yeast is immortal. In every little cell the strain of yeast which a certain prophet's people did not have time to allow to rise may even now be multiplying. A charming thought for four a.m., when charming thoughts are few.

'It's gonna be hot again,' said Jason, shaping loaves and dropping each one into an oiled tin. The first load went into the oven.

'Bugger,' I commented in a heartfelt tone. If it had not been for my new air-conditioning system, which rendered the temperature in the bakery 'hot' rather than 'infernal,' I would have melted into a large puddle with shoes in its centre.

Knead, shape, bake, knead, shape, bake. Jason took over the

challah, because he was very proud of his ability to break eggs with one hand. I started crushing spices for the fruit loaves. Bara brith today: a Welsh recipe. Everything went along smoothly. The bakery filled with the enchanting scent of baking bread. Loaves went in flabby and came out shiny.

At six I opened the door onto Calico Alley, and the Mouse Police shot out with cries of starvation. They were going to stand over Kiko of the Japanese restaurant for fish scraps. So menacing were they I would not be at all surprised to see them hauling home a whole tuna by the tail.

The sun was already striking hot and golden down the alley. Once summer arrives in Melbourne it invariably outstays its welcome. Bushfires. Parched lawns. Trudi, our gardener, swearing and collecting every drop of wastewater to keep her flowers alive. Relentless heat. I was sick of it before it started. Alas, the thing about weather is that it's compulsory.

I caught the plastic-wrapped paper as the delivery cyclist flung it at my head. I wasn't going to read it until the baking was over. Bad news makes for soggy bread, and that's all the news we get these parlous days. Best to skip straight to the crossword.

Mrs Dawson, retired society hostess and example to us all, was coming back from her early-morning walk. She was clad in scarlet cotton trousers and a hand-knitted cotton jumper with a Welsh dragon on the front. She asked for sourdough, was duly given the first loaf out of the oven, and gave me in return the exact change and a sweet smile.

The city was beginning to wake. Inside, Jason had put his challah in the oven and was compounding the muffin of the day. I could smell the ingredients: orange flower water, dates, pistachio nuts, and candied peel. Yum! Oasis muffins. The boy is a genius with muffins.

I knew I ought to go back to the kitchen and mould my pasta dura, a light, white Italian bread with a hard crust that my customers loved. But instead I remained in the doorway, brushing flour from my green apron, because down the alley came a man.

The light was behind him. He was of medium height. Stocky, with short hair. Jeans and a khaki T-shirt. Something about him said 'cop or soldier.' His eyes flicked from side to side, as if hunting for enemies. Snipers in Centre Arcade? I didn't think it likely. He was moving uncertainly. Drunk? It must have been a monumental night, to be weaving his way home at six-thirty.

He came closer, his boots ringing on the cobbles. (Soldier, then.) Close enough for me to see that he had light blue eyes with dark smudges under them, cropped black hair, tanned skin. He was shaking. No smell of alcohol, though.

He held out a much-creased envelope and I took it. It was addressed to Sgt Alasdair Sinclair. On the back was written *Daniel Cohen will help you,* the words signed *Sr Mary.* There was no way I was going to ignore anything which came from that admirable and formidable nun. What Sister Mary said went. She was, as one of her clients had told another, 'in damn big with God.'

'Corinna?' the soldier asked. Scottish voice.

'I'm Corinna,' I told him.

'I'm Alasdair,' he replied. 'They told me about you.' And then he promptly slid out of sight.

I caught him before he hit the ground and dragged him into the bakery. Jason grabbed his other arm and together we hauled him up to sit in the cook's chair.

'Who's the undead dude?' asked Jason.

'Has a note to see Daniel from Sister Mary,' I said. 'Shut and bar the door, Midshipman. Stand here, belt him with an oven slide if he gives you any trouble, and I'll go and get our private detective.'

Jason regarded him dubiously. 'What's wrong with him?' My apprentice didn't handle emergencies well. 'Has he been shot or something?'

'He's not bleeding,' I pointed out. 'On second thought, I'll watch him and you fetch Daniel—here, take the envelope. And put the coffee on before you go.'

He did as requested, then belted up the internal stairs as fast as

Heckle when a tin is opened in another room. Speaking of whom, the Mouse Police had returned, fish-scented, and were giving our guest the once-over. No danger; Heckle looked away and began his post-tuna wash. I am rather relying on Heckle to take out a burglar if necessary, probably by devouring him from the ankles up. He's an ever-hungry cat. Jekyll strolled over, put a paw on the sergeant's dusty boot then sat down on it. Right. The bakery approved of him.

He wasn't unconscious, but his eyes were shut, as though he had expended his last reserves of energy in getting to my bakery, though I couldn't imagine why. I poured out a glass of chilled water and touched him gently on the shoulder.

He flinched. Not a good reaction.

'Water,' I told him, holding the glass to his lips so that he could drink. He drained it.

'More?' I asked. He was not injured as far as I could see, but very tired.

Then his eyes opened.

Oh. Not tired. Sleepless. Haunted. I got a full-on dose of terror and nightmare.

Acting entirely on instinct, I knelt down and embraced him.

He smelt of male human, cheap soap, and fear in roughly equal proportions. He put his head on my shoulder and sighed; he seemed to find my shoulder quite comfortable, as if he could easily fall asleep, which might be difficult to fit into a day's baking. But I felt so sorry for him—he had clearly seen too many horrors for one man to absorb—that I stayed where I was. Presently I became aware that tears were sliding down my neck. He was weeping, without a sound or a sob.

Jason skidded back into the bakery and stopped on a sixpence when he saw me kneeling on the floor holding a man in my arms. A man who was not Daniel. 'Corinna?' he quavered.

'It's all right,' I assured him. 'Where's Daniel?'

'On his way. He's just getting dressed and feeding Horatio.'

'I've already fed Horatio.' That cat was an opportunist's

opportunist. He could teach classes. 'Start on the pasta dura, will you, if you've finished your muffins and challah?'

'Jeez!' he said, and dived for the oven.

The muffins came out perfect and the challah was gorgeous, slicked golden with egg yolk. The scents began to penetrate the half-swoon of my soldier. He sniffed. Nothing is more indicative of home, of safety, than the smell of baking bread. He sighed and began to sit up.

Now he would be embarrassed, and I have no patience with embarrassment. I began to talk fast. 'What will you have with your coffee: an Oasis muffin, an egg-and-bacon one, or a slice of bread?'

'Egg-and-bacon muffin,' the soldier said hungrily. 'Me mam used to make 'em. They smelt just like that.'

'Give him one, Jason,' I ordered. I rose from my knees, which creaked. That's a hard floor. 'Would you rather have tea than coffee?' I offered, reminded by his burr that he was Scottish.

'Tea,' said Alasdair Sinclair. He seemed a bit bemused. He looked around the bakery, wiping his face with the back of a scarred hand.

'Corinna Chapman,' I introduced myself. 'Jason, my apprentice. Heckle. Jekyll is presently sitting on your feet. She loves leather boots. It's some kind of fetish.'

Seeing us all watching him with interest, he started to redden. 'I'm sorry to...'

'Food,' I suggested briskly.

Jason watched with awe as Alasdair devoured an entire muffin in two bites. My Jason is a growing boy and could eat for Australia. Bets are taken on how fast he can demolish the Cafe Delicious trucker's special, which is eggs, bacon, sausages, beans, mushrooms, tomatoes, and hash browns or potato pancakes, depending on who is cooking that day. He holds the cafe record. But Alasdair looked like a worthy contender, or else he was very hungry.

Fortunately, at this point nearly all the baking was either done or in the oven, and Jason could go out for his breakfast. He skittered off and I locked the door behind him, after first scanning the alley. There was no one present who shouldn't have been.

Daniel arrived, which was a bit of a relief. He took in the ordered state of the bakery, the soldier drinking tea as though it was nectar, and, of course, the smear of flour on Alasdair Sinclair's face from resting his head on my shoulder. Hug a baker, you get floury. Daniel gave me a quick, affectionate look. There is no jealousy in him, partly because he knows there is no need for any, partly because he is an angel in tall, dark, gorgeous form. And he so firmly believes that I am beautiful that I have begun to believe it too. I cannot imagine what I did in a previous life to deserve Daniel. I must have saved a saint's life or rescued a number of deserving children from a house fire.

Daniel squeezed my hand then turned his attention to our visitor. 'Alasdair, I'm Daniel. Let's go upstairs and have some breakfast, and you can explain how I might help you.'

'I would thank the lady first,' Alasdair said, attempting a smile.

I patted him briskly on the cheek in an aunt-like manner, managing to get most of the flour off. 'My pleasure,' I told him. 'Now, off you go, I've got teacakes to make.'

Alasdair went quietly. I sent another two egg-and-bacon muffins with him, since he seemed to like them. And then I got on with the teacakes.

As I stirred, I wondered how such an obviously strong, capable man as Alasdair Sinclair had been reduced to a quivering, exhausted wreck. There were transverse scars on his wrist, I'd noticed. Not clean cuts, though; the edges were blurry. From a rope, perhaps? I frowned as I slid two trays of teacakes into the oven. I do not approve of wars.

There was a rap at the bakery door, which was still locked. As I let Jason in I scanned the alley once more. Still no lurkers or assassins as far as I could see. And Alsadair had been alone when he arrived. There was no reason for me to feel nervous.

But, unaccountably, I did. And it was time to open the shop.

Chapter Two

Open-eyed conspiracy his time doth take.
—William Shakespeare, *The Tempest,* Act 2, Scene 1

Jason began to stack the bread into the trays for delivery. I left him flirting with the rickshaw driver, Megan—a short, plump redhead with spark and drive; a much better choice than his usual languid Nordic types—and went upstairs.

Daniel and Alasdair were in close converse in the kitchen, the air redolent with fried bacon. I did not disturb them.

I changed into respectable garments: a pair of loose blue cotton trousers and a shirt. I could at last remove my heavy boots and put on sandals. My feet sang little songs of gratitude all the way down the stairs.

Goss, or possibly Kylie, was waiting at the door of the bakery when I opened it. The girls are the same height and weight— far too low—and change their hair and eye colour so often I once suggested they wear name tags. They refused, but agreed to announce their identity every morning. I like knowing to whom I am talking.

'Goss,' said Goss, and handed me her phone. I have a strict no-phone-in-the-bakery rule, though I have relented enough to allow them to put the phone in a box on a shelf, on the condition that they only text when they are having morning tea. This is, of course, tyrannical of me, relic of the Jurassic as I am. But those girls text as though their life depended on transmitting the bad news about someone's boyfriend from Kew to Hawthorn as urgently as possible, and it is not polite to the customers. It doesn't stop the customers from doing it to us, but we are required to be civilised.

'Today's muffins are Oasis, and egg and bacon,' I told her. 'There are teacakes too, plus challah, bara brith, and the usual sourdough, rye, and so on.'

'Okay,' she said agreeably. 'Meroe was asking who your visitor was.'

I considered this. Meroe is Insula's jobbing witch: a woman who might easily turn you into a toad but is careful of incurring insupportable karmic debts. She has her own shop, wherein many wondrous artefacts may be purchased if you're that way inclined, which occasionally I am. 'Indeed?'

'Just as I came in,' said Goss, presenting me with a small coarse cloth bag. It was strung on a long ribbon to be worn around the neck. 'She said…' Her brow furrowed with the effort of recalling our witch's words exactly. 'She said he's been tortured and he needs to sleep. If he wears the charm, he will sleep without dreams.'

'How did she know I had a visitor, much less one who might need a charm against nightmares?' I asked, remembering those fathomless eyes full of present terror.

'Well, duh, Corinna—she's, like, a witch?' said Goss, and slipped out of reach behind the cash register.

Duh, indeed. I left Goss in charge of the shop and mounted the stairs to my own apartment again.

Daniel and Alasdair were still in the kitchen. The soldier looked up as I entered. I dropped the ribbon over his head. His hand clutched the charm. His eyes widened.

'Our resident witch says that if you wear her charm you will sleep without dreams,' I announced, patted his cheek again, and went back to the bakery. Daniel would explain.

The usual people came in and bought bread and traded money and news. Nine a.m. brought Mistress Dread, wearing her full costume. This consisted of what are known as CFM heels (stiletto, scarlet), fishnets, and a boned and laced red French corset. Her black hair was piled atop her head and stuck with hatpins and she was carrying—of course—her monogrammed whip. She lives in 2B, Venus, and was no doubt on her way home from her dungeon.

Habitual patrons are relatively immune to surprises in Earthly Delights, but I suppressed a giggle at the reaction of a very conventional-looking young man in a good suit, who had to hide behind his bag of bread rolls to preserve his countenance. Mistress Dread nailed him in a second and flicked him her card. He blushed. But he caught it.

'Hard day's night?' I asked her.

'Brutal,' she said in her gravelly, sexy voice. 'Had to bar the doors at midnight. Every man and his woofer wants to get flogged these days. I blame the internet. Loaf of sourdough, Corinna.' She hauled up and rearranged her formidable bosom. 'If I don't get this corset off soon, I'm going to faint.'

There was a whimper from the conventional young man. He would definitely be visiting the dungeon as soon as he could summon the nerve, with his heart (or other suitable organ) in his hand and his posterior bared for the kiss of the whip. He was eyeing said whip with fascination and his bread roll camouflage was becoming inadequate.

Me, I dislike pain and do everything to avoid it, but as Grandma Chapman put it, 'Each to his own, as the old wife said when she kissed the cow.' Which now I come to think of it, is an odd thing for her to have said—both Grandma and the old wife.

Cherie Holliday came in to buy sourdough, mentioning a

picnic. When I raised an eyebrow, she told me it was to be held in our very own roof garden, where somehow the Temple of Ceres and the wisteria had been missed in the mad vandalism of the city during the sixties. Trudi keeps it alive with all the dedication of a Dutch person in a blue jumper who wants her very own linden tree and means to have it, even if she has to carry all the bathwater in the building to the roof by herself. It had been an overgrown wilderness when she came to Insula some years ago. Now the roof garden is like a little slice of paradise nine storeys up.

Cherie's family had imploded when she was very young, and though she'd been through some hard times she had done a good job of bringing herself up. She'd found a job and a place to live, and had avoided trouble, drugs, and pregnancy. Her father Andy, meanwhile, had crawled into a bottle and stayed there until she had pulled him out. Cherie was studying textile design, and was discussing it with Therese Webb, the resident of 5A, Arachne.

I got rather lost when they talked about methods of making patterns but was able to inform them that onion skins made the light golden brown shade of dye they were looking for.

'So you make soup with the insides and dye cloth with the outsides,' Cherie observed.

'Nothing as all round useful as an onion,' I informed her. 'How about a few cakes for your picnic? There are still a couple of Oasis muffins left—or would you rather some teacakes?'

'Both,' said Cherie greedily. I applaud greed. Gluttony is such a reliable sin. And you get to keep your clothes on.

'And for me,' said Therese. 'My friend Anwyn's coming to stay from Adelaide, and I've just invited another friend, Philomela, too. She was in an accident, and I've been visiting her as often as I can, though it's such a long way to go. She's in a bad way, the poor thing, but she can still sew, so I've asked her to come and stay with me to help out with my Project.' The capital 'P' was audible. 'We're doing a large embroidery for Innilgard's anniversary. We've decided we want to do Anglo-Saxon, because it was

English embroiderers who made the Bayeux Tapestry, which I might remind you was also an embroidery. We're doing The Battle of Maldon. And Anwyn's bringing Bellamy.'

'Her husband? Her child?' I guessed.

'Her cat,' said Therese. 'I am sure that he and Carolus will be friends.'

Carolus was an immaculately coloured, very imperious King Charles spaniel. I wondered. Carolus was rather accustomed to having his human to himself. So was Bellamy, probably. Though his name was propitious. *Bel ami*. Beautiful friend.

'Sister Mary's got everyone looking for a dog,' chimed in Cherie. 'I met some of her homeless in the street. They were looking for a smallish sort of border collie.'

'I hope they find him,' I said.

'If he's in the city, they'll find him,' Cherie assured me. 'They go everywhere. No one notices the homeless; people's eyes slide right over them, as though being homeless is catching.' The edge of bitterness was understandable; Cherie had been homeless herself for a period. It can't have been anything but difficult. It might even have been devastating. I didn't know. I had never asked.

'Oasis muffins and teacakes,' said Goss, putting the desired items into paper bags. Goss was good at these sorts of interruptions, even when she was speaking, not texting. They were the spoken equivalent of KTHXBAI. 'Have a nice picnic!'

'We're nearly sold out,' I commented, looking around at the denuded shelves. I always knew we were sold out when I could see the whole of Hieronymus Bosch's *Garden of Earthly Delights*, a print of which is hung on the side wall. The strange fleshly fountain was spurting. I wondered about that Hieronymus sometimes.

'I can do the banking and close up,' offered Goss, 'if you want to slip upstairs and see if everything's all right.'

'Thanks,' I replied. 'But what leads you to believe that it mightn't be?'

'Jason said you had a zombie.'

'At the beginning,' I agreed. 'He's looks much better now.'

'They do that to fool you so they can eat out your brains,' Goss told me solemnly. 'You be careful!'

I promised I would.

I do not know whether anyone has explained the concept of fiction to Goss, or if she would believe them if they did. As far as she was concerned, zombies existed. Well, anything that tried to eat my brains was going to find themselves flattened with a skillet. I had just the pan, made of cast iron and long-handled, for a good swing. Zombies, indeed.

I took a sourdough loaf I had reserved for myself and the remaining muffins and went upstairs.

There were two men sitting at the kitchen table but no zombies.

'I come bearing muffins,' I announced. 'More tea?'

'That would be kind,' said the soldier. 'You're a verra guid baker!'

'Thank you.' I put on the kettle and looked at Daniel for a cue.

He put his phone back in his pocket and frowned. 'Alasdair has lost his dog, Geordie,' he said gravely. 'A sort of spotted border collie.'

'That's a shame,' I said. And it was, but it hardly seemed like a matter of life and death.

'We were together in Afghanistan,' explained the soldier in his quiet, broad Scots. 'He's a trained sniffer. Bombs, drugs. He go' a medal. Then when…when I was taken oot, they let me take Geordie with me. We were discharged from the army in Townsville. I wasn't gonny risk him in a plane, because they don't pressurise cargo holds. Ah've been drivin' doon here for weeks. Nice and slowly, gettin' used to bein'…no' a soldier.'

'Go on,' I encouraged.

'So, I go' to the city, we're bidin' in a hostel in King Street. I was just takin' him for his evening walk when I were beltit from behind. I fell, an' Geordie…'

'Ran away?' I suggested.

His eyes flashed, his fists clenched. 'He wudn't run away. He stayed with me through aw of it, the explosions and the gunfire. He was taken. He was taken from me!' His voice was rising. Daniel put a hand on his shoulder.

'Of course he didn't run away,' he said in a soothing rumble. 'Now, you need to rest. Everyone is out looking for Geordie.'

'I walked aw night,' whispered Alasdair. 'Callin' him. He only knows the Gaelic words. That's why they retired him wi' me.'

'You walked all night and you had a blow to the head,' confirmed my adored one. 'Now you're going to lie down in the spare room and rest. Meroe's given you a charm. You won't dream.'

'I won't?' he asked, very quietly.

'You won't,' I assured him. 'She's the most powerful witch in these parts. When she bespells something, it stays bespelled.'

He clutched the charm. 'It smells like thyme,' he said, which had such an exquisitely painful double meaning that I turned around to look out the window while Daniel found Alasdair an old tracksuit and made up the spare bed.

When he was done the soldier rose and made his way to the guest room, then paused with his hand on the door. 'You'll call me…'

'The very second I know something,' said Daniel.

The door shut. We heard a weary sigh, followed by a creak as he climbed into the bed. A comfortable one. Of all creatures, Jekyll, who must have followed me upstairs, pawed at the door. She probably wanted to sleep on his boots.

'All right, fetish kitty,' I told her, and opened it enough for her to slip inside.

'Did you say muffins?' asked Daniel.

We took our tea and muffins into the parlour, so that Alasdair could sleep in peace.

'All right, tell me what's going on,' I demanded.

'Lost dog,' he replied, straight-faced.

I gave him an old-fashioned look. 'Why is this dog so important?'

'I'm waiting for a bit more info from a few friends, but Alasdair bears all the marks of a man who was tortured. At a guess, he was hung by the wrists with his toes just touching the ground—the Pathan like that one. You can relieve the pain in your arms only by increasing the pain in your feet. After a few hours, the patient suffocates. The diaphragm cannot relax.'

'Like crucifixion,' I said. I had read a book about an archaeological investigation into crucifixion and I really wished I hadn't. If you're nailed to the cross and hanging up, you have a choice between taking the weight off your feet and hanging by your hands, or easing the pain in your arms and hands and having your feet in excruciating agony. But the suffering lasts longer than the Pathan method. That's why Pilate was surprised when the messengers came to him to say that Christ was dead. His first response was 'What, already?'

Daniel looked blank. Of course. Being a Jew, he only knew the first bit of the Bible.

'Never mind.' I waved a discussion of theology away. 'So he was captured and tortured. But clearly he was either rescued, or released, or he escaped, because here he is.'

Daniel scrubbed both hands through his dark hair. 'I suspect he was invalided out of the service with PTSD.'

'Post-traumatic stress disorder?' I asked.

'Yes. Nightmares, flashbacks, hyperawareness, delusions. High risk of suicide. The only thing he loves enough to live for is his dog.'

'You mean without Geordie he's not likely to survive?' I was aghast.

'That's right,' Daniel confirmed. He took my hand. 'He might be suffering from some sort of brain trauma too, if he's had a close encounter with an improvised explosive device. He could have a contrecoup injury. The brain bounces around in the skull, leading to fugue states, pain, despair.' He made a very Jewish gesture, spreading out his hands.

'Poor Alasdair,' I said, then gave myself a mental shake. My pity wouldn't help Alasdair. He needed action. 'Right, then let's get down to it. Do you think Geordie ran or was he stolen deliberately?'

Daniel drank some more tea and bit into an Oasis muffin.

'I really don't think he would have run away. A dog who has survived Afghanistan is probably immune to nervous shock. Geordie was much more likely to have attacked whoever belted Alasdair.'

'So the assailant either wanted Geordie, or they killed him when they knocked out Alasdair and took the dog's body away to dispose of it.'

'Which is unlikely. If it was just an ordinary mugger, they would have left the dog. And anyway, I know most of the muggers in the city. I've spoken to one of the boldest, Big Charlie, who said he saw Alasdair on the street last night and actually thought about mugging him. But once he'd had a good look at him he decided not to. He pegged Alasdair as a dangerous dude. And if Big Charlie didn't dare, none of the others would. Besides, I know for a fact it wasn't him.'

'So someone stole Geordie.'

'They did—or they tried to,' said Daniel. 'If he managed to evade them, the homeless will find him. Sister Mary's spread the word. A special blessing on the ones who bring Geordie home. Also, we'll check with the RSPCA and the Lort Smith Animal Hospital and the Lost Dogs' Home. He's microchipped. And other than that…' He shrugged. 'I'm waiting for something out of the ordinary to happen.'

'What sort of something?' I asked, snitching a bit of his muffin as a punishment for being cryptic. He patted my hand and explained.

'Knocking down a soldier and stealing his dog is unusual. Whoever did it had a reason. So I'm expecting something odd to occur as a result.'

'All right,' I agreed. 'Why are you so sure it wasn't Big Charlie, by the way?'

'Alasdair was only hit on the head,' said Daniel. 'All Big Charlie's victims are belted across the knees as well.'

'Why's that?' I asked.

'Big Charlie's a dwarf,' said Daniel. 'He always brings his victims down to his level first. I'm a bit surprised that anyone managed to assault Alasdair, though. He's from Paisley, and they breed them tough there.'

'Where's that? I assume Scotland from his accent, but I've never heard of Paisley.'

'Outskirts of Glasgow, in the wilds of Strathclyde. But he's a long way from home now.'

'So the homeless are looking for Geordie. What should we be doing?'

Daniel shrugged. 'Like I said, *ketschele*, we wait.'

Daniel was waiting for something unusual. How was he going to be able to tell in this very strange city? I left him in charge of the sleeping warrior, packed my gin and tonic, picked up my cat, and ascended to the roof garden for my afternoon drink. The sole advantage of getting up at four a.m. is that you finish work early and can sit under the green leaves sipping a G and T while the peons toil in their glass boxes. Occasionally I see their poor tongues hanging out at the sight of me. I felt pity mingled with relief that I was no longer one of them. Once I too had slaved away counting other people's money and helping those who were far too rich already get even more obscenely affluent. Not anymore.

It was cool in the Temple of Ceres. Horatio sprawled out along a marble bench. I put my feet up and considered soldiers, who risked not only their lives but their peace of mind, their future, their hopes of a family and a happy life, in service to Queen and Country. All I could recall about them was a Kipling poem called 'Sappers.' Which I would look up as soon as I went back downstairs. But I would close my eyes first. Just for a moment.

Chapter Three

Your tale, sir, would cure deafness.
—William Shakespeare, *The Tempest*, Act 1, Scene 2

I was woken by a kiss, which is much the best way of being woken and doesn't happen often enough. I relaxed into Daniel's embrace—if this wasn't Daniel, I would have to get out that skillet—and murmured my appreciation.

'Any of that gin left?' he asked.

'Plenty.'

Horatio was still asleep, smearing himself out in that catlike way which seems to spread the creature flatter than a paper bag, in order to apply as much of himself as possible to the cool stone. Daniel poured himself a drink. I surveyed him. He looked frayed.

'No news of Geordie?'

'None. And the council sweepers haven't found his corpse, either. So we can assume he is alive and in captivity. For some reason.'

'Ransom?' I hazarded.

'What has Alasdair got that anyone would want? His military pension? That'd be worth two cups of coffee at a Salvo's refuge on a good day.'

'Yes, but what about information? Intelligence?'

'I don't think the CIA specialises in stealing dogs,' he answered, gulping gin.

I grabbed the bottle away from him and refilled my own glass.

'No, listen, I mean local criminals. I'm sure we've imported some along the way. That's what Australia was for from the beginning. And everyone says that the attempted reconstruction of Afghanistan is a byword for corruption.'

'That's a thought,' he said. 'I may have to consult...'

'A certain uncle?' I finished. Although there is certainly no such organisation as Mossad, and it most definitely doesn't have a local representative, the one it doesn't have is the good and worthy Uncle Solly, who runs the New York Deli in the city. He is a charming, cheerful, Yiddish-speaking darling, and not to be crossed unless you have a team of Sherpas with you. Or, on second thought, not even then. A formidable person. I am very fond of Uncle Solly.

'As you say. Let's finish this drink, no rush, then meander down to the New York Deli to buy some dinner.'

'What about Alasdair?' It didn't seem right to leave him alone.

'I've given him the keys to my office,' said Daniel. 'He has nightmares. When he was in a hostel the night manager found him hoarse and covered in sweat. He was disturbing the other guests. Which is also deeply humiliating for him.'

'Meroe's given him a charm to ward off nightmares,' I pointed out. We really had to find this dog.

'Well, yes; but he'll be better off with me. And because he has to make the place secure. Every lock. Every window. My office even has shutters and iron grates. He'll feel safer there than at a hostel. He doesn't like a lot of people around.'

'Right,' I said. Daniel's office is actually a small flat. It's clean enough and has all the amenities and because it's right in the city centre it has very heavy security. In Melbourne's heartland if you don't, you can experience all the joys of aggravated burglary. I would trust Daniel's locks with my life.

I drained my gin and Daniel held out his arm. 'Now, Madame, if you would do me the honour...'

I rose and took it. I picked up the esky, he elevated Horatio, and we went downstairs to de-cat. Then, leaving Horatio to continue his post-lunch pre-dinner nap, we went out into the street.

It was a filthy day. The heat had settled down on the city like a lid on a saucepan. I was soaked in sweat within seconds.

So it was with great relief that we stumbled into the New York Deli. Uncle Solly was sitting in his usual chair in his white cook's apron, drinking a tall glass of something pink.

'Dollinks!' he exclaimed. 'You look melted! Come, sit, drink a little cool drink with me.' He snapped his fingers and one of his multitudinous 'nephews' poured and carried. It was Campari and soda, icy cold and bitter.

Daniel dispatched his in one long draught.

'Good, Ari, you got the proportions right—give the man another,' ordered Uncle Solly. He eyed me with his bright, penetrating gaze. 'Corinna, dollink! Are you okay? This weather—what can you do? And how about this ox?' He gestured to Daniel. 'He been treating you right?'

'Yes, Uncle, dear,' I said. 'He's a mensch. But we've had a sad case come our way. A soldier who's been in Afghanistan.'

'That's a sad case indeed,' said Uncle Solly. 'There are no good stories coming out of that place.'

'We wondered...' I began delicately.

'If you could get a good dinner from the New York Deli?' he finished, jumping up. Several people had come into the shop. 'Of course! For you, everything. The good sausages, the salt beef, the salads, the olives! You step in the back, ask Eph about the new pastrami.'

I can take a hint, so I collected Daniel and we stepped around the counter and into the back room.

Which was a surprise. The first section was the kitchen, with refrigerators and boxes of produce and a lovely long counter with bowls and knives and other implements. Behind that, though, there was a computer installation which looked like it could run the International Space Station all by itself.

Staring at the oversized screens, fingers poised over keyboards, was a pair of twins. Small, dark, undistinguished-looking. Both female. Both with that faraway gaze as if half of them is always still in the Matrix.

One twin removed her radio headset and said, 'I'm Eph. Uncle sent to you ask about…?'

'Afghanistan,' I said. 'A returned soldier called Alasdair, a missing dog, and possible local involvement.'

'Geordie,' she said.

'You know about it?' I asked, surprised.

'It's our business to know everything that happens in the city,' she said, matter-of-factly. To her left was a bank of screens showing what had to be police CCTV. This was hacking of a high or Lone Gunmen order—the Lone Gunmen being Insula's IT Miracles While U Wait consortium. Their knowledge of computers was only equalled by their incomprehension of almost everything else, including nutrition or basic housekeeping.

'All right,' said Daniel patiently. 'What can you tell us?'

Which is, I noticed, not the same as 'What's happening?'

'Go and tell Ari to give you two more Cokes,' she ordered him. 'And tell him more ice this time. I'm lining up the images. It will take a couple of minutes.'

Daniel went. I sat beside her. She smelt very sweetly of something like patchouli oil and cola. The film flowed. The life of the city, running backwards, light/dark/light. The Mouse Police would be scampering out to ram-raid the Japanese restaurant at… that one. I would be opening the door of my bakery at about… that frame. It was fascinating.

Daniel returned with the supplies. The silent twin reached for hers without ever taking her eyes off the screen. She was watching something altogether different. Several youths tipping over rubbish skips. Youthful high spirits, their defence counsel would say to the magistrate. Who wouldn't believe it, either.

Refreshed with Coke, Eph clicked a key.

'This footage is from outside a club in King Street that is of interest to us,' she explained. 'It has political people visiting it. Here's your soldier.'

Alasdair went past, Geordie at his side. As Big Charlie had noted, he looked like a dangerous dude. Shoulders straight, gaze flickering from right to left and up and down, alert, wary. I wondered if he had brought his sidearm back with him. Geordie was a smallish, vaguely border collie-esque black-and-white dog. He stuck close to Alasdair's heel, watching him all the time. They were not just comrades, they were a partnership. Man and dog strolled out of shot.

'Next camera's not as good,' said Eph. 'Sorry. But here—' she clicked it along frame by frame '—is when it happened.'

Two men—no, three. One pounced on Alasdair from behind and hit him with a small club. I didn't recognise the weapon. Geordie launched himself off the ground, teeth bared, as his master crumpled to the footpath. He sank his fangs into the forearm of one man before he was stuffed into a sack and the three men hurried away. A few seconds later Alasdair sat up and looked around groggily. He put a hand to his head then got gingerly to his feet. He opened his mouth, as if calling out. Then he staggered out of the frame.

'I'm printing all we can see of those faces,' said Eph. 'Which isn't much. Hoodies are the height of fashion for every crim in this city.' Her tone was dispassionate as she continued, 'We pick your man up again at McDonald's. Soup Run.'

I saw the admirable Sister Mary direct that night's heavy, a huge Maori called Ma'ani, to carry Alasdair into the back of the van for first aid. The doctor was Jorgen, who had also just come back from a war zone. That must have helped. Alasdair was in the van for some time. When he emerged, he was clutching the envelope on which Sister Mary had written the directions for my bakery. He went on his unsteady way, his lips moving as if he was still calling for Geordie. I was almost in tears as I watched.

That settled several things. The dog had been kidnapped. Alasdair had been deliberately targeted. That meant they wanted something from him. Now we just had to find out who did it and get Geordie back unhurt. Eph handed Daniel a printout, which he scanned quickly and thrust into his pocket. He must have been thinking along the same lines, because he asked Eph, 'Did you recognise the men who took Geordie?'

'They're not on our database. Not political, as far as we know. But we couldn't see much of their faces so we can't be sure.'

'Is there anything connected with Afghanistan, sappers, or dogs that we should know?'

'Afghanistan is rotten,' she said in her expressionless voice. 'We're keeping an eye on several people. Here are their names and a summary of what we know. You should call Ari on the special line before you approach any of them.'

'All right,' said Daniel. 'I'm a bit surprised you had all this ready for us. Did you know we were coming?'

Eph gave him a quick grin of satisfaction. 'It wasn't hard to guess that Alasdair would find you, and you'd come to us. That's how come we had all this ready for you.'

'I'm grateful, believe me. What else?'

'Strange stuff,' said Eph's twin, speaking for the first time. 'They're tipping out all the skips along King Street. That's hard work. They don't usually do that.'

'They?' Daniel asked.

'Youths,' she said contemptuously. I would have put her own age at about fifteen, if that. 'Also, there's a nasty assault happening on Swanston. Right in front of the cops. Both men now arrested.'

'Did anyone recognise that weapon they used on Alasdair?' I asked.

'It was a sap,' said Daniel. He looked from one twin to the other. 'Do you know anyone who uses such things? Or sells them?'

'They sell them in Knives and Fishing Supplies in King Street,' replied the twin.

'Sorry,' I told her, 'I didn't catch your name.'

She smiled at me. 'Raim.'

The two girls then said in unison. 'Our code name: Ephraim.'

'Lovely to meet you both,' I said, smiling in return. Though it did seem like I was talking to one person. Ephraim being one of the Twelve Tribes, it seemed an appropriate name for them both.

'All right, Agent Ephraim, will you keep me informed?' asked Daniel.

They giggled. 'Certainly, Agent Daniel.' Then they added a crisp phrase in Hebrew which made Daniel laugh.

We went back out through the shop, carrying the documents in a New York Deli tote bag into which I also gathered some of Uncle Solly's marvellous potato salad, a green salad with a sachet of Thousand Island dressing, and some sausages. 'With good sourdough bread,' announced Uncle Solly, kissing the tips of his fingers. 'A feast.'

We kissed him goodbye and plodded home through the steamy heat.

Insula had never seemed so cool and clean. We met Trudi in the atrium. (Of course we have an atrium, with an impluvium and goldfish. What else?) She was down to navy cotton shorts and a blue T-shirt with a modified leather glove strapped to her shoulder for her kitten, the diabolically inspired Lucifer. He was a small orange cat whose karma, Meroe says, is already indelibly smirched and who lives for trouble. He was presently swimming in the pool, diving for—but not catching—goldfish. Trudi reeled him in and he came up grabbing with both clawed front paws.

She put him on her shoulder and he dripped all down her T-shirt.

'Can I dry him for you?' I asked. Her trolley stood nearby and she always had cat-drying towels. A wise precaution, given Lucifer's propensities.

She smiled wearily. 'No, it's nice and cool. Maybe one day we'll be cold again, eh?'

I fervently hoped this was the case and left her to continue reasoning with the freight elevator. It only obeys Trudi.

I won the game of scissors paper stone and got first shower. I dressed in a loose green batik robe with blue butterflies; Jon—our resident overseas aid worker and inexhaustible mine of information about the world and everything in it—had brought the fabric from Bali and Therese had made it into a garment for me. We work on a barter economy in Insula. Then I yielded Daniel the shower and went to cook the sausages. Instantly Horatio woke and reminded me that it was cat food time. Actually, I had remembered that all by myself. It was always cat food time. Horatio munched, I cooked sausages, and Daniel washed.

He came out of the shower dressed in a rather abbreviated towel. I still gasp at the sight of him. The muscular lines of his body, the scar where a Palestinian shell had nearly scooped out his insides. The very gleam on his kneecaps is strong enough to peel paint off walls and does terrible things to my libido. I didn't even know that libidos notched up that high. But his eyes were glowing with another kind of hunger.

'Food,' he said, getting out plates and doling out salad.

'Yes,' I agreed. I was hungry too.

He poured me a glass of Marlborough Sound sauv blanc and we sat down to eat.

'Just one phone call first,' he said. He made a call, and spoke fast to someone called Mike. 'Dog bites,' he explained as he picked up his fork. 'Geordie sank all his teeth into one thug's forearm. He would have needed a doctor. Mike has access to all the hospital emergency departments. That bloke would have had a very sore arm.'

'Not sore enough,' I said, biting vengefully into a sausage. It was a very good sausage. 'And I hope his tetanus jab stung. Bastards. Are you in contact with Alasdair?'

'Yes, he rings me every couple of hours. At least I can tell him that Geordie is still alive, though captive. I need to know when he gets a ransom demand.'

'Will he give them what they want?'

'I don't know,' said Daniel slowly. 'He might. I think he might. He really wants Geordie back and he may not care what he has to do, or how far he has to go. The whole campaign was one long nightmare, and Geordie is all he has to remember it by with any pleasure. I'm meeting a mate of a mate tonight. Another engineer. He might be able to explain Alasdair's service to me, what he's likely to know. He was with him in Helmand Province.'

'A pesthole?' I guessed.

'And that's throwing roses at it,' agreed Daniel. 'It's easier for me. I'm an Israeli: I defend Israel from her enemies, which encompass her just like in biblical days. It can all get questionable and political, but that's the basis of being an Israeli soldier. Self-defence. I'm in front, and behind me are the people. It's my duty to defend them, even with my life, because Jewry must survive. Clear?'

'Crystal,' I agreed.

'But we—that is to say, the Western Alliance, of which Israel is possibly a member—got into Afghanistan, a war that no one since Alexander the Great has ever won, a war that cannot be won, and we are in the same position as the Russians, who thought they could beat up a bunch of ragged tribesmen and got horribly beaten up themselves. Bad guys, bad guys, and slightly less bad guys. Add to that a lot of Western capitalists screwing everyone over, and it gets murky. Like Vietnam. The fight is not against soldiers in uniform, but against the people, and every road might hide an IED, and the people you gave medical care to this morning will cheer when you are blown up this afternoon.'

'Horrible,' I commented.

'Never get involved in wars in the Middle East unless you are already there,' Daniel said. 'Some more salad?'

'Thank you.' I crunched a leaf. 'Where are you meeting this mate of a mate?'

'His name's Russell,' said Daniel, 'and I thought I'd take him up to the roof garden.'

'Good idea,' I approved. 'I'll sit quietly in the Temple of Ceres and listen.'

'And you'll hear everything I miss,' he said, and kissed me at last.

Chapter Four

Said dog I stay and hear
And none shall know my fear
While lord and lady sleep whom I hold dear
—David Greagg, 'Cat and Dog'

A couple of hours later I took another shower, re-donned my blue butterflies, and watched Daniel sleep. He lay flat on his back, spread-eagled. Leonardo's Vitruvian Man. He breathed deeply, his chest rising and falling. I noticed with a certain vicious pleasure that the mark of my very own teeth were outlined in purple on his columnar throat. That mark said, as unequivocally as a cat's foot on a stolen piece of smoked salmon, Mine. Though, of course, once it has been under a paw, there is usually not any serious attempt made to repossess the smoked salmon. I was getting foolish with staring at Daniel, so I picked up my novel. I was rereading Elizabeth Ann Scarborough, *The Healer's War*. Engrossing. And utterly brutal.

Daniel was still sleeping. I picked up another book which had been defying me to read it. It looked more than a little bit weird, but hey: who knew? It was called *The Spear of Destiny*, and it purported to tell the tale of Longinus's spear, which had pierced the side of Jesus on the cross and was some sort of holy relic for everybody who was anybody. Including Hitler. I had delayed reading it on two grounds. The first was that I didn't want to think about crucifixion. But the fact that poor Alasdair had endured something very like that at the hands of the merciless Pathans was quietly digging at me. Come on, Corinna! I told myself. If Alasdair can have it done to him, you can at least read about it.

My other reason for avoiding the book was my aversion to the Führer. Surely the world had dragged over the inglorious career of Adolf Hitler sufficiently by now. On the History Channel, I knew, they spoke of little else. But as I got into the book I found myself enthralled, despite the excessive mysticism of the author, who was obviously a True Believer in psychic powers. I wasn't, but I could suspend disbelief. Who knew that a fair whack of Hitler's entire career had been devoted to finding the spear of Longinus? I speed-read to the end, and realised with a small shock that, assuming the spear in Vienna was the real thing, Hitler had achieved his quest.

I dragged myself out of my cogitations in time to ascend to the roof garden. I would cache myself in the Temple of Ceres and Daniel would bring his engineer to sit in the jasmine bower. Thus I could hear, and the engineer would not be constrained by a female listener.

In due course, the lift doors opened to disgorge Daniel, a tallish, muscular man, an esky and a middle-sized dog. Daniel settled his visitor—the aforementioned Russell, presumably—with a beer in hand. The dog looked up at Russell. 'Yair, all right, Bill—go for a walk,' said the man to his companion. The dog, possibly a blue heeler/greyhound cross, pottered off into the undergrowth. I knew where Horatio was, but hoped that Trudi was not still up here gardening. Lucifer would leap on that poor dog's face and ride him like a bronco. But I heard no squeaks of feline excitement, which might be interpreted as 'Ride 'em, cowboy!' nor any shrieks of displeasure. Good. No cats. And, as a bonus, this dog looked perfectly capable of eating Mrs Pemberthy's rotten little doggie, Traddles, should he be infesting the garden. Though that would not do Bill's digestion any favours.

'You wanted to ask me about Scottie,' said Russell warily.

'Geordie has been kidnapped,' said Daniel, coming straight to the point.

'Fucking hell,' said Russell.

'My thoughts precisely.'

Russell put a hand on his arm. 'No, look, mate—this is serious. Chris said you'd been a soldier?'

Daniel nodded. 'Israel Defense Forces.'

'Right. Then you'll know. What it does to you, I mean.'

'I know,' said Daniel.

'Afghanistan's a running fight against enemies you can't see because, given the right situation, they're everyone.' Russell paused to take a sip of beer, then resumed. 'And we're fighting and dying and getting blown up, and for what? Fuck all. You know Kipling?'

'I do,' said Daniel.

'"The Young British Soldier"?'

In reply, Daniel began to recite: *'If your officer's dead and the sergeants look white…'*

'Remember it's ruin to run from a fight…'

'So take open order, lie down, and sit tight, and wait for supports like a soldier.'

'When you're wounded and left on Afghanistan's plains, and the women come out to cut up what remains…' Russell's voice was slow and quiet.

'Jest roll to your rifle and blow out your brains…' Daniel finished, *'An' go to your Gawd like a soldier.'*

'All true. Today we'd call in ARTY—air support or artillery. But it's the same. The same war, too.'

'That bad?' said Daniel sombrely.

Russell popped the lid off another beer, leant back, and sighed.

'Yes. It's that bad.' Then, in a more animated tone, he said, 'Look. I brought you a little present from the Battle of Maiwand.'

Daniel bent to peer at something small in the palm of Russell's hand but I could not see what it was.

'A homemade bullet?' he guessed.

'From 1880. A Jezail bullet. Made of all the bits of iron lying around and covered with lead. Acted like a fragmentation round. That's what got Sherlock Holmes's Dr Watson. Poor bugger must have been crippled.'

'You're a historian,' said Daniel.

'And this,' said Russell, and Daniel bent forward once more.

'It looks ancient,' he observed. 'The hinge from scale armour, perhaps? We have found such things in Israel. They usually come from...no, not Alexander?'

Russell thumped the beer bottle down for emphasis. 'He was the last general to win at Maiwand, and he wasn't conquering—he just wanted to get through. Everyone else who's tried it over the centuries has been fucked. And so are we. Jeez, I'm glad we're bringing the boys home! And the girls, of course. All of us.'

'So the campaign has failed?' asked Daniel gently.

'It was always going to fail. Politics.' Russell spat neatly into a bed of irises and I did not blame him. 'Americans. Specifically, presidents. Not the poor grunts' fault. But their money men have fucked the war over, and still are. Only thing we can hope for is to make all sides hate us so much that they unite to drive us out. Then we put a big wall around the Pashtun, and they'll kill each other. Their longest period without feuds is twenty-six years—their golden age. You know the Pashtun word for "cousin" is also the word for "enemy"?'

'That is an interesting language,' said Daniel.

'The only people who understand what Afghanistan's like are people like your mob—the IDF—and the Vietnam vets. Same sort of war, really: an invisible, hostile enemy united only by their hatred of us. In Vietnam our lot were sappers, just like in Kipling.

That's what I do, or did. We build things, we blow things up. We were the tunnel rats in Vietnam. They always give the impossible jobs to the engineers.'

'And the impossible just takes you a little longer.' Daniel smiled and quoted Kipling again. *"It's all one," says the Sapper.'*

'But IEDs can break anyone's nerve,' said Russell. 'Could be anything: a string, a wire, a rock, a cowpat. You can't sit down, you can't travel, you can't relax, ever. Like you blokes and suicide bombers.'

Daniel nodded.

'But we've got the dogs and we've got good mates, so we manage.'

'I understand,' said Daniel.

'I'm all right,' stated Russell, stretching his legs out in front of him. 'Bill?' A faint woof came back from the other side of the garden, where Bill had found something to engage his interest.

'Good,' said Daniel.

'I mean, I'm all right, I've got mates, I've got a wife and a baby, I've got something to come home to—I've even got Bill. He's a hero, got a medal to prove it. Found fifteen IEDs. Saved hundreds of lives. I've got the nightmares, of course; we've all got the nightmares. But I'm okay. Alasdair, though...'

'Hasn't got anyone else?'

'That's right. Oh, he was famous for a little while, for all the good it did him.'

'What do you mean he was famous?' Daniel sounded as surprised to hear this as I was.

Now Russell sounded surprised. 'You didn't know? I guess you don't spend a lot of time looking at social media.' He pulled his phone out of his pocket, played with it for a bit then handed it over.

Daniel peered at the screen. 'How long ago was this?' he asked.

'Two years. The army's generally not over keen on letting out any information about what goes on in theatres of war, but this was such a good propaganda piece that they let it through.' I was dying to know what they were talking about, but it looked as though I would have to wait. Russell seemed like a good bloke, but he'd fallen into the All Blokes Together habit of leaving the womenfolk to catch up as best we could.

'Perhaps,' Daniel suggested, 'the government was in a spot of bother back then and welcomed the distraction.' He frowned. 'Though this is an English journal, isn't it?'

'Yep. He was still serving with the British Army then. But we got to know each other in Helmand and he decided he'd rather be an Aussie. After he was demobbed he applied for citizenship and it was granted overnight. Ministerial prerogative. I guess the minister is more into social media than you.' Russell brought his beer to his lips and tipped his head back to drink. 'So maybe Alasdair has some information that the kidnappers—dognappers—want? There's a lot of drugs in Afghanistan. Maybe this is connected to the drug trade.'

'That's a promising idea, Russell. I'll keep it in mind. Tell me more about him.'

'Poor old Scottie. Not interested in girls. Or boys. Just him and his dog. He used to spy for the English. He had a serious talent for passing himself off as a local, and he found out lots of intel they'd never have found otherwise. I knew he was going to drive down from Townsville to spare Geordie the journey in the plane's hold. Well, I did that, too. Bill and I went on the train. It was fun. Picked up my family in Sydney and came down together. The kid loves Bill and Bill thinks Tommy's his puppy. But what Scottie will do without Geordie…' He shook his head. 'He was caught in a bad ambush; jeep ran over an IED. Everyone else was killed, but Scottie was captured. They had him for three days. Three days before anyone noticed that he wasn't among the dead. 'Course, it can be hard to put together all the pieces. That's why a lot of us put one of our dog tags on the laces of our boots.'

'They tortured him?'

'Bastards,' Russell spat again. 'Only one who knew he was gone was Geordie. Whined, dragged, tried to pull people by the sleeve, did everything short of actually running off the base, because he knew he needed help. Finally some fuckwitted squaddie worked out what Geordie was about and got a patrol on to it. The bastards had had a lot of fun with Scottie. The medics didn't think he'd live, but he did. Still, I reckon he's got no reason to trust anyone in the world except his dog. His mates didn't come looking for him. It took one of our patrols to find him.'

'What do you think will happen to Alasdair if we don't find Geordie alive?' asked Daniel.

'I dunno, mate,' said Russell heavily.

A head was reposing on my knee. I patted. It was Bill. He grabbed my sleeve in his teeth and pulled me to my feet. I valued my caftan so I rose and came into view.

'Who you got there, Bill?' asked Russell. His hand dropped to where the stock of his gun would have been; on a sling, I suspected. In the same manner as Daniel, he looked suddenly extremely dangerous. I held up both hands.

'Friend,' I told him.

He relaxed back into the chair.

'All right, Bill, loose,' he told the dog. Bill, wagging his tail, un-fanged my dress and went to sit by his master's side.

'You see, these dogs are like brothers,' said Russell, making room for me on the bench. 'Sorry about that, he's a bit protective.'

'A very good thing to be,' I agreed.

'This is Corinna,' said Daniel. 'She's helping me to find Geordie.'

'Your partner, eh? Okay.'

'How do you find the dogs in the first place?' I asked.

Russell scratched Bill's ears absently. 'In refuges, lost dogs' homes. We look for a smallish dog with a real good nose.'

'Why small?' I asked.

He grinned at me. 'Because sometimes we have to carry the dog, along with the pack and the gear and the rifle—and you do not want a St Bernard strapped to your chest when you're leaping out of a copter.'

This struck me as eminently sensible.

'We go through all the training together. We devise our own orders, so no one can mislead the dog. Dogs have got amazing noses. Haven't you, Bill, eh? Amazing. They can sniff out a microgram of explosive in air. And Geordie was a drug dog, too. Whereas if you want a bloodhound, you can't go past my Bill here.'

Bill wagged his tail again. I could practically see the halo around his ragged ears. He was a shabby, ill-favoured dog, but clearly very happy. His master was rubbing those ears and Bill was slavering happily onto his thigh.

'Anyway, will you let me know if I can help in any way?' Russell asked. 'I feel bad about Scottie. Someone should have come for him. And they didn't.'

'I'll call you,' promised Daniel, and he rose to escort Russell and Bill out.

I stayed on the bench, looking out on the flowery, fragrant garden. Alasdair had probably known that he would not be rescued, that no one would notice him missing from that heap of body parts and destroyed machinery. He was captive, in the hands of his enemies, to be killed in the cruellest way possible, at their sadistic leisure. He must have despaired.

And who delivered him from his enemies and the pains of hell? Not his mates. His dog. His only friend in the world.

We absolutely *had* to get Geordie back.

But how?

Chapter Five

Flout 'em and scout 'em; and scout 'em and flout 'em.
Thought is free.
—William Shakespeare, *The Tempest*, Act 3, Scene 2

'So tell me about this article,' I prompted. Daniel took out his phone, rummaged in the depths of cyberland for a moment then handed the phone to me.

On the screen was a photo of Alasdair holding a smallish black-and-white dog in his arms and grinning. My heart turned over to see the change in him. Back then, he looked absurdly young and filled with ebullience. Now, the face was the same, but haunted and filled with terror. The banner headline read HERO GEORDIE SAVES PATROL.

The accompanying text was somewhat overwritten, but the gist was clear enough as I flicked downwards. A patrol had been driving along the highway in an armoured car, when Geordie had begun barking furiously. Rather than telling the dog to shut up, the driver had braked hard and stopped. The patrol had disembarked and fanned out on both sides of the road. They found an IED almost immediately, not ten metres from where they had stopped, right in the middle of the road. The bomb squad disarmed the

IED and great had been the rejoicing of everyone, and presumably there'd been extra rations for Geordie. I handed the phone back and we exchanged one of those Significant Looks.

'All right. So maybe we have a motive after all?' I suggested.

Daniel glanced skywards as he thought this through. 'I see what you mean. Alasdair, it transpires, is no longer an anonymous squaddie with a dog. He's a social media hero from two years ago, and maybe he knows something, and they're using the dog to put pressure on him? Look, I know that's tenuous logic at best. It's verging on cargo-cult thinking. But kidnappers don't usually specialise in Clear Thinking 101.'

'Maybe. I can't imagine why anyone wants the dog except as a means of getting to Alasdair. But there is a problem with that.'

He took my hand in his and squeezed it gently, something which always sends a shiver of delight up my spine. 'How do they get a message to him to issue their demands? That really is a problem, isn't it? He's staying with me, but I'd be very surprised if anyone knows where I live.'

I patted his hand reassuringly. Daniel's flat is in an utterly anonymous grey block near the market. Thus far, apparently, not one of his nefarious acquaintances had managed to trace his whereabouts. Daniel had been trained in an exceedingly hard school, and I suppose that ordinary crims are less gifted trackers than Hamas gunmen.

He kissed me and rose. 'I'm going to make the rounds of the rest of inner Melbourne's underworld in the next few days. And I may have another talk with Big Charlie. He may not have attacked Alasdair himself, but I suspect he knows more than he's letting on.'

I stood also and embraced him. 'Be careful, my love.'

He pressed his body close to mine and kissed me again. 'I will.'

I watched him depart, then returned to my apartment to feed Horatio. I spent the rest of the evening in quiet contemplation and retired to bed early. My dreams were troubled by barking dogs and the haunted faces of soldiers. Then the scene changed, and

I was chained up with my hands above my head. Someone was pushing sandpaper across my face and leering at me.

I awoke, drenched in sweat and fear, to find Horatio washing my face. I switched on my bedside light and hugged him. Normally he would not permit such liberties, but tonight he lay patiently in my arms. I felt his even breathing and relaxed my grip. At once he struggled up onto my pillow and washed himself. Then he pushed his nose against mine and nuzzled me. I stroked his beautiful flank and he relaxed again, tucking his face into his paws. I switched the light off, and subsided into dreamless slumber.

Four a.m.

I have probably mentioned how I feel about four a.m. I breakfasted, fed Horatio, fumbled into my baking clothes and felt my way down the stairs.

Jason was there, whistling. He saw me. He stopped whistling. I gestured to him to continue.

'There must be something wrong,' I told him, with the poet Frost, 'in wanting to silence any song.'

'Er, yeah, Captain,' responded Jason. 'Sourdough mixing, olive bread on the go, making pane di casa.'

'Carry on,' I said, with a Picardian wave. There was also freshly brewed coffee, I noted gladly. This was going to be a day for high-octane caffeine. I poured a cup and sipped. All that emotion from yesterday was lying heavily on me. I watched Jason as he moved, sure, strong. I could see the muscles in his back shift as he hauled a sack of flour to the mixer. A beautiful piece of nature, healthy, comely, curly-headed and cheeky. Which could so easily be reduced to its component atoms by one improvised explosive device.

'Cap'n?' he asked, catching my gaze. 'What's wrong?'

'I was thinking about soldiers,' I said. 'And wars.'

He grinned at me. 'It's not doing you any good,' he told

me. 'Think about bread instead. Should we make bara brith again today?'

'Good advice, Midshipman. Bara brith it is, so get out the spices. And later you can have a go at making baklava if you like. Ask Yai-yai for some tips.'

I would much rather think about bread than wars. Thinking about wars just makes me angry and sad, but thinking about baking means that there is, in the end, bread. Which can be eaten.

We baked busily. The Mouse Police displayed their prey. Five mice, one rat, and a couple of moths. The moths were not strictly vermin, but I decided that they might have flapped into my precious Mother of Bread and inconsiderately drowned, in that annoying way moths have, which made them a legitimate threat to public health. I distributed munchies and disposed of the corpses.

The bakery filled with the pleasant noise of mixers mixing, Jason whistling, air conditioner whirring, and cats crunching. My mood improved.

By the time I let my cats out into Calico Alley, the sun was rising, but there were no distressed soldiers walking down it. Just Ian of the Rising Sun putting on Radio Nippon and speaking politely to the moggies who had collided with his door as he was opening it. And required compensation in the form of tuna, of course. I went back into the scented bakery to sift spices. Cinnamon, cloves, allspice, the perfumes of paradise.

Just as we were settling into our comfortable, unthinking routine, there came a shriek of feline fury, the one that tears eardrums and shatters wineglasses, and a frenzy of barking and yelping.

I ran out into Calico Alley. This hadn't happened for ages. Most of the local dogs knew enough to stay away from the Mouse Police. The battle-scarred faces, deckle-edged ears, the rolling seaman's gait all indicated to the wise canine that here was Trouble with a capital T and they suddenly remembered urgent appointments in quite another part of town.

However, here they were: two large, lolloping, curly-coated black dogs, bailed up against their door by Heckle, who was shrieking like a soul in torment and had every hair on his scruffy body raised. The poor dogs didn't dare to move. They had never seen anything like this enraged, heavily armed porcupine. With attitude.

'Heckle, if you please,' I said to him as I walked up the alley. 'They're just nice dogs and this is a public throughway, you know. And Ian has some tuna scraps with your name on,' I added.

Ian held out the plate of scraps, and Heckle smelt his favourite fish. I could see him decide, Well, all right then, but you've got off lightly: I could beat you with a tram tied to my tail and don't you forget it, as he snapped his mouth shut, shook himself, and strolled over to the Rising Sun to reunite with his fellow police officer and the tuna.

I swallowed. Now I had to face the owner of the dogs, who might be justifiably annoyed. The poor creatures were shivering. They hadn't expected something like Heckle to rise out of the cobbles. They'd probably have nightmares.

'Is that thing a cat?' asked a pleasant, sceptical voice. A short, dark, very pretty young woman, accompanied by a slightly taller, dark, equally pretty young woman, was opening the shop door. The dogs bolted in, tails between legs, and mobbed their owners, wagging frantically and trying to explain that it wasn't their fault, the door had been open and it all looked really interesting until suddenly…(sob)…there was this *thing*…

'Darlings, sweethearts, it's all right,' said one pretty young woman, patting and caressing. 'It's not your fault! It's mine!' Turning to me, she explained, 'I left the door open while I put the paper away and they just slipped out. They're spoodles, so they do tend to be a bit scatty. I'm Marie, and this is Kate.' She gestured to the other woman then extended a hand.

We shook.

'I'm Corinna. That's my bakery on the corner. I hadn't noticed your shop.'

'We just moved in,' said Marie, taking her friend's hand affectionately.

'Music?' I looked around, taking in scores and discs and books and a cheerful jumble of things which would be hours of fun to sort through.

'That's the name,' said Kate, pointing.

I looked up. A newly painted sign bore the blazon HEARD IT BEFORE.

'Lovely,' I said. 'And these poor darlings?'

'They'll be all right as long as I remember to keep the door closed,' said Marie. 'Let me introduce Allegro and Biscuit.'

The dogs had calmed down in the absence of Heckle, and each licked my hand politely, though that might have been the remaining traces of flour.

'I let the Mouse Police out every morning at six,' I said. 'They're usually back as soon as they run out of tuna. I'm so sorry. Can I offer you something by way of apology? A loaf of bread, perhaps?'

'That sounds fair,' said Kate, grinning.

'Right, then, I'm still baking, but come along later and you shall have whatever you like. Even some of Jason's muffins.'

'Did he make the astounding one I bought yesterday that tasted like Turkish delight?' asked Marie.

'He's a master when it comes to muffins,' I agreed.

As I left, I heard Marie say, 'Now, if we let them out every morning at six, we'll be in muffins for life.'

I smiled to myself. They were charming and I was delighted to meet them. I hoped their shop did well.

The day was looking up. I returned to Earthly Delights to take the sourdough rolls out of the oven before they scorched. Heckle returned, shoving Jekyll with his shoulder in an 'I showed them who is the dominant mammal in this lane, me hearties' piratical manner which I found extremely funny.

Jason and I completed the baking, and I sent him to the Pandamus family's Cafe Delicious for their trucker's special breakfast. I suspect they keep adding extra bacon and hash browns and toast and so on to see just how much Jason can eat before he literally explodes. They haven't managed to daunt him yet. He has years of abuse, heroin addiction, and related malnutrition to assuage. Also, he has just discovered a cable TV program called *Man v. Food*. The champion eater is his new role model. I preferred it when he wanted to be Marvel's Thor.

Jason returned, replete for the present, and we loaded the rest of the bread into the ovens. I was just peacefully arranging shop bread into racks when Goss ran in (I think it was Goss, she was too over-wrought to announce herself), screaming, 'Del's gonna kill Taz!'

I don't know what she thought I could do about it, but I dutifully ran to the second battle of the day, telling Goss to bring her phone in case we had to summon help. A silly thing to say. She would naturally bring her phone and film anything exciting. It would be going viral on YouTube before lunch—assuming we got to lunch, at this rate.

When I arrived at the cafe, I found the situation adequately exciting. Del Pandamus, who was one of those stocky middle-aged peasant men who can, if the need arises, haul a tractor out of a ditch or prop up a fallen horse all by themselves, was holding Taz—one of the nerds collectively known as the Lone Gunmen—up against the wall by his throat. He didn't look like letting him down any time soon.

Taz was turning an interesting shade of purple. I like Del. I didn't want him to go to jail for nerdicide. I stepped up and enquired as to the bone of contention.

Del shouted that the little *malakas* had sent rude pictures to the Kyria. That was beyond unlikely, the nerds being acquainted with sex only in theory and probably really happy with their Black Widow blow-up doll. So I poked Del under the armpit and said 'Put him down! Now!' in my firmest voice. Del did. Jason calls it my captain's voice. Works on dogs, too, though never on cats.

'Taz, are you all right?' I asked.

I let him lean on my shoulder while he fought to get some breath back. When he could speak he gasped, 'No, no, it wasn't us! Really! No!'

'All right, it wasn't you, I believe you,' I assured him. 'Del? What's this about?'

'This little wanker, he fix my accounts for me!' shouted Del. All Greek arguments must, by law, be conducted at the highest possible volume. 'He sneak something into the machine, and when the Kyria log on, she saw…she…' He made a broad, Promethean gesture of horror and despair.

'All right,' I said, 'this is clearly some sort of glitch. Taz and I will look at the computer, Taz will fix it, and no one needs to die today; it's already far too wearing for a Tuesday.' Then I added, 'Del, you have customers,' which is the only thing guaranteed to divert a Greek patron from homicide.

Loudly calling on St George to defend his honest house, Del rushed into the cafe.

'It was just a real simple accounting program,' said Taz hoarsely. 'Shouldn't have thrown up any pictures at all.'

'Come on, let's have a look. Goss, can you open the shop? Show's over. You can show me the vid later.'

'Okay,' said Goss—I had guessed right—and I escorted a quivering Taz into the little office at the back of the cafe, picking up a can of Diet Coke for him as I went. Nerds run on caffeine, as do bakers, just via a different delivery system.

There sat Kyria Anastasia, a pillar of black salt in the office chair. The screen showed a complicated writhing, spurting, moaning mass of bodies, limbs everywhere, mouths, hands, both sorts of genitalia…no wonder Del had gone up like a rocket. Actually, I would have liked to inspect it further, if only to work out who was doing what to whom, because they sounded like they were really enjoying it, but now was no time for amusement.

'It wasn't him,' I told the old lady. 'Come and have a strengthening ouzo and a sit-down, Kyria.'

She yielded the chair to Taz and allowed me to escort her into the family room, where she pointed out the ouzo and the fridge. I poured her a good dollop and we watched it turn pearly as the ice melted. This reminded me irresistibly of certain biological substances in which the video had been liberally doused. I bit my lip and poured myself a small tot. The Kyria took the glass, winking at me as she took a healthy swig. Then we both broke down and started giggling. Old ladies aren't all that easy to shock, generally.

'Harvest festival,' said the Kyria nostalgically. 'Those were good days.'

I drained my glass and bade her sit for a moment, to preserve her fiction of being shocked, then went back to the office. Taz, cola-fuelled, was attacking the keyboard with fingers that moved faster than sound.

'Anything?' I asked. 'I have to get back to the bakery soon.'

'Can't nail it down,' muttered Taz. 'I'll have to get onto my own system. They're good, whoever they are. I expect we'll find some ransomware; but I can fix it. Er, thanks, Corinna. Saved my life.'

'Any time,' I told him. I ought to return to Earthly Delights, I knew. But Jason could look after things without me for a while. Instead, why should I not spend a little longer here, relaxing while others worked?

I reached into my bag and pulled out *The Spear Of Destiny* again. It had been sitting there ever since the previous night, and now seemed a good time to remind myself about it. Some of Professor Monk's latest enthusiasm (Biblical scholarship) had rubbed off on me, which is why I had bought it. While I couldn't do ancient languages, I felt able to cope with this one. Even though the author was a bit over the top in his descriptions of Mystical Experiences, which he treated as matters of fact rather than fancy.

I might not believe much in magic, but there is one thing most people would agree on, and that is the idea that you can sense when someone is staring at you. I was sensing it right now:

someone behind me was staring at my shoulder blades. I didn't want to turn around quickly and alert whoever it was that I was onto them. If only the cafe had an appropriately situated mirror, like the ones that turn up so conveniently for detectives in novels. But as it turned out the mirror wasn't necessary, because the sensation ceased as the starer rose and walked past me, pausing for a moment to look at my book, then left.

I did not get much of a look at him. Smallish, vaguely Eastern European, and utterly unmemorable. Was it me or the book that interested him? I had never seen him before, of that I was certain.

I returned to the bakery, where all was well, although Jason was cross at missing out on the fun. Goss was consoling him by showing him the video on her phone. I must say I did come across as commanding.

'You go, Cap'n!' exclaimed Jason.

'Is all the bread loaded?' I asked quietly. I really needed another cup of coffee. I wasn't used to drinking ouzo at this hour of the morning. Jason jumped and practically saluted.

'All the restaurant bread's gone, Cap'n. All the muffins are shipshape.'

This reminded me of my earlier encounter. 'Oh, by the way, Kate and Marie who've opened the music shop will be in for some free muffins I promised, so leave a few aside for them.'

'Okay.'

I got some more coffee, Goss put her phone away, and the day proceeded gently, with bread sales and quiet conversation, rather than by leaps and screams. It was most soothing. Boring, perhaps, but sometimes I just like boring.

The lunch crowd cleaned us out of almost everything. I saved a loaf and some cakes for myself, not knowing if I would have visitors. I still felt a bit guilty about those poor dogs whom Heckle had probably startled into permanent conniptions. There were enough cases of PTSD around as it was.

Chapter Six

Thy head is as full of quarrels as an egg is full of meat.
—William Shakespeare, *Romeo And Juliet,* Act 3, Scene 1

The panic alarm sounded at three o'clock.

The residents of Insula had agreed that our collective security needed some beefing up. It wasn't as though any of us had put in a requisition for Adventures, with a side order of terror and kidnapping. Most of us just wanted to grow things, make things and, in my case, bake bread. But Adventures kept on happening, and as a result we had installed panic buttons in every unit, with displays showing in whose apartment the alarm had been triggered. Dion Monk's red light was flashing on my wall, and the insistent beep-beep screamed from the speaker. I pressed the mute button, wrapped myself around with my dressing-gown, grabbed my bag and left the apartment. I had just closed Earthly Delights and had been looking forward to a pleasant afternoon nap. It did not appear that I was going to get it.

Professor Monk's door was ajar. Mrs Dawson and Trudi were already there. Trudi—once again in shorts and a blue T-shirt—was brandishing a large garden fork and looked ready to use it. The ginger kitten Lucifer was perched in his harness on her shoulder, sniffing excitedly. Mrs Dawson—elegantly dressed despite the

heat in a summer skirt, cream-coloured blouse and mauve jacket—
had disdained weaponry. She nodded to me. 'Well, Corinna? The
three of us will have to manage for now.'

Trudi led the way in, preceded by the points of her weapon.
And there was Professor Monk in the middle of his parlour, standing agape over a recumbent body. Nobody I knew, and no one
else seemed to have any ideas as to how he had come to be so
unexpectedly among those present. There was blood, though
not enough to suggest imminent danger of death. The smell of
it filled the room, and Lucifer was taking it in and pawing the air
in excitement. It was a young man, so far as could I could see,
wearing nondescript pants and a hoodie the colour and texture of
decaying vegetation. I bent down beside him. He was motionless,
but a faint suggestion of respiration seemed to be happening.

I looked up at Professor Monk, but his presumably unwelcome
intruder was not at the forefront of his mind. He shook his head,
wiped his forehead with a white handkerchief, and called out in
tones of anguish and concern, 'Nox? Where are you, my little
friend? Where is my little darling? *Basilissa!*'

I stood up in time to see Therese Webb and an unknown
woman join the gathering. Professor Monk ignored them. An
expression of devotion and relief passed across his face as a small
black kitten emerged from the bedroom. She was affronted. She
stomped heavily across the fallen intruder towards her protector
and clambered up him, pausing only at his shirt-fronted chest.
She dug all four sets of claws into him as he cradled her in his
ancient arms and began to coo soothingly to her in what I could
only presume was Ancient Greek.

I looked again at our visitor. Still nothing happening there.
I supposed we should do something about him, though I was in
no hurry. Mrs Dawson watched the Professor indulgently for a
while, and laid her slender hand on his arm.

'Come along, darlings!' she commanded. 'Come and sit in my
apartment. You shall have a stiff drink, Dion, and so shall Nox.'

The kitten looked at her with a moment's surmise then climbed onto her shoulder. Professor Monk allowed himself to be led away, and I looked at Trudi. She was leaning on her garden fork, but the substantial muscles in her bare arms were tensed. She glared at the fallen youth as if he were an unwelcome sprout of deadly nightshade. I felt that he would be well-advised to play dead so long as she was anywhere near him.

I reached for my phone and began to dial Detective Senior Constable Letitia White, known to me as Letty through long and not always pleasant association. I thought it would save time and needless explanation if I called her, rather than having to introduce a brand new cop to my cast of thousands. At least Letty knew who we were and what we all did for a living. While I waited for the call to be answered I turned to the recent arrivals.

'Hello, Therese. And you must be Anwyn?' Therese's two guests had been named as Anwyn and Philomela, but I recalled that the latter had been in an accident. This one was a plump, sturdy woman wearing an Indian skirt and blouse and adorned with a great many silver bangles and necklaces. She grinned at me.

'Hello, Corinna. Yes, I'm Anwyn. Therese has told me so much about you!'

I nodded politely as a grumpy voice came on the line. 'Corinna? What can I do for you this bloody awful day?' Just for a moment I wondered if she ever regretted giving me her phone number. Then again, perhaps I was brightening up her working life and giving her diversion from the diurnal run of boring crimes and equally boring criminals.

'Hello, Letty? Look, I'm sorry to bother you, but you did say to ring next time something untoward happened. We seem to have a body.' I gave it a nudge with my foot. 'I think it's still alive, but we should probably have it seen to.'

A squawk of scandalised interrogation sounded in my ear.

'Yes, well, we don't know anything about him. He's in Professor Monk's apartment. Trudi is standing over him with a garden fork, so if anyone's in danger it isn't us... Yes, an ambulance is probably indicated. I'll stay here until I see you.'

I put my phone back in my pocket and smiled.

Anwyn was gazing at me in some astonishment. 'So this sort of thing happens a lot here?'

'All the time,' I told her, then turned to our gardener. 'Trudi, are you happy to keep an eye on our little friend here?'

She nodded, and waved her weapon suggestively. 'Oh yes. My grandmother used to do this when we had Germans.' She pronounced the word as though it rhymed with vermin, which seemed fair enough considering that the Nazi occupation of the Netherlands had been brutal.

'We'll keep you company, Trudi,' Therese said. 'I'll fetch our embroidery.' Trudi pulled over some chairs from the side of the room and sat in one of them, still balefully glaring at the Professor's unwelcome guest.

Therese headed for her apartment and I trooped towards the stairs to Mrs Dawson's. With three sceptical women and one four-foot garden implement to watch over him, I didn't think our friend would be any trouble. Then I had a sudden illumination and doubled back to Professor Monk's apartment. In his study I found his precious leather-bound commonplace book, which contained all his working notes. The front page was in plain English, and began with the title The Gospel of St Joseph. My Biblical knowledge was nothing special; but I'd never heard of that one. Flicking through the pages, I saw Latin, and Ancient Greek, and who knew what else, handwritten in orderly rows. I stuffed it into my bag. I didn't know how long his apartment would be embargoed, and he would fret without his pet project. Then, prompted by I knew not what instinct, I went into the kitchen. The fridge door was open, and so was the freezer cabinet. Odd. I didn't want to interfere with a crime scene more than was needful, but this was a bit unusual. I had a closer look. The ice cubes were melting in their plastic trays. So that meant that the doors had been open for...how long? Maybe an hour?

Now this was strange. Why would Professor Monk have left his fridge door open for that long? You cannot read anything into that, I could hear a sceptical detective constable opine; old people can be forgetful. Perhaps he had opened the fridge and freezer doors and then been distracted by something, like his cat. Except that Professor Monk's mind was still razor-sharp, and he showed no signs of age-related inattention at all.

It seemed to me that this was an extremely thorough burglar. Most burglars are happy to make their visitations as evanescent as possible, but this one had been here nearly long enough to grow a spare beard. I peered into the freezer and found a plastic packet of prawns beginning to thaw. I slipped them into my bag as well. I knew someone who would be very glad of them, and I did not think they were any sort of Clue. Even for the Famous Five. I left the rest of the Clues untampered and left the apartment.

I found Professor Monk reclining in a most elegant armchair, wrapped in a gorgeous Chinese silk robe (red, with golden brocade dragons) that would have been far too big for the elegant Mrs Dawson, and was doubtless the property of the late Mr Dawson. The Professor's shoes and socks had been removed, and his slippered feet luxuriated in the deep carpet. He held in his hand a tall gin and tonic, complete with a lemon slice, and he appeared recovered from his ordeal.

'Ah, Corinna,' he remarked. 'There you are!'

It was a scene of ultimate comfort. At his side sat Mrs Dawson (in matching armchair), also sipping a G and T. On her impeccable Chinese carpet was a blue china bowl filled with milk. A small black kitten was attending to it, with both ears pinned back. So far as Nox was concerned, Outrages had been committed and she was owed compensation. The tiny sound of furious lapping could be heard from the bowl's interior.

Mrs Dawson smiled at me and rose. I presented her with the packet of prawns and her mouth curved in a smile. 'I know someone who will be happy to receive some of these,' she said. 'And the remainder will be paella this evening.'

She disappeared into the kitchen with the prawns and returned, taking up a protective position on the left of the reclining Professor Monk. He beamed at her.

'Gin and tonic?' Mrs Dawson offered.

'Not yet, but later would be wonderful,' I answered.

What I had had in mind for the afternoon had certainly included a G and T or so, relaxing in the Temple of Ceres on the roof, but I was resolved to have it only after the alarums and excursions had been satisfactorily concluded.

'Professor, you may want to keep this by you,' I suggested, producing his notebook from my bag.

His eyes lit up, and he patted the small table by his right elbow. 'Leave it there, Corinna, if you would be so kind. Many thanks! I have no idea when I am likely to regain the use of my apartment, and I do not want policepersons morrissing through my notes. I do not believe for a moment they are pertinent to the crime scene.'

'We may probably assume that they are not. Professor, if you do not mind my asking, what can you tell us of your intruder? Had he an introduction, or did he simply barge in without so much as leaving his calling card on a silver tray?'

'It is a mystery,' the Professor admitted. 'We have not met before. I am sure I would have noticed. I had left my front door open, since my *basilissa* wanted to explore the building. I was consulting a Latin dictionary in my study when I heard what sounded like the arrival of several tonnes of coal into my parlour. Goodness knows what he meant by it.'

'Are you certain he was alone?'

His deep blue eyes exchanged a piercing look with mine. 'No. I cannot be certain, but I believe he was. Had he been accompanied, there would have been, at the very least, footsteps running away down the stairs.'

'All right, I won't ask you any more for now. I'm going back to your apartment, Professor. And this time I shall search it as thoroughly as I can without getting fingerprints everywhere.'

'And we shall remain here, Corinna,' Mrs Dawson stated. 'Do keep us informed, Corinna.'

The door to Dion Monk's apartment was still open. I looked through it towards the parlour. It appeared that the audience for today's pageant had grown rather than diminished. We had Visitors, standing mostly in a clump along the far wall, looking down at our burglar. The young man appeared to have regained consciousness. But he lay where he was, with three kitchen chairs placed around him at equal intervals. Trudi had her garden fork poised, and it appeared that Anwyn and Therese were armed with pins, needles, scissors and stilettoes. Trudi waved her free hand at me.

'All in order here, Corinna,' she announced. 'We have an agreement. He lies quietly on the floor, and I don't stab him with the fork. Please shut the door.'

Taking out my handkerchief, I wrapped it around my hand and lightly closed the door on the burglar and his guards. Then I gave the newcomers the once-over. Standing apart from the others, and looking at me without expression, was Meroe, dressed in one of her usual gypsy wraps. She nodded, but did not speak. Her eyes were taking everything in, but she preferred silence until she was sure of herself. I surveyed the remainder of the crowd. There were two men and three women—though there was more than a whiff of intersex in their attire and attitudes. All were in their early twenties as far as I could tell. Four were dressed informally in long trousers and white T-shirts emblazoned with RMIT PERFORMING ARTS. The fifth sat in a wheelchair a little away from them. She appeared to be watching everyone else. She was mousy-looking, and wore a pale blue shirt and jeans. Her hands grasped the wheels of her chair. In her lap was a loop of crewel, half finished, in bright colours. I could not see what it was going to be as yet. But it looked good.

They all looked at me expectantly. Clearly I was required to make the introductions.

'Hello, I'm Corinna, and I live here. I'm the local baker. If you like bread, or bready products of any kind, please ask me. And you are…?'

'We're actors,' announced the tallest of the five youths in a voice brimming with self-assurance. A salesman's handshake was proffered, and I duly accepted it. He reeked of private school and privilege with a capital P, though he looked decent enough. Grammar rather than Scotch, I guessed. 'I'm Stephen, though I'm Trinculo for the duration. We're from Mars,' he added helpfully.

'I'll take your word for it,' I said, though I knew what he meant. Mars, also known as apartment 3B, was generally vacant. I deduced, without evidence, that it was an investment property owned by someone's parent. Probably that of Stephen Trinculo. I turned to the others.

'Luke, currently being Prospero,' said the next, encasing my hand in a slender, elegant palm. You could have fooled me, but there it was. I had it from his own exquisite lips. He was very dark-skinned and looked decidedly Caribbean, though without the dreadlocks.

Next in line was Claire, it seemed, though she introduced herself as Caliban. I was getting the idea by now. I had never imagined Caliban as short, neat and blonde, any more than I had imagined such an ethnically diverse aristocratic sorcerer, but it was evident that my horizons were going to be forcibly broadened. I suspected the presence of the late Bertolt Brecht in somebody's dramatic studies.

Then there was Sam (presumably Samantha, though one never really knows): tall, slender, and olive-skinned. 'I'm Ariel,' she explained. 'We've moved in here while we're rehearsing *The Tempest*.' She exchanged glances with the others then said, 'Would you like to come to a rehearsal? We're doing act 2, scene 2 this afternoon.'

'I would be delighted,' I said, curious to know what brave new world was this they were inventing. 'Where and when?'

'Mars, four o'clock?'

'I'll be there.'

I turned to the last of our newcomers, sitting up in a wheelchair against the wall. 'Hello,' I said. 'I don't think we've met.'

She shook her head.

'Her name is Philomela,' said Meroe quietly. 'She is unable to speak. She's staying with Therese and her friend.'

I looked questioningly at Philomela, who nodded. She had short, dark, bobbed hair and beautiful brown eyes which looked intelligent and perceptive.

'Would you care to join your friends?' I asked her.

She nodded again. I opened the door and wheeled her inside next to Therese.

'Well, people,' I said to the actors, 'I'm afraid there's nothing much to see. The police are on their way and until they've done their bit they'll want to keep the crime scene as clear of people as is reasonable.'

'Is anyone hurt?' Claire asked. 'We heard the alarm go off, so we left the play and came to see if anyone needed help.'

'I'm glad you did,' I told them. 'Did you hear or see anything apart from the alarm?'

Apparently they hadn't. 'Well, in that case, as soon as we know anything ourselves, we'll let you know. All I can say is that we appear to have a mysterious intruder who is being held under guard in the parlour. And that's all I know. Splendid of you to be doing Shakespeare. Well done. All right, let's bring the curtain down on this act, yes?'

At that moment the intercom buzzer sounded. 'On second thoughts, could one of you go down and open the front door? If it's a police officer, let them in.'

'And if it isn't?' Claire wanted to know.

I was going to say 'Hit them with a brick,' but you never know if new acquaintances are going to take you literally. Instead I pressed the speaker. 'Who is that?' I enquired.

'Detective Senior Constable White, as requested. Corinna, let me in, will you? It's like a pizza oven out here.'

'I'll go,' said Meroe, and disappeared down the stairs.

The actors exited stage left, and within the apartment all was quiet. Presently, up the stairs came the awful majesty of the law, in the form of Detective Senior Constable Letitia White, accompanied by a whipcord figure whose identity badge proclaimed her to be Det Constable Helen Black. She refrained from introducing herself, but contrived to project an atmosphere of calm authority. I liked her slender face and short black curls, and her deep brown eyes. They were in standard summer plain clothes: hovering somewhere between Italian Bespoke and Maison Target. Matching summer slacks (grey), blouses (ecru), jackets (oyster), and sensible flat shoes (slate). There was a definite statement of Grey in their attire, and their faces matched their outfits. They nodded politely, but they didn't seem all that pleased to see me.

Philomela: When they took me to hospital, they said I wouldn't be able to see again. My glasses were destroyed. But when I got new ones I could see perfectly. And I found I could read. Then they told me I'd never be able to walk again. And I can, in a way. And they told me I'd never speak again. And it's true I cannot speak, nor write. Not yet. And that is the worst loss of all. When you are in a wheelchair and you have aphasia, people think you are an idiot. But while I may be rendered dumb, I am no fool. And I will find a way to tell my story.

Chapter Seven

The god of my idolatry.
—William Shakespeare, *Romeo and Juliet*, Act 2, Scene 2

I looked around for Meroe, wanting moral support, but she had disappeared. I suspect she has access to secret dimensions and can come and go as she pleases.

I opened the door to the parlour to find the scene unchanged. Trudi, Anwyn and Therese looked like the Three Fates. Anwyn even had the shears of Atropos, and was holding them meaningfully. In the corner of the room, Philomela sat unnoticed in her wheelchair. She was hunched up, but taking it all in. None of them took their eyes off the youth on the floor. Remarkably, he still had not moved.

Letitia took in the scene with a glance, and gestured to an empty sofa.

'You may as well sit in on this, Corinna. I'd rather have you where I can see your hands above the table. All right. Whose apartment is this, for starters?'

'Professor Monk's,' I answered. 'He is currently upstairs in Minerva—that's 4B—being attended to by Mrs Dawson.'

The detectives exchanged a glance, and Helen left to interview the victim of the incursion. Letitia glared down at the figure on the carpet.

'All right, son. What's your story? What the hell is this about?'

The youth goggled at her. His pale lips opened, but no sounds emerged. Nothing, in fact, but a rasping choke. His eyes were wide and terrified. Letty White looked at me. 'Is this bloke armed?'

'I really don't think so,' I said. 'He looks frightened.'

'Good. Can you hear me, son? Here's what I want you to do. If you can manage to sit on the floor with your hands above your head, I'd like some answers to some questions. If you're a good boy, I won't even handcuff you. If you do anything I don't like the looks of, this lady here is probably going to stick a fork in you, so I think you're going to be good. What do you think?'

Trudi grasped the fork meaningfully, but lowered it so the tines rested on the carpet. Not for the first time, I was quietly pleased that Letitia's gun—if she indeed had one—was well out of sight. I didn't think we'd even need Trudi's gardening fork, but you never knew.

The youth uncoiled himself slowly, as if everything hurt. It probably did, though I wondered why. Surely the peaceable and gentle professor hadn't belted him? Here was a mystery over and above how he had come to be here at all. He sat himself in a morose little huddle in the middle of the carpet and stared at his shoes. Battered runners, with laces coming undone. He held both hands to his hoodie for a moment. Splitting headache, I diagnosed. There was a hint of St Sebastian awaiting the receipt of his fourteenth arrow. He shook his head, allowing the hood to fall to his shoulders. Unkempt black hair straggled down the back of his neck. He smelt of terror, dirt and something else I couldn't get a handle on. As requested, he clasped his long, grimy fingers on top of his head.

His eyes darted around the room. Take away the dirt and the fear and he might have been beautiful. Surrounded by malevolent women as he was, it might well be that Letty White was the least scary person in the room. Again his mouth opened, but no sounds came out.

Letitia rolled her eyes. 'Have any of you got a bottle of water? I don't want anyone going into the kitchen yet.'

Trudi had a spray-nozzle water-bottle tucked into her belt. I recognised it at once. She used it to spray delicate shoots. I hoped she hadn't put any fertiliser in it. She handed it to the youth, who helped himself to several sprays' worth of refreshment. He handed the bottle back to Trudi warily, still mesmerised by the gardening fork apparently.

Letitia fixed him with a piercing eye and said, 'Okay, son, what's your name?'

He flinched as if someone had flicked a paper pellet at him. 'Jordan King. I—'

And that appeared to be it for the present. Something was happening in his throat, but no more sounds emerged. He seemed to be trying to swallow a cricket ball, and failing.

Letitia White's voice grew softer, as if she were trying to entice a twitchy stallion out of its stall and into harness. 'Look, Jordan, this isn't a proper interview. We're not at that stage yet at all. We're just talking. All that formal stuff happens down at the station. I can arrest you right now if you like, but I'm beginning to think you want to be helpful. You're just a bit embarrassed by all this, aren't you? Was it all your idea, or did you have a mate to help you?'

His head shook violently. 'No! I'm alone. No one else was here.'

She almost purred. 'See? You can talk, can't you, Jordan? Now, why did you pick this apartment in particular? Did you try every door until you found one that was open?'

'No. Just this one. I found the door open.'

'And what were you looking for, Jordan? Money? Easily convertible goods?'

Head shake. 'No. I'm not a thief.'

'You could have fooled me. And do you know who lives here?'

That got a reaction. Jordan's long, oval face flooded rose, and his eyes positively flickered with lightning. 'A heretic.'

'I see. Any particular heresy you have in mind, or are you just generally hunting for heretics you like the look of?'

My breath shortened. I assumed that Letitia was making a joke, but it seemed to have got in amongst him. Surely not? Does anyone *really* expect the Spanish Inquisition?

'Just this one. He has something that doesn't belong to him. I came looking for it.'

'And then? How did you finish up on the floor?'

'I don't know. I think someone hit me.'

Ms White looked meaningfully around the room, and we all shook our heads. 'No, I don't think so,' I suggested. 'Any of us might have done that, if we'd seen him menacing our dear friend. But we really didn't.'

'Jordan, stay quite still. I want to look at your head. You were wearing your hoodie when you came in, were you?' Nod. She leant over him, examining his head and the interior of the hood. Both were marked with blood. While Letty White looked around the room, I took a closer look at our intruder. He was far from clean. But there was more than grime in there. He bowed his head, and he seemed to be praying. I leant a little closer and saw that inside his jacket was far more chest hair than a youth his age could possibly possess. A distressing miasma began to fill the room. From within that hoodie arose a reek like the interior of Count Dracula's underpants. If that was what I thought it was...

Meanwhile Letitia found what she was looking for on the low coffee table: a smear of dark blood staining one of the corners. I hadn't noticed it before. She turned to Jordan. 'Might you have slipped over, do you think?'

'Yeah, maybe. I don't remember anything except being hit over the head.'

DSC White looked at the carpet. It was securely fastened to the floor.

'May I?' I put in.

Letitia nodded.

'Is it possible you tripped over a cat?'

'Maybe. I remember there was a cat.'

I nodded. This seemed only too likely. I was glad that Nox had survived the encounter unharmed.

'So you possibly tripped over a cat and hit your head on the table there.' Letitia pointed, then pulled out her radio and walked to the side of the room, muttering into it. Then she turned back to the youth. 'What were you looking for, Jordan? This thing you claim doesn't belong to the person who lives here?'

'It's a book.'

All the blood must have drained out of my face, because I saw Letitia White give me a penetrating stare. This was definitely Not Good News. I had tampered with a crime scene, and the one thing I had thought could not possibly be relevant to the investigation had turned out to be crucial. How could I possibly have known that?

There was a soft knock at the door, and presently Professor Monk was with us again, accompanied by Detective Constable Helen. He was still dressed as before, but carried his *déshabillé* with studied nonchalance.

'Professor Monk.' Letitia indicated the seated Jordan. 'Can you imagine what this young man might possibly be trying to burgle your flat for?'

I noticed that the rosy blush on Jordan's face had mutated into a glare of silent hatred.

The Professor blinked benignly. 'I'm sorry, but I haven't the foggiest. Perhaps he can enlighten us, hmm?'

'Well?' Letitia prompted.

'He knows what it is,' Jordan growled. His lips had peeled back from his dazzling white teeth in a snarl. I hoped he wasn't turning canine on us; we were most of us cat people in Insula.

'Well, no, young man, I'm afraid I don't.'

The youth almost howled with anguish. 'Don't lie to me! You've got something that belongs to the Church! You should give it back!'

'Ah, you mean this?' Professor Monk held up a small USB stick. Thank the goddess for that. I was filled with admiration for him. With a little creative misdirection he had saved his manuscript from confiscation, and got me off the hook as well. Without even looking at me, he turned to Ms White. 'I carry it with me all the time, you know. And despite what this deluded youth appears to think, if it belongs to anyone at all, it would be the University of Tel Aviv. It is the Gospel of St Joseph of Arimathea. Or so we think. We don't precisely know yet, but it's all very exciting. I'm having such fun with it.'

Jordan gave him a Torquemada look of utter loathing. 'It is full of erroneous doctrine!' he protested.

I kept having visions of Michael Palin in his red robe, mugging for the camera with Diabolical Acting.

Professor Monk gave him a considering look. 'And how would you know that, young man, hmm? Do you read Ancient Greek? Latin? Hebrew? Aramaic?'

'I can read Latin.'

'*Ain tu? Mirabile dictu.*' He scanned Jordan's face for a moment then shook his head. 'No, you probably wouldn't know that. And who sent you to my apartment? The Dominicans? I doubt that. They're rather keen on learning these days, you know.'

Jordan relapsed into obstinate silence, and Letitia White gestured angrily. 'All right, this is getting a bit too mystical for my liking. I'm sorry, Professor, but I'll have to take that USB away as evidence. You will get it back. And I'm sending for the SOCOs, the scene-of-crime officers. This isn't just a normal break-in anymore. Is there somewhere you could go until they've finished here?'

'But of course,' said Mrs Dawson. Though uninvited to our little conference, she had nevertheless materialised at the appropriate juncture. 'Do please join me in Minerva. I shall put the kettle on. I think tea all around might be just the thing.'

'Before you go,' interposed Letty. 'Professor?' She held up a small plastic ziplock bag. 'The memory stick?'

'Ah, of course!' Professor Monk handed over the USB, and DSC White sealed the bag.

'All right—Helen, could you stay here until the SOCOs arrive? Jordan, you're coming down to the station with me. When we get there, you'll make a full statement, sign it, and show me some ID—which you had better have on you, by the way. And then... well, we'll see, won't we? Be good and I might even let you go home today.'

'K.'

As Jordan King was escorted down the stairs by the stern detective senior constable, we trooped up the stairs to Mrs Dawson's apartment. I looked back to see Detective Constable Helen Black standing in front of the open door like Cerberus guarding the gates of hell. All she was lacking were the two extra heads.

When we were comfortably ensconced in apartment 4A, Dion Monk looked at me with a confiding eye and held up one finger. 'Now that our friends have departed...' He grinned.

I held my breath in anticipation.

'I do have some news for you about our little friend.'

'Do tell,' I urged.

He leant comfortably against Mrs Dawson's arm and nodded. 'I thought he looked familiar, but I couldn't track down the memory at first. But I seem to recall he was in one of my first-year classes. Most of one's first-year cohorts come and go, passing by like the idle winds, but a few stick in the memory. Jordan is one of them. A most conceited boy: quarrelsome and argumentative. I was obliged to reprove him on one or two occasions.'

'That must have been a few years ago,' I pointed out. 'You've retired from teaching.'

'Yes, it would have been a few years ago. But I'm sure I've seen him somewhere more recently. Perhaps when I gave a public lecture last year about the Dead Sea Scrolls.'

'Did you mention anything about the Gospel of St Joseph?' I asked.

He blinked. 'I may have done. That would explain his uncalled-for irruption into our lives, perhaps?'

'Except that we still have no idea why he thinks you're a heretic, do we?'

'I fear not.' I wasn't sure why, but a certain gleam in the Professor's mild and gentle eye made me think that he knew more about this than he was letting on. I let it pass. After all, it was his project. And his burglary.

Mrs Dawson clasped his arm. 'Never mind, dear. Doubtless we shall find out in good time.' And she poured the tea.

Philomela: When Therese asked me if I wanted to come stay with her, I nodded as vigorously as I could. What I wanted to do was to shout: YES, OF COURSE! Because I've heard about this Corinna Chapman. She solves mysteries and I wish she would solve mine. But for that I will need to speak—and for now all I can do is sew.

Well, if Corinna can't help me, perhaps that is the answer. When we have finished the Battle of Maldon embroidery, I will begin a new design. I will make an embroidery about what happened to me and show it to the police. It's been done before. There was a medieval role player in Sydney who made one to describe what happened to him at his university. It's beautiful, and terrible. His church should die of shame for letting that happen to him. We're Greeks. We don't let our priests do that. One whiff of scandal and the priest is sent away to a monastery, like the one on Mount Athos. But his embroidery helped my friend Gary, even though the priests died before they could be punished properly.

So, if I cannot speak, I will do that. But if I should recover my voice, well, I will shout my story with all the rage that is trapped within me. I will be furious. For a long time.

Chapter Eight

The fringed curtains of thine eye advance
and say what thou seest yond.
—William Shakespeare, *The Tempest*, Act 1, Scene 2

By now, I'd pretty much had enough for one day. I thanked Mrs Dawson for the tea and returned to my own apartment, hoping to find Daniel within.

Disappointed, I checked my phone. One unread message, from my dearest beloved. I scanned it hungrily.

Expect me after 4, ketschele.

It was now three forty-two p.m. My heart quickened—then I recalled that I had promised to sit in on the actors' rehearsal today. Perhaps they wouldn't mind if I stayed for only half an hour. That would be long enough for me to get some idea about them. We lived in very close quarters here at Insula, and I liked to have a sense of the measure of the men and women within our midst. Reluctantly, I texted Daniel back.

I'll be busy till 5.

I wanted a drink now. But virtuously deciding to forgo my G and T until Daniel's arrival, I opened the fridge door and took inventory.

I felt against my knee the gentle headbutt of Horatio, who'd decided that he'd like a look too. Reading from top to bottom I found the following: butter, cheese, brandy (what was that doing in my fridge?), eggs, cream, milk, bacon, creamed corn, half an onion, dejected ham, depressed tomatoes, suicidal spring onions, a sobbing remnant of chutney in a sad little jar, and precisely three beans. I wondered if I could make a three-bean salad out of them. This had been one of the many culinary banes of my girlhood, thanks to the over-optimistic kitchen habits of my tree-hugging parents.

On the very bottom shelf I found a sealed plastic dish containing leftover roast leg of lamb. I unpeeled the lid and inspected the interior, while Horatio looked at me with a wild surmise. His expressive tail flicked upwards, and he meowed a lot: just cut me some of that intoxicating meat and I'll let you have the rest.

This sounded like a deal I could live with. I began to slice the meat. One for you, one for me, and three for the pot. Soon the leg bone gleamed white in the afternoon sunshine. I watched Horatio settle down on the kitchen floor to give the lamb his full attention. What could I make for dinner with these scraps and remnants? I recalled one of my grandmother's favourite recipes. 'Never waste food!' she had admonished me. 'When it looks like all you have is leftovers and ingredients, cook them up together.' Grandma's pot-luck, I said silently. This one is for you.

I chopped, sliced, diced and excavated, and soon my big pot was nearly filled. I ground pink rock salt and black pepper on top with nutmeg and allspice, and placed it on the stove with the heat on low and the lid firmly covering it, so that Horatio would not be able to assist me any further. By now he had slipped away to wash his paws and radiate general pleasure from his favourite chair. I reached into my storage pantry, pulled out a picnic basket and filled it with sourdough, cheese, the gin bottle, sliced lemon, tonic, and a small portable ice box.

It was twenty past four. My esky would be fine for the half-hour I was intending to spend with the actors, I decided.

Back downstairs I went to the door of Mars. I rang the bell, and the summons was answered by Luke, who wore a tight-fitting plain white T-shirt which showed off his muscles to excellent effect. I could sense him noticing my admiration. He didn't seem to mind. 'Hi, Corinna,' he said in a bass sort of voice. 'I'm not in this scene, so I'm on Door instead. Come and watch.'

I caught my breath. I had been expecting just a plainclothes run-through rehearsal with books or scripts. What I saw was a darkened room with one brilliant spotlight. It certainly hurt my eyes to look at it. I looked at the floor instead. Wriggling slightly inside a voluminous black cape appeared to be two bodies, giggling. Four shapely legs protruded from the cape. They were moving in a highly suggestive manner. A clear contralto voice announced itself, and Sam entered, wearing jeans and a black leather jacket and carrying a box of cask wine under one arm.

'*I shall no more to sea, to sea, here shall I die ashore.*' She stared down at the bodies, did a double-take, blinked, and muttered: '*This is a scurvy tune to sing at a man's funeral. Well, here's my comfort.*' She pretended to drink from the cask, and blinked again as the bodies on the floor continued to wriggle. Then she began to sing in a deeper pitch, tenor heading towards baritone:

> *The master, the deck-washer, the boatswain, and I,*
> *The gunman and his friend*
> *We loved Moll, Meg, Marian, and Margery*
> *But none of us cared for Kate.*
> *Kate had a gutter mouth—*

Sam paused as renewed giggles erupted from beneath the coat. Another double-take, then the song resumed. I saw Luke press a button somewhere and accordion music played in the background as Sam continued:

> *Would cry to a sailor, 'Go hang!'*
> *She loved not the savour of tar nor of pitch,*
> *Yet a tailor might scratch her where'er she did itch.*
> *Then to sea, boys, and let her go hang!*

Another pause as Sam looked down at the bodies in the cape, and poked experimentally at one of the protruding legs. Wriggling of some sort was still happening. She shook her head and continued. *'This is a scurvy tune too. But here's my comfort.'* Another pretend drink, and an agonised cry came from within the cape.

'Do not torment me. Oh!'

Sam knelt down and made a dumbshow of elaborately counting the four legs. *'What's the matter? Have we devils here?'*

'Cut!' Luke called out. He switched off the spotlight and raised the lights in the room. The cape unrolled to reveal Stephen, wearing jocks and a white T-shirt, and a grinning Claire dressed in black underwear.

Luke put his hands on his hips and glared at them. 'I'm really not sure about this scene at all, Stephen.'

Stephen stood up, grinned complacently, and watched as Claire wrapped the cape around her body. It was a very attractive body, I had to admit. He appealed to me with arms outspread. 'For an Australian audience, you can't avoid thinking of Caliban as Indigenous. We're trying to deal with themes of exploitation here.'

'Without having me as the token blackfella, because I'm not interested,' Luke put in. 'And yes, I totally get that we're having a serious nod towards sexual exploitation on top of all the other forms of exploitation the First-Worlders inflict on Caliban. Just no.'

I looked at Claire, who shrugged. 'I don't know about that. It works for me. First I get friendly, then I get drunk, then I get angry.'

Sam laughed. 'Don't forget you start angry.'

At once Claire's eyes flashed, and she all but spat the following:

> *All the infections that the sun sucks up*
> *From bogs, fens, flats, on Prosper fall and make him*
> *By inchmeal a disease! His spirits hear me*
> *And yet I needs must curse.*

Sam nodded. 'You see? You're making it too complex. It's an interesting idea, but it makes the themes too muddled. Just stick to drunkenness and power plays. Also, you're upstaging me. No one likes being upstaged.'

I remembered something from our first introduction. 'Sam, I thought you were Ariel?'

She grinned. 'I'm doubling Stephano at the moment. I think this could work.'

Stephen laughed. It was a good-humoured laugh: complacent but equable. 'We don't have a director, either. Whoever isn't onstage gets to direct. I like the idea. Look, we're short of money for this production, so we're trying to do it as a four-hander. If we can raise some more, we can afford more cast members. We're still thinking that over. Okay, we leave the sexual overtones out? What do you think? Long shorts? I think we need the bare legs.'

Luke rubbed his chin. 'Yes, we do. Frayed cuffs, just below the knee?'

'For both of us?' Claire nodded. 'I've got some jeans I can cut down.'

'Sure.' Luke switched on the spotlight again. 'This one's borrowed from the theatre department, by the way. A lot of actors rehearse in normal light and get thrown by the reality of spotlights. We're getting used to doing it as though we were in the theatre. Okay, roll the scene again, but lose the sexual politics. Go!'

He brought the house lights down, and Claire began by slinging on a sizeable backpack and grimacing. Her face grew more pointed, and her eyes flashed.

> *All the infections that the sun sucks up*
> *From bogs, fens, flats, on Prosper fall and make him*
> *By inchmeal a disease! His spirits hear me*
> *And yet I needs must curse. But they'll nor pinch,*
> *Fright me with urchin-shows, pitch me i' th' mire,*
> *Nor lead me like a firebrand in the dark*
> *Out of my way, unless he bid 'em. But–*

She paused, flinging the pack to the floor with a thump of frustration. In a more moderated tone she continued:

> *For every trifle are they set upon me,*
> *Sometime like apes that mow and chatter at me,*
> *And after bite me, then like hedgehogs which*
> *Lie tumbling in my barefoot way and mount*
> *Their pricks at my footfall. Sometime am I*
> *All wound with adders who with cloven tongues*
> *Do hiss me into madness.*

Enter Stephen, still in his jocks and T-shirt. Claire flinched, and continued:

> *Lo, now, lo! Here comes a spirit of his, and to torment me*
> *For bringing wood in slowly. I'll fall flat.*
> *Perchance he will not mind me.*

She lay down, wrapped herself in her cape, and was still.

Stephen delivered his lines with a casual air, speaking easily and well. Then he wrapped himself in Caliban's cape and he too lay decorously still. I had to admit Luke was right. With added concupiscence the scene had been uncomfortably wrong. Funny, yes. But not in a good way.

The scene wended its way: fast-paced but with appropriate pauses. When Sam reached the line *Can he vent Trinculos?* she held up both Claire's legs and shook her head slowly in bewilderment. I laughed. It was impossible not to. Claire edged out from under the cape and faced me.

> *These be fine things, an if they be not sprites.*
> *That's a brave god and bears celestial liquor.*
> *I will kneel to him.*

Back she went to pay homage to the demigods of cask wine, and I watched, fascinated. All three were natural actors: far better than the student performers I remembered from productions run by friends at uni. Attendance was compulsory, but it gave little pleasure at the time. I noted also that the soundtrack was continuous now, with sea sounds and the odd crack of thunder. I presumed that lightning would be added, if funds permitted. But Claire was stealing the show. Her desperate vulnerability was poignant as she uttered the lines:

> *I'll show thee every fertile inch o' th' island.*
> *And I will kiss thy foot. I prithee, be my god.*

All the more so for her state of comparative undress. I saw whence had come the idea of sartorial vulnerability, but Luke and Sam were right. The infra-cape cuddles would have got laughs, but discordant ones. The scene wound to its conclusion, the spotlight went off, Luke turned up the living-room lights and looked searchingly at me.

'What did you think, Corinna?'

'Excellent! You're doing brilliantly, all of you.'

There was a general easing of tension all around the room.

I had to say something like that anyway, but I must have carried enough conviction to put their minds at ease.

Claire and Stephen unselfconsciously resumed their jeans and they sat around in armchairs, talking over the minutiae of the scene. I tuned out a little, looking around the apartment. Serious money had gone into interior decoration. There were expensive-looking prints and artworks on the walls. The kitchen, visible at the far end of the expansive lounge room, was straight out of *My Kitchen Rules*. The couch looked big and comfortable enough to be a party venue all by itself. I felt emboldened to put the question to Stephen. 'This is a very impressive place. Is it yours?'

He grinned. 'No chance. It belongs to my father. He lives out in the Western District, but he comes up for football finals and the Melbourne Cup. He said we could use it while we were rehearsing.'

It sounded like Daddy was a man with more money than he knew what to do with. Yet had they not said they were short of cash? Perhaps this was the extent of Daddy's generosity.

I stood up. 'Look, that was brilliant. I have to go, I'm afraid, but thanks for the invitation. That was seriously good.'

They made appropriately modest noises and I made my way back to my apartment. While that had been an enlightening experience, it didn't cast any light on our manifold mysteries. Our lost soldier and his missing dog. The break-in at Dion Monk's apartment, the kerfuffle at Café Pandamus. I stared at my hamper. Being unenlightened makes me hungry and thirsty. I was tempted to start without Daniel. Just then, the door opened behind me, and there he was at last: tall, muscular, and smelling of lime and frankincense. I threw both arms around his muscular chest and felt his delicious lips on mine. 'I am so pleased to see you,' I breathed into the curls over his ear. 'I have had A Day.'

He did not ask any questions, but flicked his eyebrows upwards.

'Oh yes! Please. Ceres will be beautiful at this hour.' I grabbed my keys in one hand, and my basket with the other. 'Horatio? Would you like to come too?'

Curled up on his chair, my beautiful cat blinked at me. He stretched out all four paws and alighted with care onto the floor. The three of us made our way to the lift. Horatio sat in front of it, as if willing the doors to open with his expressive whiskers. The doors slid open soundlessly—not trusting to whiskers alone I had pressed the button—and he allowed us to enter first. Then he parked himself just next to my feet, placing one forepaw on my slippers. Just to make sure I didn't try anything too adventurous.

It was uncomfortably hot at street level, but up on the roof light breezes played around the shrubs and pots. Horatio ambled up to the mint, gave it a solid examination and looked back at me hopefully. I really must see about getting a catnip plant for him. This herb, he seemed to be telling me, is almost right. But it's not good enough. *Come on, human! Do something about this inexplicable oversight.* Having expressed his feelings, he progressed slowly through the garden. Sometimes he stood up on his back paws to smell the flowers. There were roses (four different shades of red and a few fragrant whites), sweet peas, blood-red fuchsias, geraniums, pelargoniums, marigolds, tomatoes, and basil. Having given them all the paw-print of approval, he sauntered into the parsley forest. It really was a forest. We had started with a few small plants and with very little encouragement it had become our own little wilderness. Umbelliferous seedpods crowned most of the saplings, but there was plenty of broadleaf left. I handed Daniel my picnic basket.

'Could you handle this, my beloved? I need more herbs for dinner.'

When I had returned with handfuls of mint, parsley, and basil, Daniel had organised two gin and tonics with ice cubes. I had packed my two biggest matching tumblers, handmade by a medieval-inspired potter. After a long day's labour the last thing I want is to be footling around with dainty glasses. We sat down on adjoining seats and sipped contentedly, inhaling the aromatic spices, the crisp lemon juice, the quinine-flavoured soda, and the pleasant, cushioning embrace of high-quality alcohol. We munched bread, cheese and olives, and admired the perfect afternoon. Every now and again Horatio brushed his tail against us, and we took turns to caress his cheeks and under his chin. He accepted morsels of cheese and lay down underneath my chair.

'*Nu*, what sort of day have you had?' Daniel enquired at length.

I told him, omitting nothing. His eyes registered surprise, but he did not interrupt until my tale wound to its conclusion. 'So we think the maniac who broke into Professor Monk's apartment is a religious fanatic who's after the Professor's notes. What's so important about the Gospel of St Joseph, anyway? Assuming that's what it is.'

'I've had a look at it,' Daniel said. 'How these scrolls work is that someone starts at one end, someone else starts in the middle, and what you get is a compilation of different versions of the same stories, often in different languages. I can manage the Hebrew bits and it's interesting reading. We have our own views about the carpenter's son, which I might tell you about some other time.'

'Did you see anything in it that might inspire burglary?' I wanted to know.

'It depends. Could your young man be a Palestinian sympathiser? Some of the local Arabs in Jerusalem want to lay claim to everything historical. I think their idea is to airbrush Jewishness from Israel.'

'Good luck with that.'

'We just laugh and tell them no thanks. When the Dead Sea Scrolls were found, the Vatican wanted to hang on to them all and control the release in case inconvenient facts might arise.'

'So what did Israel do?'

He smiled. 'We talked to them for a while, but they were quite intransigent. So we decided to release everything to anyone who wanted it. I thought the Catholics had got over it. A fundamentalist Protestant, maybe? What did he look like?'

'I don't know. But he smelt bad. And I'm not sure, but I think he was wearing a hair shirt.'

His eyes opened wide. 'That really is unusual. Did he mention heresy, by any chance?'

'He talked about erroneous doctrine,' I recalled. 'And he did call the Professor a heretic.'

'Catholic, then. If he really was wearing a hair shirt, that makes him a very unusual Catholic, though. I've met quite a few, and not one of them would wear anything like that.'

'Do we still have a Spanish Inquisition?'

He laughed, but with an undertone of caution. 'Once upon a time that was nothing to joke about. These days it's called the Congregation for the Doctrine of the Faith. The worst they do is post people to unpleasant parishes and tell them they're not allowed to preach anymore.'

'Maybe he's a splinter group of one, like the People's Front of Judaea? But really: What could there be in this scroll that would upset anyone now?'

'Would it surprise you to know that Jesus was almost certainly married?'

This sounded a bit Dan Brown to me. 'To Mary Magdalene?'

'Why not? She does kiss him a lot in your Bible. And some of the Dead Sea Scrolls are a bit more forthcoming.'

'Are we talking about children as well?'

'What I've read seems to suggest so. And yes, our *Da Vinci Code* guy seems to have been right. Mary Magdalene went with St Joseph of Arimathea to the south of France. Though I doubt that the Merovingian kings were descended from them.'

'That does seem a bit weird. Look, I'm not really any sort of expert on Christianity. It didn't play much of a role in my life except by accident. But does it matter if Jesus was married and had children?'

He thought about this for a while. '*Ketschele,* how likely do you think it is that a man could reach the age of thirty back then and not be married? Unless he was an Essene.'

'Who were they?'

'The people who wrote the Dead Sea Scrolls were Essenes. They were separatists and mystics, and what we know about them is not all that pleasant. Although there is a definite suggestion that Yeshua—Jesus to you—might have been one of them. When we hear that he spent forty days and nights in the Wilderness, he probably went to stay with them. Think Haredi on steroids. They wouldn't even share the same city with women, which explains why they finished up around the Dead Sea.'

'And also why they died out?'

'That too. But we knew about them before the Scrolls, from Josephus. He was a contemporary historian. He was the only survivor of Masada, and managed to talk his way out of it.'

'Masada? Sorry, I think I know who the Haredi are. What was Masada?'

My love grimaced. 'One thing we really learned about Imperial Rome is that you don't mess around with them. The last Jewish revolt took three years to quell, and Vespasian used four legions to crush it. The last fortress to fall was Masada, and all nine hundred and sixty defenders killed themselves rather than surrender to be crucified.'

'All except this Josephus character?'

'All except him. He became a friend of Titus—Vespasian's son—and wrote two books called *Antiquities of the Jews* and *The Wars of the Jews*. He says that some of the Essenes weren't so anti-woman. Jesus could easily have been one of them. Anyway, I can imagine that some Christians would be very angry at the idea.'

It was my turn to mull over this. 'But it's been suggested before, surely? And not just by Dan Brown?'

'It is…puzzling. Anyway, the Gospel of St Joseph is probably by St Joseph of Arimathea, who put Jesus into his own tomb. I didn't know he'd written a Gospel, but Biblical scholarship isn't my forte. Anything new about Biblical times is probably bound to upset somebody. Especially someone as inflammable as our little friend Jordan.'

At that moment, the lift doors opened and Meroe wafted towards us. It is what she does, as if her feet are only touching the ground for the look of the thing. She was wrapped in a blue silk shawl with white clouds painted on it. 'Blessed be,' she said with a beatific smile.

I certainly felt blessed, with my Daniel at my side and my adored cat asleep under my chair.

'I want herbs for cleansing the Professor's apartment,' she explained.

We watched her stately progress as she gathered all manner of herbs I knew and some I didn't even know were here. She put them into a small calico bag and came to sit with us. I offered her the gin bottle, but she shook her head.

'Meroe,' I said, 'do you have any idea why anyone should want to steal Professor Monk's manuscript? We've talked it over and we're still confused.'

She folded her neat hands in her lap and closed her eyes. 'The Rom have many stories about Jesus that you may not know. We left India long ago and went to Egypt. Then we came to Palestine. A gypsy boy is supposed to have stolen the nails for Jesus's crucifixion. Unfortunately, they found some more. But we have His blessing for that.'

'Would it surprise you to know that Jesus may have been married to Mary Magdalene?'

She looked at me with her dark eyes unblinking. 'Of course they were married. After Jesus was taken up, St Joseph took her with him. She had one child, and was carrying another unborn. They went to France, and we went with him. Have you not heard this before?'

Daniel shook his head. 'This is gypsy lore, known to all your people?'

'Not to all, perhaps. Why? Is it important?'

'It may be. What else can you tell us, Meroe? It would seem that there are more stories than we knew about Jesus of Nazareth.'

She closed her eyes for a moment. 'Have you heard the tale of the robin?'

We shook our heads.

'When Jesus was on the cross, a robin flew down from a sycamore tree and tried to pick out the thorns from His forehead. But the crown of thorns was buried too deep, and the red blood stained the robin's breast. And that is why all robins have red breasts, in memory of the kind bird. Robins may not be hunted, for any reason. The fowler may take any bird save the hawk, the eagle, and the robin.'

'No, I never heard that either.' Daniel bowed his head, and Meroe stood up.

'I think the police must be done with Professor Monk's apartment by now,' she said. 'Perhaps we should go there now, and I will perform the cleansing ritual.'

Daniel went with Meroe while I escorted Horatio back to my own apartment. I had just put the herbs I'd gathered in my pot and settled Horatio down with some kitty dins when my phone rang. It was Daniel.

'Corinna? You'd better get up here right now.'

When I arrived, the door was flung open. Meroe, Daniel and I stared at the interior. It looked like there had been an invasion of Visigoths.

Philomela: My body hurts all the time. I'm used to it now. And while I would love to be able to dance again, I can live without that. Without my voice, though, I am utterly lost.

Chapter Nine

These violent delights have violent ends.
—William Shakespeare, *Romeo and Juliet*, Act 2, Scene 6

'Hello? Letitia? You're not going to like this, but…'

No, she didn't. Within fifteen minutes she was back, with the SOCO team and Detective Constable Helen. Surfaces were dusted for prints, disturbances examined, assurances given that none of us had tampered with the crime scene and so forth. Helen played with Nox, who was enjoying the attention and allowing his sense of personal outrage to be soothed into comfortable oblivion. Within half an hour the besuited ones had gone, together with Detective Constable Helen. Meroe too had departed. Thus far we had not gathered any more of an audience, which seemed fair enough; the residents of Insula had had enough adventures for one day. I certainly had.

Detective Senior Constable White leant against the wall of the corridor and called upon her Maker to save her.

'Corinna, this time it really wasn't our little friend Jordan—he's still in the cells. On that basis, I'm letting him go for the time being. Even if our Second Burglar is connected with Jordan, there is no way he could have told them he'd failed in his attempt. I am going to assume they're still after the same thing. Bizarre as this may seem. Now can any of you explain to me what is so special about this damned gospel? Don't tell me you've discovered the secret identity of Jesus's descendants? Please tell me this isn't a Dan Brown mystery.'

I exchanged glances with Daniel. 'I really don't know,' I confessed. 'But I'm beginning to think it might be. Why two separate burglars, at least one of whom appears to be a religious fanatic, chose today to break into the Professor's apartment to find his USB stick is more than I can understand.'

She reached into her pocket and held up the thumb drive. 'We probably won't know anything until the Professor has deciphered whatever is on here, so I'll give it back to him. And of course I'll ask everybody else in Insula all over again. But I'm assuming none of them have heard anything, since they're not here gawping. All right, carry on. You can help the Professor clean up.'

I leant on Daniel, feeling both shaken and stirred. Very soon we could hear sounds on the staircase. Then the lift purred its way upwards and the doors opened to reveal Anwyn, standing by Philomela's wheelchair. 'Hi, Corinna,' said Anwyn. 'We've just heard, and we thought we'd both help out. Therese is cooking dinner.'

I wished I was.

Mrs Dawson and the Professor entered together from the stairwell. He looked resigned, as though he'd just been invaded by Spartan hoplites for the fourth time this month and it was only to be expected. She looked furious. 'This is utterly monstrous!' she fumed, patting the Professor's arm. 'We are all going to help clean up.'

And so we did. But as my beloved began to put things back where they should be, which would be a long process, I had eyes only for Philomela. She rolled her wheelchair over to a pile of books, and leant down to pick up several old Penguin classics. I had no idea what she was doing, but her eyes were flashing like thunderbolts.

'That splendid lady detective has asked me to call her if anything is missing,' Professor Monk was saying. He took off his glasses and gave them a quick polish. 'But I don't think there is.' Eventually he too noticed Philomela, and he walked over to gaze down at the small collection she had made. 'Ah, yes, well done,' he said. 'You have collected all my Ovids. Very kind of you.'

She placed five of the six books she had garnered on one of his bookshelves. The Professor held out his hand to take the last, but she shook her head violently and began flipping through the pages. When she had found what she wanted, she held it out and jabbed her finger urgently at the text.

The Professor craned his head forward for a moment then drew in his breath sharply. 'Oh dear,' he muttered. 'Very well, my dear. Yes, I understand what you're trying to say.' He stood in front of her and reached out his right hand as if to soothe a frightened animal.

Reluctantly, she put out her own right hand, briefly squeezed the Professor's, then dropped her hand back in her lap.

'But this is going to require some careful thought and a good deal of understanding and patience from both of us,' he continued. 'Would you mind if we leave this for now? I've had several shocks today and I'm not exactly at my best. But yes, I do understand. You didn't pick up that book by chance, did you? You wish to draw my attention to the tale of Philomela, your namesake— because Philomela lost her tongue, and had to write things down to communicate with her sister Procne. Am I right?'

She nodded. The fire in her eyes had subsided to a steady gaze now.

'Very well, Miss Philomela. We shall discuss this tomorrow. Is that acceptable?'

Philomela hung her head for a moment, then nodded once more.

I exchanged glances with Anwyn, who gave a shrug of incomprehension that mirrored my own feelings. It looked as if ancient manuscripts were taking over my life. Perhaps my future was written on a copper scroll somewhere in the West Bank. I looked forward to finding it and having someone translate it for me.

Mrs Dawson decided it was time to take charge. 'Now, Professor,' she announced in her best Luncheon Is Served voice, 'I really do think that we've all had enough excitement for one day. Do, please, come and stay under my roof tonight, in case anyone else should wish to disturb your rest. Anwyn, will you take your friend back to your apartment? I will lock the door here.'

This was absolutely fine with me, and Daniel took my arm. Fortified with gin, we walked back downstairs to my apartment. I closed the door, locked it, slipped the deadlock, and put the chain on its hook. I was going to have an evening with my Daniel and I didn't care if they brought a battering ram. Then I went to my bedroom for a quick change of clothes. I wanted to surprise him.

It certainly had the desired effect. His eyes widened with delight when I re-emerged, and he kissed me, running his hand down my back as he did so. I had thrown off my street clothes and most of my underwear and attired myself in my blue, purple and gold caftan.

'This is new?' I watched his face calculating, wondering if he should have registered this creation already in his sartorial memory bank.

'Indeed it is. I made it with batik cloth presented by Jon and Kepler. I gave them some wow-wow sauce.'

'Is there really such a thing? I've read about it in Terry Pratchett's books, of course. Doesn't the Archchancellor say something about his father swearing at wow-wow sauce, and exploding after a charcoal biscuit?'

'There really is. And since Kepler is from South-East Asia, where they like their tastebuds scarified, I thought they would like it.'

'And they did?'

'Very much so. I'll be refilling the jar when I get a spare moment from burglaries and lost animals. If my kitchen explodes suddenly one day, you'll know why.'

I removed the lid from my slow-cooking pot and inhaled. The eggs were sitting on the kitchen bench in their carton, so I broke two into the pot.

'They are certainly idiosyncratic eggs,' Daniel commented. 'The yolks are different colours.' He opened the box and looked at the remaining eight spheroids. 'Different-coloured shells, too.'

'They came from named hens reared in hotel-standard accommodation,' I assured him.

'The hens really have names?'

'Oh yes. Ophelia and Juliet, apparently. And you can taste the difference.'

'And the roast lamb I see you have in the pot? Raised in a health spa, no doubt?'

'Oh yes. After all those horrible exposés of mass-produced meat, I can't even look at cheap supermarket stuff. It's more expensive, of course. But I don't care.'

He ran his finger down the side of my cheek. 'Very proper. Animals understand about being killed and eaten. But we owe them a happy life up until their unfortunate finale. Are you thinking of raising chickens in Ceres?'

I laughed, stirred the pot a few times, and began to set the table for two. 'Raising dough for the bread keeps me busy enough. But Trudi is talking about getting a hive. We shall have homegrown honey.'

Daniel sat down in his chair and shook his head. 'I wonder how Lucifer will cope with swarming bees.'

I turned off the pot, took my biggest ladle and served up two steaming, fragrant heaps of casseroled leftovers. 'We may expect the odd mishap, I expect. But Lucifer can find trouble anywhere.' I laid the plates on my table and gestured at them. 'Grandma's Pot-luck, just like Grandma used to make. I hope you like it.'

He leant forward over the table and kissed me lightly on the lips. 'It smells wonderful.' Then he ate a spoonful and smacked his lips. 'And it tastes even better.' A cook always likes an appreciative audience. He grinned at me. 'Is wow-wow sauce this good?'

'Oh yes. It's from a nineteenth-century recipe from *The Cook's Oracle*.' I consulted my internal recipe index. 'Butter, plain flour, beef stock, white vinegar, parsley, pickled cucumber, Worcestershire sauce, salt, black pepper. Oh, and English mustard.'

'Really? That alone would render it incandescent. No wonder the British built such a vast empire. Being brought up on English mustard would make anyone want to take it out on somebody else.'

We ate companionably, chatting of this and that. And we admired Horatio's casual elegance as he sauntered in, sniffed his bowl of fishy kitty dins, curled his tail around his front paws and looked up enquiringly. Daniel gave his head a friendly stroke, and raised an eyebrow.

'I think he wants mice pie,' I explained. 'I'm hoping he will accept kitty dins in lieu.'

With an all-but-audible sigh, Horatio bent his head to work. We did likewise. When our bowls were empty, I looked at Daniel. 'More?'

He shook his head. 'No, *ketschele,* I need to be light on my feet tonight. I'm off in search of Alasdair's poor little dog.'

'Any word on the streets today?'

'None. Frankly, we have too many mysteries on our hands. I'm trying to think of a connection between them, but I don't think there is.'

'I don't think so either,' I said ruefully. 'Unless—could our double burglary have anything to do with the ransomware problem at the Cafe Delicious?' I suggested.

He shook his head. 'I can't think of any reason why it should be related. There's a lot of ransomware around these days. It's usually Russians or East Europeans.'

'Other people hack computers, surely? The Chinese?'

'No. Oh, the Chinese are brilliant hackers, but they're more concerned with espionage, either industrial or political. I never heard of any of their hackers putting porn on anyone's computer. They're a bit fastidious like that. No, this says Slavic countries to me.'

'Is there a reason why they treat everyone else as prey?'

'The Pan-Slavic Brotherhood has legitimate grievances. But I can't see how our other crimes might be connected with the Russian Bloc. Surely not the break-ins. Our boy Jordan with the hair shirt is surely Catholic, isn't he?'

'I can't imagine what else he could be. But I thought Catholics were law-abiding.'

'Except the mafia, perhaps. But yes, you're right. Anglo-Catholics are frighteningly law-abiding as a rule. It's a mystery. And what is up with Philomela, I have no idea, although the good Professor seems to have an inkling. But one puzzle at a time! I need to find a dog, and quickly.'

He made as if to rise, but I put my hand on his arm. 'Could I persuade you to stay for dessert? It does go in a separate stomach, you know.'

He sat down again at once. 'Of course. What is it?'

'Wait and see.' I covered my pot and put it in the fridge, then removed a tray from the freezer and put it on the table. 'Strawberries and lemon sorbet, with a light soupçon of gin.'

He clapped his hands in delight, and I watched him eat without haste as I sampled my own bowl. I longed to take him to my bed and ravish him all night long. Sometimes on weeknights this was feasible. Usually not, since he works late hours, while mine are so early they're almost the previous night. On Friday night, however, my wonderful man, I will take you in my arms and ravish you until morning. I hope.

He stayed to wash my dishes for me, hugged me lovingly and set off on his quest of canine rescue. I considered a look at the TV, but decided against it. The world has grown so impossibly strange. I cannot be bothered with pay TV, and free-to-air is filled with depressing explosions and orange-haired clowns pretending to be world leaders. Nowadays the television is chiefly for watching DVDs. But tonight I retired to bed with the *The Healer's War*. A strange book for bedtime reading, you may say, and normally you would be right, but I was finding it oddly therapeutic. As I closed the cover and laid the book on my bedside table, I believed I understood poor Alasdair Sinclair a lot better now. I sighed contentedly as Horatio took up his customary position on my bed (curled up with his back to mine), and fell into a dreamless sleep.

Have I mentioned how my heart leaps at four a.m.? Alarm clock rings its clarion call to arms, alarm clock is flung to the carpet and trodden underfoot by somnolent baker, Horatio looks up in affront and goes back to sleep. Slippers are donned, shower administered, heavy boots booted, overalls overcalled; coffee, ovens, dough, and I experience the darkness of the soul in the early dawn, brightened only by the invincible cheerfulness of Midshipman Jason.

I was only a few minutes into my routine when there was a loud disturbance outside. Angry voices could be heard: baritone and bass. One of them sounded familiar. 'Midshipman? I'm all over dough here. Find out what's going on, will you?'

'Aye-aye, Cap'n.' He opened the street door and disappeared.

Conversation seemed to be happening, but it didn't sound dangerous. I administered kitty dins to Heckle and Jekyll, despite their low body count (no rats, three mice and something I couldn't identify and didn't want to; even the rodents were too hot to want to forage much in this weather), watched them wolf it down and saunter off, tails in air, in search of further patrons. Dawn was just glimmering in the sky above the skyscrapers, and a procession loomed dimly towards me, led by a huge, dark figure holding a smaller shape by the collar, Jason bringing up the rear.

As they paced towards me up the dim alley, I recognised the gigantic form of Ma'ani from the Soup Run, gentle enforcer to the down-and-out community of inner Melbourne. He doesn't look for trouble. Trouble just evaporates as soon as he hoves into sight. He is about nine feet tall and nearly as wide.

I turned my attention to the specimen he was escorting. Both sandshoed feet were trailing off the ground. A distressing miasma of studied unwashedness preceded him by a couple of metres. As my eyes became accustomed to the dim light I realised it was none other than our uninvited guest, Jordan King.

Philomela: At last. Somebody understands.

Chapter Ten

Thou art wedded to calamity.
—William Shakespeare, *Romeo and Juliet*, Act 3, Scene 3

There are moments when words fail me. This wasn't one of them. All the accumulated frustrations of the previous day boiled over, and I let myself go more than somewhat.

'Why, Jordan, how nice of you to drop in again. Actually, no, I don't know why I said that. I am far from pleased to see you. Is there something you forgot to do during your last visit, like turning on the fire hydrants or pouring yoghurt on my first editions? Perhaps you would like to redecorate my apartment by throwing paint on the walls and smearing apricot jam all over my carpets?' I paused for a moment. 'No, wait, that wasn't you, was it? There seems to be a queue to break into our apartments here in Insula. I suppose there's some sort of roster, is there? You and our other burglar are taking turns? Do let me know so we can accommodate you as far as is possible.' I showed him my teeth.

Since Jordan seemed neither willing nor able to say anything for himself, Ma'ani grumbled into life, like a front-end loader preparing to level a building site.

'What's this bloke doing hanging around here, Aunty Corinna?'

Ma'ani shook Jordan, as gently as possible, while still holding him well off the ground.

My unwelcome guest shivered like a sapling in a hurricane. He now resembled one of those pole-squatting Stylites who had fallen off his pillar. He still didn't speak, so Ma'ani continued in a low, menacing rumble. 'You trying to burgle our aunty's bakery, son? 'Cos if you are, I'm gonna give youse a belting. Aunty Corinna is a friend of ours. Why don't youse go and break into some rich bloke's house in Toorak? What're ya doing here, anyway?'

I could have asked Ma'ani to put Jordan down so he could explain himself, but I didn't feel like it. I was beginning to find Jordan as a hanging basket more tolerable than his previous incarnations.

Finally, he coughed into life. 'I'm here on God's work,' he gasped.

Ma'ani laughed. It was like water splashing in an underground sea cave. 'Yair, well. I'm here on God's work too, son. Feedin' the poor's what we do. What do you think you're doing that's so important?' The mighty hand waggled his captive slightly, and gently lowered him until both feet were on the footpath. But the iron grip on his hoodie, at the scruff of the neck, did not loosen.

Jordan recapitulated his sorry tale of Hunt the Heretic and Ma'ani laughed again. 'What do we do with this bloke, Aunty Corinna?'

I shook my head in frustration. 'I don't know, Ma'ani. Short of clubbing him to death, it looks like he's going to keep on coming.'

'I could cook him and eat him for you,' he suggested. 'It's no trouble, really. I could turn him into a *hangi*.'

'That is a very kind offer, Ma'ani. I'll think about it.'

Jordan unleashed a torrent of what seemed to be frenzied Latin, and Ma'ani bent his ear to listen. Then he grinned.

'Right. So yer a Catholic, are ya? You're coming with me, son. I'm taking you to see Sister Mary. She's a Catholic, too, and she's in damn big with God. Youse can explain yourself to her.'

I handed Ma'ani the sack of bread we reserved for the Soup

Run, and he hoisted it over one mighty shoulder. With the other hand, he picked up Jordan again, without any apparent effort, and carried him off into the growing dawn.

Jason and I looked at each other. My apprentice grinned at me. 'Problem solved, Captain?'

'I hope so, Midshipman. And we may as well begin with the bread. Today's specials: fig, almond, and apricot sourdough, and potato bread.' I paused, remembering where he had been yesterday. 'And you can try your hand at baklava.'

'Aye-aye, Captain!'

And so we slipped into our routine. Autopilot is a dangerous thing when surrounded by large ovens, but we did all the standard things and admired our handiwork busily turning itself into yeasty delights. The potato bread was simple enough. The fig, almond, and apricot I had done before, and I knew what changes to make so it would not get too soggy. When all the breads were well underway, I turned to my midshipman.

'Jason? Ready to show me what you learnt yesterday?'

'Yai-yai says I'm getting the hang of it,' he told me proudly.

Yai-yai was right. I admired considerably as Jason removed three sheets of filo pastry from the fridge and laid them out. I noted with approval the fact that each sheet had a damp tea towel spread over it to keep it from drying out and flaking. He combined almonds, walnuts, caster sugar, cloves, and cinnamon in a bowl, and seized a sharp knife and held it up next to his mouth. Last week I had caught him putting it between his teeth like a pirate's cutlass. I had forbidden this, and he understood why. This was his Pretend-I'm-A-Pirate moment and, so long as the gesture remained incomplete, I was okay with it. He winked, and I nodded tolerantly. He whipped off the first tea towel, smeared the surface with unsalted butter, sliced the sheet into three, and expertly shovelled on the nut mixture. Almost before I knew it, he had a huge aluminium tray filled with baklava cigars.

Removing a tray of bread, he loaded his confection into the

oven. 'Fifteen minutes, Captain,' he sang out, and I set the timer accordingly.

After that, I watched him make up a syrup with lemon zest, cinnamon sticks, cloves, sugar, and water. Finally, he produced a large plastic jar filled with crushed pistachio nuts and shook it like a maraca. 'Yai-yai says these come from Aegina,' my apprentice told me. 'They used to be pirates, but after Greek independence they decided to grow pistachios instead.'

'I'm sure their neighbours appreciated the career change,' I suggested.

When the timer went off, Jason slipped the tray from the oven, poured his syrup over the baklava and topped it with a thick dusting of pistachio crumbs.

'Most people put the pistachio in the middle,' Jason informed me. 'But Yai-yai says not to overdo it. A little pistachio goes a long way.'

I reached out for a slightly burnt one at the edge and bit into it. Feeling his eyes fixed on my face imploringly, I took my time before speaking.

'Jason, that is truly excellent,' I told him. 'It is possible that they were a little too long in the oven, but even so, I'll bet there's none left by closing time.'

'It's hard to scale up with baking time,' he commented, leaning back against the sink. His hand took another of the slightly burnt cigars and devoured it. 'Yep. Yai-yai said twelve minutes, but I thought fifteen because our ovens are bigger and I'm making more than she would. It's triple the quantity she makes. Should I have gone for twenty?'

'Too long. Maybe seventeen. But a brilliant first try, Midshipman. By the by, how are things at Cafe Delicious?'

Jason nodded. 'All right. Seventeen minutes next time. Del is fine now that their computer is clean again. Taz, Rat, and Gully took care of it.'

'Was there any indication of who was responsible?' I wanted to know.

'Nah, these guys don't leave prints. Just standard ransomware, though. Gully said he could clean it off with his eyes shut.'

This was probably true. Of the three members of Nerds Inc., Gully was the most dreamy. Of late, he seemed to be sleepwalking. The result, no doubt, of too many late nights staring at monitors, laptops and phones. Taz had decided to specialise in Android, which I assume is to do with phones. Rat had branched out into the ills and ailments of something called Ubuntu. I didn't ask. But Gully still did what Gully always did, which was to vacuum up computer viruses and malware better than anyone else. But if we didn't know where the ransomware had come from, then we didn't know if it was related to any of our other mysteries. Of which we had far too many for my liking, I thought, frowning as I recalled Jordan's reappearance.

'All right, Midshipman. Potato bread, ho!'

'Aye-aye, Cap'n.'

By one o'clock we had finished for the day. I dismissed my work-force, keeping back a dozen of Jason's baklava cigars. We had sold around fifty, but they still needed a little fine-tuning. He had gone back to see Yai-yai with two of the remaining cigars, to see what she thought of them. And I made up a platter of six and carried them to Mrs Dawson's apartment.

She answered my knock at her door, still in her dressing-gown. Well, well. Now here was an unexpected turn of events. She seemed flushed, and more relaxed than I had ever seen her. There was a certain Something in the air it seemed to me. She ushered me into the dining room and disappeared into the kitchen to make a pot of tea. Presently I was joined by Professor Monk, also in his dressing-gown, and looking complacent and happy.

'My dear, how splendid to see you looking so well,' he ventured.

'And you also,' I returned without a hint of insinuation in my voice, or so I hoped.

I laid the platter of baklava on the dining room table, and the Professor sniffed appreciatively.

'Jason's latest experiment?' he enquired.

I nodded.

'Splendid. And how are things at the Cafe Delicious?'

Before I could answer, Mrs Dawson entered with a pot of tea. She poured tea and disbursed baklava, while I brought them up to speed with yesterday's doings at the cafe. I then told them about the return of the prodigal early this morning.

Mrs Dawson pursed her lips, and Dion Monk's eyebrows raised a full centimetre. 'How extraordinary!' he exclaimed. 'What a persistent young man he is. But you say he is now neutralised as a threat to my apartment?'

'That may be so…' Mrs Dawson leant back in her chair and beamed at him. 'But let us not forget that the second burglar is still at large.'

'Indeed not,' I put in, eyeing them both. There were odd under-currents to this conversation. 'The second break-in could not possibly have been Jordan, so it is not safe for you to return to your apartment as yet.'

'Ah,' he answered mildly. 'Well, in that case, if I may trespass on your hospitality a little longer, my dear…?'

'Indeed you must. I insist upon it.'

They exchanged a look best described as melting and I had the distinct feeling that I wanted to be elsewhere, as soon as possible. However, I had one more question to put to them.

'Professor, have you had a chance to talk to Philomela?'

He shook his head. 'No—at least, I have attempted to, but all we have achieved is an agreement to speak when she feels up to it. I rather gained the impression that she is mute by means of trauma rather than disability. But that is still a formidable obstacle. When she is ready to converse with me, she will call. Until then…' He sighed. 'Oh dear. I do hope to have an end to these irruptions into our quiet, blameless lives. And this Maori enforcer? He will keep young Jordan suppressed?'

'Oh yes. Ma'ani did offer to cook him and eat him, which seemed to make an impression.'

'I remember hearing about the liberation of East Timor,' Professor Monk said. 'Apparently one of the Indonesian commanders was very unhappy about it. So the Australians crept into his tent one night and left an army badge pinned to his pillow. And because the Maori cannot help but go one better, they did what I believe is termed a creepy-crawly next night and left a knife pinned to the ground on one side of his pillow and...' He paused.

'Oh no. Really?' I could see where this was going.

'Oh yes. And a fork on the other side. I think a recent reputation for cannibalism can be very useful when used sparingly. Sister Mary might be more effective in doctrinal matters.'

'I really hope so. But all the doctrine in the world is better when bolstered with bowel-knotting fear.' I rose. 'Thank you for the tea, Mrs Dawson. I must go and rest.'

And with that, I left them to their own company, let myself into my apartment, and curled up with Horatio. I was asleep within minutes.

I woke up suddenly and uncomfortably, threshing around in the blackness. Horatio protested, and I heard him jump down onto the carpet in offended silence. I glanced at my digital clock and saw it was 2:11 a.m. What sort of time was that?

I checked my phone. Daniel had not called. No one had called. I had slept for nearly twelve hours, and theoretically I should be bounding out of bed, ready to take on the day and wrestle crocodiles if necessary. Instead, I felt as though someone had beaten me about the head with a shillelagh with nails in it.

Horatio jumped back onto the bed and mewed at me. I switched the bedside light on. Normally after such a rude awakening he would be eager to go back to sleep, but he stayed in a crouch, staring pointedly at the door. 'What's wrong, little friend?' I whispered. I touched his flanks. His whole body was tense. Quivering.

This wasn't good. I put on my dressing-gown, tied the cord around my middle and looked around for a weapon. In the absence of anything resembling a shillelagh, I grabbed a folded umbrella, grasped it firmly in my left hand and gave it a few practice twirls. My expensive girls school had provided me with many opportunities in sport and recreation. The only one I enjoyed was fencing. It had only been offered for one term, but I had taken my revenge on many of the slim bullies who were astonished to discover that the despised Fat Girl had quicker reflexes than they did, and packed a weighty left-handed punch with a foil. I often wondered if I had been responsible for fencing's removal from the curriculum. But my reflexes were still adequate, and they might be needed now, because my ears had detected stealthy movements in the next room.

And there was more. Unbelievably, I heard the sound of quiet singing, or possibly humming. It was very soft, as though someone were playing an Arabic instrument at the bottom of a very deep bathtub. The same little phrase, droning on and on but starting from a lower point each time. I froze—not out of fear, because by this point I was very angry indeed and was wanting to spread it around a little, but to await the optimum moment. When the droning hum subsided gradually into silence, I prepared to act.

Urged on silently by my cat, I paced across my bedroom carpet, opened the door and flicked on the living room light. I took in the scene with mounting alarm. My bookcase was half-empty, and books and DVDs were strewn all over the floor. Standing in the middle of the floor, holding a substantial torch in one hand, was a black-clad ninja. Black trousers, black skivvy, black mask, black slippers. Only the hands and a pair of deep brown, fathomless eyes were visible. They blinked.

'All right, Mr Ninja. Hands up!' I bellowed.

I ran across the room to stand between him and the exit. Yes, I know: the safer option would have been to encourage whoever it was to leave. But a boiling rage had erupted inside me. I had had altogether enough of this nonsense, and someone was going to be very sorry. The eyes followed mine. The chin nodded. He—I had to assume it was a he—lifted the torch and waved it in menacing circles. I slid towards him and jabbed him in the chest with the end of the umbrella. It must have hurt, for he grunted, and danced away towards the bathroom. I managed to stab him again in the side as he moved. My bathroom had a double-sided lock. If I could lure him in there I could turn the key on him and imprison him until help arrived. But his eyes flicked over the lock with the key still in it, and he pirouetted away from the door and back towards my bedroom.

'Stay out of there!' I growled. No ninja was going anywhere near my cat!

I moved to block his passage to the bedroom door, and he darted at once towards the front door. I managed to land another jab in his stomach, and he fell to the carpet. I knelt over him and reached for the ninja mask, and what I saw beneath made me gasp with a feeling of vast, numbing surprise. Then I was headbutted with an old-fashioned Glasgow kiss, and all the lights went out.

Philomela: Now that an opportunity has presented itself, I find I am not ready. But the Professor is a kind man. I will tell him everything. Soon.

Chapter Eleven

A very ancient and fish-like smell.
—William Shakespeare, *The Tempest*, Act 2, Scene 2

My alarm went off, and I reached out to suppress it. Instead of my bedside table, my groping hand touched carpet. Since when had I installed carpets on my nocturnal furniture? Oh. I hadn't. What Rupert Brooke has styled the rough male kiss of blankets were entirely not in evidence anywhere to hand. The smooth male kiss of Daniel was also not apparent. I wished it were. The light appeared to be on, so I opened my eyes cautiously, ready to close them again on general principle if the prospect were too dire. Why was I lying on the floor? Most importantly, why did I feel as though I had experienced the entire percussion ensemble of the Melbourne Symphony Orchestra playing toccatas and fugues on my battered body?

Since I appeared to be still alive, I groaned. The last time I had woken up on the carpet had been when my former husband James had introduced me to tequila. This was not something for which I had volunteered. In any marriage there is generally one person being held hostage by the other's mood swings, and sooner than watch him pout like a disappointed toddler I had done my wifely duty. I had sucked that lemon, licked that salt, and slowly melted into a cactus-flavoured heap on the floor. Next morning he had complained of a hangover, and I had nursed him with liquid infusions and as much sympathy as I could muster. Which, given that my own head felt as though it had been bathed in the interior of a Hawaiian volcano, was not very much.

I lay where I was and attempted some form of recollection. Little by little, the events of the preceding night leaked back into my mind like a muttered confession. Disturbed shelves, check. Books and DVDs no longer on floor. My nocturnal visitor had put them back, though (as far as I could tell) out of order. My eyes flicked to the front door. Mr Ninja had thoughtfully shut it behind him. I remembered that he wore a mask, and that I had made a determined effort to remove it. When I had accomplished this, I thought I remembered feeling shock at the face beneath it: sufficient to throw me off guard and give my burglar an undeserved opportunity to knock me out. Unfortunately, all I could remember was the surprise. Of the features revealed beneath the mask, I recalled nothing.

My hand patted around me, and touched fur. I looked beside my prone body to discover my devoted Horatio, hunched up and alert, next to me. I stroked his head and ears, and he mewed at me. This wasn't his usual morning mew of: What do we want? Breakfast! When do we want it? Now! This was solicitude, pure and unalloyed by personal greed. He began to purr. Then he wriggled northwards and began to wash my face. This was a thing he did on occasion, when he thought I needed it. I never really knew whether he was telling me I love you, human! or I'm going to keep doing this until you feed me.

After a couple of minutes of tender exfoliation I dragged myself to my feet. Panadol and cold water seemed to be called for, and I availed myself of both. Horatio wrapped himself around my ankles and mewed up at me again. Are you all right? he wanted to know. And what about breakfast, now I have fulfilled my maternal duties?

I went to the kitchen, fed him kitty munchies and a small tin of fish (extra rations for standing guard over me beyond the call of duty), turned the kettle on, and checked my apartment quickly. So far as I could tell, nothing was missing. My handbag was untouched. Whatever he wanted, he had not found it. I made coffee, inhaled the bitter, bracing scent of roasted pick-me-up and considered my predicament.

Point the first: surely not Jordan King again? I thought this highly unlikely. He had shown no interest in me at all. He had displayed a truly Jansenist contempt for women in every fibre of his repellent body when we had spoken. He might suspect me of hiding the Dead Sea Scroll of Doom or whatever it was, but those who have been suppressed by Polynesian giants tend to stay that way. And Sister Mary should have him well in hand. She intimidates most people. I have seen her cow and berate a government backbencher without breaking stride. While I am by necessity unfamiliar with religious zealots, surely the Jordan Kings of the world would be all the more likely to hearken to the admonitions of nuns.

Point the second: did Jordan King have an accomplice? Was Mr Ninja his backup? Or was this related to one of our other mysteries? And if so, which one? The missing dog? The Gospel of St Joseph? The Café Pandamus ransomware?

Point the third: why could I not remember what I had unveiled when I ripped down the ninja mask? What could have been so incredible as to make me completely drop my guard? After all, I had gained much the better of our duel until then. Yet I had been so taken aback that I had allowed this vile intruder the chance to give me a Gorbals kiss. My forehead still throbbed like a long-remembered insult.

Point the fourth: unlike Miss Marple, Sherlock Holmes and all the televisual sleuths with nothing to do all day but solve crimes, I had bread to bake, staff to administer, and a business to run. I drained my coffee, staggered into the bathroom and examined myself. External blood? None. Complexion? Pallid, verging on sepulchral. Eyes? Far too much Count Dracula there, with added bruising manifesting around the margins even as I watched. The phrase Black Eye never does justice to the multi-coloured splendour which often occurs. I was due for a pair of beauties. I washed my face, changed into my work clothes and returned to the kitchen for boiled eggs and sourdough soldiers.

Down in the bakery I resumed my morning rituals. Heckle and Jekyll were rewarded for their haul (three mice, one undersized rat and two moths) and had sauntered out for their morning adventures. It was now Thursday. I fervently hoped that I might make it to the weekend without another attempted burglary. Jason seemed sleepier than usual, and had not paid me much notice at first, but when at last he did he stared as though I had turned into someone completely different.

'Captain? How's the other bloke?'

I explained, in brief, and he shook his head in bewilderment. 'But why? What's so special about Insula every burglar in Melbourne wants a piece of us?' he demanded. 'Why does this keep happening?'

'If I knew, I would tell you, Jason. I'm working on it.'

He made me another cup of coffee and we set to work. By the time the first loaves emerged, I felt a little better. We inserted the Thursday olive bread, and I was just mixing the date scones when I laid down the wooden spoon and gasped.

'Captain?' Suddenly he was at my side. For some reason he reminded me irresistibly of my beautiful tabby cat Horatio. I have no idea what's happening to you, he seemed to be saying, but I'm here, at your side, ready to repel boarders. I resisted the urge to stroke his hair and ears.

'It's all right, Jason. But staring at all this white bread dough has triggered my memory. I've remembered what I saw when I dragged down the ninja's mask.'

'What was it?'

'There *was* no face under it.'

Jason's mouth twisted at the corners. 'Really no face?'

'I assume he has a face in there somewhere. But all I saw was a pure white mask, with two eyeholes, and deep brown eyes glaring through them.'

'Whoa! That's really creepy.'

'It certainly was. But that is how I come to be sporting a pair of black eyes. I dropped my guard because you just don't expect someone to have another mask underneath their mask.'

'No. I can see that. Let's have some bread and honey,' he suggested.

We had a moment or two to spare, so we did that, as dawn grew bright outside the louvre windows.

Shortly after dawn broke its bleary way through the somnolent fug of inner Melbourne, I heard scratching on the outer door. I looked up from my mixing bowl. 'Midshipman? Go see who that is, will you? And if it's Jordan again, dong him one with the ladle.'

As always, Jason took me completely at my word. 'Aye-aye, Captain.' He selected the largest ladle we had, and opened the door.

It was the Mouse Police, smelling of Japanese takeaways. Heckle and Jekyll were still licking their lips, but they had decided that they were better in than out this morning. I had no idea why they wanted in so early, but...whatever. I saw Jason look down, and then askance. It was the most completely askance look I'd seen in my vicinity all week, and we'd had a few.

'Jason? What is it?'

He walked back inside, picked up a tea towel, bent down to pick something up in it, then walked back to me with a wild surmise in his eye. 'Captain? Look what I found in the alley.'

I stared at it. Yep, that was the mask all right. The plain white one with two eyeholes and nothing else. I noted with approval that my redoubtable apprentice had not needed to be told to preserve the purity of the DNA samples that the Victoria Police were possibly going to extract from it. Assuming that Detective

Senior Constable White did not simply wash her hands of me and my constant home invasions.

'Well done, Midshipman. Box it up and we'll hand it over when the cops get here.' I watched with approval as he stowed the mask in a half-carton and sealed it up with masking tape.

I looked at the wall clock. (Analogue, not digital. I wanted one clock in my workspace that told the time using hands and angles. I don't know why.) Nearly seven a.m. In an hour, it would be time to ring the police—again. Letty White might be expected to be at work by eight a.m. Just time to get the paprika and onion bread baked and ready—because it was Thursday, and Thursday was goulash day at Magyar Kitchen. But first, I had to get into my Meeting the Staff and Customers clothes. I had another quick wash upstairs, donned my summer trousers and a light blouse, and descended to the shop to see Kylie and Goss settling in to work. They gaped at me.

'How was the bus?' Kylie asked.

So much sympathy from my staff. 'Long story, and I'll tell you some other time. Exec summary: yes, I got burgled this time. Our persecutors are clearly equal opportunity crims and they thought it was my turn. Yes, the guy got me a beauty. But I've left several dents in him and with any luck he'll remember me with a curse for the next few weeks. Time to sell some bread, ladies.'

At eight sharp I called Letitia White again and outlined my early-morning adventures. There was a long silence on the other end of the line, punctuated by heavy breathing. I believe there were muttered remarks addressed to her Maker, calling on Him to give her strength.

'*Again*, Corinna?'

'I'm afraid so. And no, I have no ideas. Oh, by the way, there was one other invasion I didn't tell you about.'

The strangled yelp on the other end of the line suggested that Senior Constable White had been attacked by feral ducks. 'What?! When was this?'

'Yesterday, early. Look, I'm sorry. I just forgot, because Ma'ani dealt with it, and…it's hard to keep count these days.'

'Who the hell is Ma'ani?'

'Maori enforcer for the Soup Run. You've probably come across him.'

'Oh, him. Right. Six axe-handles across the shoulders; looks like he bench-presses Mack trucks. Okay, I'm on my way.'

The rest of my working day passed in a blur of faces. I tried to give Letty a reasonable account of myself. It didn't help that she took one look at me and said, 'What does the other bloke look like?' But she made extensive notes, accepted Jason's gift of the mask and told me that the SOCOs would be around, yet again, in due course and that I should keep my apartment locked until then.

Meroe came into the shop mid-morning to give me a quiet blessing and a quick but remarkably soothing hug before drifting out again in a waft of incense. Megan the courier came for the bread; customers came, went, shopped, and slowly emptied my shop of comestibles; Kylie and Goss chattered of this and that, and more personal remarks were made about my multicoloured eye shadow. I allowed these to pass. Every time I passed a mirror my black eyes seemed to be more spectacular. In a brief lull I rang Daniel and apprised him of my misadventures.

There was a short, pregnant silence then he said, 'I think I might go and see Uncle Solly. This is getting out of hand.'

Near closing time, Gossamer was adding up the day's takings while Kylie, reunited with her phone, scanned it anxiously for any world-shattering news she might have missed. And apparently there was some. 'Goss!' she shrieked. 'Come and look at this!'

At once, Gossamer was at her side, and they both began to coo like a pair of pigeons discovering an unexpected source of free grain.

'What is it?' I enquired.

Kylie showed me the phone and I read the following:

BEST FRIENDS REUNITED

Two years ago Geordie saved Alasdair's patrol by barking furiously and causing the driver to stop just short of an IED buried in the middle of the road. Today they were reunited in Townsville, after Sinclair decided to settle in Australia after leaving the British Army. 'I love Aussies,' he said. 'They're great to have beside you in a scrap.' Geordie was his sniffer dog in Afghanistan and was discharged along with his master. The pair will settle in Melbourne. 'Geordie doesn't like aeroplanes, so we're going to drive there.'

Underneath was a photo with the caption: *Returned soldier Alasdair Sinclair with his devoted canine Geordie.*

I wondered for a moment whether I should tell Kylie and Goss that Alasdair and Geordie had since been parted, but decided against it. I love them both, but as far as they were concerned discretion was something that happened to other people, and the fewer people who knew about our lost dog the better. I noticed there was nothing in the article about the traumatic end to Alasdair's tour of Afghanistan. The journalist had not discovered it, and presumably Alasdair didn't want to talk about it. I smiled at the girls and contented myself with saying, 'Very sweet.'

As soon as the shop was closed, and Gossamer dispatched to the bank with the day's takings, I went back to bed and slept until six o'clock. I awoke to find Daniel leaning over me and offering a gentle hug. '*Ketschele,* you look very well for someone as much in the wars as you have been,' he whispered.

Since I now felt about two hundred years old, he carefully helped me out of bed and escorted me to the kitchen. We drank coffee and ate croissants spread with plum jam, and I looked at him with adoration.

'The world has gone a bit random on us,' he observed.

'It certainly has.' I put down my cup and sighed.

'But I do have some additional information.'

'Which mystery? The dognapping?'

He nodded. 'Yes. I found Big Charlie and had a Serious Talk with him.'

'Don't tell me he did it after all?'

'No. But he did witness it. He refused to say much about it, though, except that they were Bad Men and he didn't want to get involved.'

'Does he have any idea where they come from?'

'All he said was "up north". I pressed him harder, but he clammed up completely. I think he knows the men who assaulted Alasdair and took Geordie, and he's scared of them.'

'I thought you said Big Charlie wasn't scared of anyone?'

He scratched the side of his forehead and frowned. 'Until now I would have said so. It would appear these are serious villains. And I've been to see Uncle Solly. I mentioned that Alasdair was a fellow spy. Or, rather, "a fellow member of the intelligence community". I thought it might help. But I didn't learn anything much of consequence, I'm afraid. Tell me more about your ninja visitor.'

I told all. He didn't interrupt, but took my hand and held it tightly in his own. When I'd finished my recital he kissed me and smiled. 'You must have been a considerable shock to him. Most people don't fight back when they have home invasions, you know.'

'I don't even know if it's advisable to fight back. I just did it.'

'And I think you did splendidly.' He grinned. 'I've known even very old ladies to get stroppy when their houses were being bur-gled. One of them belted her teenage attacker with a bedside lamp and tied him up with the power cord.'

I laughed merrily. 'Good on her! I'm with that. Why the hell should we let perfect strangers help themselves to the contents of our homes?'

'Why indeed?'

'The question is: who was he? And what was he after?'

Daniel shook his head. 'I don't know where your ninja visitor fits in with our other mysteries. Is he is connected to Jordan's one-man Crusade? It's hard to imagine our burglars aren't looking for the same thing. But why? Who even knows? As for the rest?' He put both hands in the air and gazed heavenwards. 'Who knows? Maybe they're looking for Alasdair? Maybe they're looking for Philomela? It's wildly improbable, but it looks like all bets are off. Any updates on her, by the way?'

'Nothing about her, I'm afraid. But I do have something else. Kylie found it today.'

I took out my phone and searched for 'best friends reunited.' After trawling through a few false leads I found it, and handed the phone to Daniel. He read the article and pursed his lips.

'I see. So we can probably assume that our dognappers have read this, and that's where they got the idea. The fact that Alasdair and Geordie are famous for being best friends may point to an attempt to pressure Alasdair into…what? As far as we know no one has sent him a ransom demand. Then again, since he's at my place and nobody knows where he is, that would be hard.'

'They could leave a ransom demand here,' I suggested.

'Only if the dognappers and the burglars are the same people. Otherwise there's nothing to connect Insula with Alasdair. And what are they after? Drugs? Probably. We don't have anything like enough information, do we?'

I shook my head, and he shook his, shaggy curls fringing his beautiful face like attendant cupids. 'We have too much evidence, too many cases, and we don't know where we stand. It's…perplexing, *nu?*'

'Let's go to Ceres,' I suggested. 'And there we shall rest from our labours.'

Five minutes later, we were sitting side by side inhaling the mixed aromas of the garden. I poured out two gin and tonics, with lemon and ice, and handed him one.

'Are you sure you should be drinking after being concussed?' he wanted to know.

'I was not concussed! Anyway, even if I was, the hell with it. This G and T has my name on it.'

'And this has mine.'

We clinked glasses, and he reached into his shoulder bag and produced a paper package. He unwrapped it and revealed an oblong block of honey cake. It smelt intoxicating: of summer bees and thyme thickets. 'I got this from Uncle Solly,' he explained. 'He says it will make you feel better.'

I ate a piece. It tasted every bit as good as it smelt. He nibbled at a piece himself, and kissed me. 'When I started to learn Hebrew, my parents gave me honey cake just like this.'

'Because learning should be sweet?'

'Oh yes.'

Philomela: Soon! But I have lost my words, and I cannot find them! But I must, and will.

Chapter Twelve

Remember thy swashing blow.
—William Shakespeare, *Romeo And Juliet*, Act 1, Scene 1

'All right, Daniel, how was your visit to Alasdair?'

We were sitting in my kitchen/living room. Dinner had been savoured: gnocchi with pumpkin sauce, a light garden salad, and crème brûlée, washed down with a Marlborough sauvignon blanc. For once I'd had a completely uneventful day at work. Bread and other related farinaceous products had been baked, delivered, bought, and taken away by eager customers. The shop had experienced a busy Friday, and by one-fifteen Kylie had been dispatched to the bank with the day's takings. I'd had one of my diurnal ambitions abundantly fulfilled: a day entirely without crises or attempted burglary. My other ambition, I hoped, would soon be fulfilled too. I looked across at my brown-eyed love and saw that he was smiling.

'Good and ill, but better than I expected,' he announced, picking up his half-empty glass of New Zealand's most famed bottled sunshine. He clinked it against mine. 'Poor Alasdair is still pining, and close to despair. But he brightened up a little when I told him what I suspected.'

'Don't keep me in suspense! Tell me!' I implored.

The corners of his mouth turned up in an adorable crinkle. 'Last night I scoured the local streets again and turned up nothing of interest. If Alasdair's doggie were being kept anywhere in the middle of town, I think I would have found him by now. So we have to look further afield. One of the things you may have heard about criminal investigation is that people usually remember more than they know. It takes time for the subliminal memories to well up from underneath, especially if something you've heard makes no sense at the time. And Alasdair now remembers something about the gang who nabbed his dog. He says they spoke to each other in a language he couldn't recognise. That means we can probably rule out any connection with Afghanistan. He knows enough Pashto and Dari to get by; he's pretty good with languages. And that's not all he has remembered.'

I do love Daniel, but his way of approaching his point with slow relish can be infuriating. I reminded him of this. 'Daniel, if you don't get to the point right speedily, I may brain you with a pepper grinder. That one.' I indicated my foot-long polished-wood top-loader, which had been in frequent use during the gnocchi phase of dinner. It was sitting in the middle of the table lording it over the other condiments. He grinned, took my hand in his, and clasped it firmly.

'One: someone mentioned the name Kilmarnock. He forgot about that at the time, because Kilmarnock is in southern Scotland and he didn't think it was relevant. Two: he now recalls that they said the word 'Insula.' At the time, that meant nothing at all to him; but when I mentioned your apartment was called Insula he had a light-globe moment and said he was sure they had said something about a building called Insula. And the other thing he overheard was something that sounded like *vorteh nizaky*. It was said in a hissing whisper, but he has no idea what it means and nor do I. But Kilmarnock on the other hand…'

I shook my head. 'Sorry, but that's not ringing any bells for me.'

'That's because you're an innocent inner-city girl and the far-flung suburbs of Melbourne's badlands are a closed book to you. But far to the north, across many miles of dusty, windswept plains and shopping malls, lies the mythical land of Kilmarnock. A new and rapidly growing suburb within the City of Hume. And I now think that somebody in this building comes from there, and has inadvertently brought trouble with them.'

I leant back in my chair. 'All right. Who's new here? The actors?'

'They'd be my first guess. And your task for when you next have a free moment, my dearest, is to get talking with them and see if you can discreetly find out which of them comes from there. But we have another candidate, too, though we can't talk to her—or, rather, she can't talk to us.'

'Philomela?'

'Who else? She's been traumatised by something horrible. It may have happened to her, or it may just be something she's seen. We need to find out more about Philomela if we can.'

'I'll have to leave that with Professor Monk, I think. And what about Anwyn? She's new here too. Could she be involved?'

Daniel got up and paced around the room, rubbing his sinewy hands through his hair, which was longer than usual and beginning to come over all corkscrews. This is something of an occupational hazard with the Children of Israel unless they guard against it ceaselessly. He shook his shaggy head and sighed. 'This is getting too complicated. Let's start from the beginning again and talk our way through it all.'

I made herbal tea (peppermint for Daniel, rosehip for me) while Daniel stroked Horatio's face and ears. My guardian cat had wanted to know when he was getting his supper, and had put in a silent but trenchant protest. Daniel watched me turn out a packet of salmon mix into his bowl. Horatio sat down in front of it, wrapped his tail around his front paws and offered up a fervently silent prayer to Bast, goddess of cats. I hoped his prayer also included us, his devoted servitors. Grace concluded, he addressed himself to the fish and licked the bowl clean. He gave us both a thoughtful look while washing his face and paws, then sauntered off towards my bedroom.

We sipped our tea and went through the whole bizarre series of events again. I brought out my favourite Spirax notebook and wrote careful notes, using an actual ballpoint pen. Eventually I looked up at Daniel, smiled, and began our summary.

'Item the first: Sergeant Alasdair Sinclair—late of Her Majesty's armed forces serving in Afghanistan—turns up with his tale of mugging and dognapping. We have CCTV footage of said assault, and he's definitely not making it up. They leave him on the footpath and take his dog Geordie. This makes no sense at all because the streets of Melbourne are crawling with dogs of every conceivable breed, size, shape, disposition, and fur colour. What's special about Geordie?'

Daniel shook his head. 'I can't imagine. The only thing that occurs to me is that this is a drug cartel and maybe they think Geordie can smell out drugs.'

'That would make sense.'

I turned a page in my notebook and briefly admired my calligraphy. It was better than I expected, given that like most twenty-first-century folks I hardly ever write with a biro. 'Geordie, meanwhile, has vanished off the face of the earth, and the only clue we have is two words that sound like somebody clearing phlegm from their throat, and mention of a borough town in the Scottish borders that may or may not also refer to a suburb on our city's outskirts. But it could also mean *You have a big nose and exceedingly bad breath* in whatever eldritch tongue the gang was conversing in. And so far, that is all we have.'

'So far, that is all we have,' Daniel confirmed.

'Item the second: Cafe Delicious. A ransomware attack, cured by our resident Nerds Inc. Suspects? Could be anyone, really.'

Daniel nodded without comment.

'Item the third: lots of new people come to Insula, to whit Anwyn from Adelaide, a bunch of actors from RMIT, and Philomela, who could be from anywhere.'

'And tomorrow being Saturday, Corinna the baker–sleuth will be able to find out all sorts of things about all these people without attracting suspicion. What do we need to know?'

I ran my forefinger down my list. 'Has Anwyn ever been to Kilmarnock, and has she any information that might shed light on these strange happenings? Also, I am to cultivate the actors if possible and see if they know anything or have any connection to Kilmarnock themselves.'

'Correct. And we must ask the same question of Philomela, and hope she can be induced to answer.'

'Yes. Which leads us to item the fourth: that something traumatic has happened to Philomela and we have no idea yet whether there is any connection with our Happenings. But we wouldn't be surprised because neither of us trust coincidence as an explanation of our concurrent weirdness. Professor Monk seems to be our best option there. If she talks to anyone, he will be the one, I think.'

Daniel's agate eyes gleamed. 'Yes. But really, why should that be, I wonder? Is it something to do with his classical library? There may be other reasons, but I can't think of any right now.'

'Neither can I. Items the fifth and sixth: the serial break-ins. Now here we definitely do have two different sets of burglars. The ineffable Jordan King is currently in the protective custody of Sister Mary and the redoubtable Ma'ani.'

'Are we sure about that?'

Daniel grinned. 'Yes, we are, because I asked. Sister Mary isn't letting him out of her sight. You can rely on a devout Catholic to obey orders from nuns. And in his case, at least, we know what he was looking for.'

I paused for a moment's recollection of Jake and Elwood Blues and their insane devotion to the Penguin. 'The new scroll, which he has determined is filled with a heresy so dreadful that there was nothing for it but inept burglary. Can we find out more about that?' He took my hand again and held it. 'I think you can. Go and see Sister Mary, if you have time. She will be able to get more out of him than any of us could, and she may pass it on to you.'

'Unless it's under the confessional seal. No, wait: Nuns can't do confession, can they?'

Daniel lifted his hands and gazed at my white plaster ceiling, which was accumulating some long strands of cobweb. Yet another reminder to me of my interrupted life of late. 'Who knows? I can't see why a creepy parish priest can take confessions, but a nun of invincible virtue can't. But, then, Christians are a mystery to me. Anything he's willing to let on to her, she will probably tell you. And your sixth item?'

'My ninja burglar, who was a lot more efficient than poor deluded Jordan. And this is the bit that I don't understand at all. Do you, Daniel?'

He frowned. 'I can't connect the two burglars. I can't match Jordan's medieval obsession with heresy with your ninja. I doubt he cares about missing gospels. He was after something different. And he hasn't found it. If anyone here is a coincidence, it has to be Jordan King. But an efficient burglar, targeting this apartment block, is far more likely to be connected with one of our other cases. But which? Not the dognapping, surely. You don't have a dog, you have cats. And I can't envisage a crime gang trying to use a cat for anything at all.'

On cue, Horatio strolled across the kitchen floor and sat pointedly in front of his munchies bowl. Daniel reached for a packet, shook some of the contents into the ceramic bowl and watched devotedly as Horatio began to munch his way through the endangered species of the Southern Ocean. And I admired my beautiful lover, reaffirming my conviction that men who love cats are far more trustworthy. My ex-husband James refused to have cats in the house. As part of my Declaration of Independence from the squalid, petty tyranny of my marriage, I had acquired Horatio within days of moving out.

Daniel resumed his seat and folded his hands on the tabletop. 'No. There's something else here. And we have no idea what it is. Yet. It may not even be a thing we actually have on the premises. But it would be well worthwhile to see if any of our inhabitants, new or old, have acquired something that could be noteworthy. Ask around, please.'

'All right. But if you don't mind my asking, my beloved, what will you be doing while I spend my precious weekend sleuthing around here and at the Soup Run?'

He grinned. 'I shall divide my time between my own flat, where I shall give aid and comfort to Sergeant Sinclair; and Uncle Solly, to see if he knows anything new; and scouting around for information about Kilmarnock. Which may be the most scarlet of red herrings, but we have to check it out anyway.'

Suitably mollified, I said, 'Tell me more about Kilmarnock. Who lives there?'

'All sorts. Anyone who wants to buy a house and can't afford the ridiculous prices closer in to the city. I've heard whispers about an Azeri crime gang. There's some sort of turf war happening. There aren't many Azeris there; and most are, as you would expect, law-abiding but not exactly willing to talk to strangers. But they're a possible lead. They might feel that all this crime is bringing down the neighbourhood and giving them all a bad name.'

'Daniel dearest, please pardon my utter ignorance, but who are these people? I've never heard of them.'

'From Azerbaijan, one of the former Soviet republics. They're not as terrifying as the Uzbeks, but you don't mess with people like that without a really good reason. And the Eastern Bloc countries specialise in cyberwarfare.'

'Do you think they could be responsible for the ransomware attack on Cafe Delicious?'

'Why not? If this little community of ours has attracted their attention, why would they stop at burglary? Crime gangs always need money, for girls, guns, gambling habits, and the rest of it. And it may also be a deliberate distraction, to keep us off balance.'

'It worked, then. No, wait. What religion are the Azeris?'

Daniel leant over and kissed me. Hard, on the lips. 'Corinna, you are a genius. Of course. They can't have kidnapped the dog, can they?'

'Because they're Muslims, and dogs are haram?' I ventured.

'Yes. So even if the Azeris are behind all this, someone else took the dog. Damn! Still, all information is useful. All right. You talk to the actors.'

'Oh, one more thing?' I tried to recall the melody, or whatever it was, from the ninja burglar. I hummed it as best I could, while he looked at me steadily. 'Does that mean anything to you?' He shook his head.

'No. Where did you hear it?

'From ninja guy. He was intoning while casing my apartment. It sounded unbelievably creepy, no? Daniel, we really have more than our fair share of mysteries, don't we?'

He gave me a wry smile. 'We do. Are any of them connected to each other? I don't like coincidences any more than you do, my beloved, but really: how could any of these things be related? I can't see it at all. So, let's concentrate on Geordie, shall we? And that can wait till tomorrow, because right now I have other things on my mind.'

And thereupon he lifted me to my feet, and without further ado, he carried me to by bedroom. I do so admire strong men.

Philomela: So close today! He is such a kind, patient man. He just sits with me, and brings me cups of tea and biscuits. And he talks about anything and everything: Herodotus, Thucydides—whom he does not admire at all, and I admire him for that—and stories from all over the world. Maybe he's telling me stories his dad told him. He seems to have the idea that I was attacked by a gang. He didn't say the word 'rape,' but that's what he was thinking. And of course that's all wrong. It's worse than that. But I can't get the words out. We'll try again, though. And we will get there. We must.

Chapter Thirteen

'Tis an ill cook that cannot lick his own fingers.
—William Shakespeare, *Romeo and Juliet*, Act 4, Scene 2

Four a.m. again. My least favourite time of day. I blinked wearily at the digital alarm clock as it flickered from three fifty-eight to three fifty-nine. I have taken to waking a couple of minutes early so I can forestall the alarm with my finger. Otherwise, sooner or later, I am going to forestall it with a ballpein hammer.

My bed was so warm! I stretched out my toes and found they were impeded by Horatio, who moved in his sleep for a moment. I could feel his tight body stretch out then subside gratefully back into slumber. And my back was also warm: far more so than normal. Sometimes I dreamt that Daniel was with me in bed, warm and chocolate-scented and utterly adorable. The alarm clock ticked over to four. I reached out my hand, but there was no stentorian clangour. I felt Daniel's achingly warm stillness, and realised that (a) yes, Daniel really was here in bed with me, and (b) the alarm had not been set and therefore (c) it must be Saturday. As my drowning senses subsided into grateful oblivion, the last remnant of my conscious mind provided me with the inevitable conclusion that (d) it really was Saturday and I could go back to sleep.

I awoke refreshed and invigorated by the gentle, yet persistent scraping of what appeared to be a small strip of bacon-flavoured sandpaper. I opened my eyes to find Horatio giving me the benefits of a thorough dermabrasion. His paw was resting on my cheek, and I felt him applying the finishing touches to my nose. Usually you have to pay good money for this. Mostly he stops there, though if I manage to sleep through the facial he has been known to proceed to pedicure. This gets me out of bed and vertical in seconds. I stroked him, and he arched his back in luxurious contentment and sauntered down to the end of the bed to resume what was manifestly going to be a post-breakfast nap. Which also meant that Daniel was up and about, and had already performed this most essential service. He was nowhere to be seen, but the delectable scent of Someone Doing Things to Bacon began to waft from without. I arched my back in sympathy with my cat and wrapped my arms around a pillow. I opened my eyes long enough to take in the clock face telling me it was now 9:32 a.m. and all was tremendously well with the world. And suddenly I was asleep again.

'Corinna? Breakfast is ready.' I opened my eyes again to find Daniel kneeling by the bed and holding my hand. His hands are always warm. I lifted my head and kissed him. He carefully kissed me around my eyes. I imagined I could feel the bruising retreat under his kisses. I stood up and he held out my dressing-gown for me so I could climb into it. I tied the cord around my waist, and he led me into my kitchen, drawing out a chair for me. On the plate in front of me was a perfect eggs benedict on light rye toast with fresh broadleaf parsley from Ceres and a side order of bacon—several rashers thereof—along with a glass of freshly squeezed orange juice and a steaming mug of coffee. I fell upon it like Saul smiting the Philistines, admiring as Daniel sat opposite me and tucked into not so much a big breakfast as a breakfast to feed a medium-sized school canteen. There were poached eggs, grilled tomatoes, sautéed mushrooms, Cumberland sausages, spinach leaves, guacamole, and a double helping of fried bread.

I drank my coffee thoughtfully and wondered if I dared to raise the subject with him. Jewish dietary laws were matters we had skirted around and never really discussed. Most people know the word kosher, though I gathered it was far more complex than pork and seafood. These were undoubtedly *traif,* or forbidden, but there was a lot more to it than that. I wondered how modern Jews felt about rules that probably made a lot more sense when you were wandering around in an unrefrigerated desert. I had no memory of raising the question of *traif* before, and debated the respective merits of asking, or keeping a tactful silence. I decided upon the former. 'Daniel, darling, I hope you don't mind me bringing the subject up, but I'm curious. This bacon is amazing. Made no doubt from animals raised in a spa and massaged daily by muscular youths in exciting loincloths, but…what *is* the story here?'

My beloved smiled his most melting, sloe-eyed smile. 'Oh, you mean the zebra? Yes, it's really good, isn't it?' And he shovelled another strip of it into his delectable mouth.

'Zebra? Black-and-white-striped horses with attitude? Those zebras?'

'Oh yes. Just outside Tel Aviv there are huge zebra farms. And it tastes just like bacon, or so I believe.'

I considered this while helping myself to more of it. 'So, as you drive past these zebra farms, do the inmates make any noise in particular?'

He gazed at the ceiling. 'Oink?'

I gave up. His personal interpretation of Judaism's dietary laws was no business of mine anyway. I gazed at the *Saturday Age* to see if anything took my fancy, but after a few minutes of that I folded it up and put it face down on the chair. I exchanged a look with Daniel and his chin inclined. 'Quite right too. I think I would prefer to read a book. The News from Abroad will only spoil your breakfast, and that would be a pity.'

'A tragedy,' I concurred, but made no move towards my book-shelves. First things first…

Before long I was gazing at a platter swept clear of everything that had so recently adorned it. Even the hollandaise sauce had been mopped up with my toast. 'And so…before you set out upon your adventures, Daniel, let us consider our sources. Is there anyone we have forgotten who may be able to help us?'

Daniel thought about this and blinked. 'Kylie and Goss? I don't think so. Nice girls, but they're from Nunawading, aren't they? But maybe worth a shot.'

'Keep guessing,' I suggested, and his dark eyes opened wide.

'Of course. If anyone knows anything about the drug scene, it is your worthy midshipman. Why not summon him?'

I did so, with the promise of breakfast, and Daniel and I exchanged glances. Jason would more likely divulge confidences to me, so without a word my beloved returned to the kitchen to prepare a midshipman-sized breakfast. My doorbell rang almost immediately, and I opened the door on my devoted second-in-command. He looked offensively healthy. He had filled out wonderfully from the emaciated junkie I had adopted. His hair, formerly limp, broken, and filthy was now aggressively blond and curling. His skin shone with healthful vitamins. And his eyes! Blue as cornflowers, with dazzling white instead of yellow as their backdrop. He was wearing a tight black T-shirt (plain, for once) and the muscles on his biceps seemed to be fighting to escape. He saluted smartly, though I saw his eyes widen at my particoloured eyeshadow.

'At ease, Midshipman. Your breakfast will arrive as soon as Daniel can cook it for you. Please, take a seat. And what would you like to drink?'

'Got any Coke?'

'Sorry. But I have juice. Made from fruit and everything.'

I gave him some pineapple and mango in a long glass and he gulped it down in one long, slow slurp. I watched, fascinated. Not for the first time I wondered where teenage boys manage to store all the food and drink they consume. He set the glass down, wiped his mouth with the back of his hand (reminding me at once of Horatio), and grinned at me.

'You seem to have slept well?' I suggested.

He nodded.

'Yeah, Cap'n, I always sleep well these days. And I love the weekends. I wake up at four, same as usual, have a Coke and go straight back to sleep again. I'd just woken up when you called.'

'Same here. Jason, I'm happy to feed you today, but I was wondering if you knew anything about our home invasions.'

His face instantly clouded over, with possible thunderstorms later on. I realised I had not expressed myself with anything like the delicacy requisite to the occasion. I plunged in at once before his feelings could be hurt any further.

'Jason, let me hasten to assure you that I do not believe for a moment that you're involved in anything untoward. I'm sorry. It probably sounded like that, but that was not what I meant at all. We think we have some possible clues, and we were wondering if you could enlighten us.'

The atmosphere lightened visibly. Jason was so easy to read. Every passing thought showed in his face. It was just as well he was on the straight and narrow. He has no talent for dissembling.

'Okay, I'm listening, Cap'n. What have you got?' He leant back in his chair and stretched. His T-shirt rode up, showing his flat belly and navel; he was as unselfconscious as a cat.

'Jason, what do you know about Kilmarnock?'

That brought the thunderclouds back to his face, but a different set. This was fear rather than outrage.

'You're not thinkin' of movin' there, are ya, Cap'n? Don't do it! It's a bad place.'

'No, we're not going anywhere. We're staying right here in Insula. But we think someone in Kilmarnock might be looking for us, and not in a good way. And we thought you might know people who know people…' I left the sentence hanging. He caught on at once.

'Well, yeah, Corinna. I've heard stuff.' He placed both hands on his head and rubbed his scalp, for no reason I could see. 'See, most people come into town to score. It's still the biggest source of…stuff. There's still lots of hangout places the cops don't know about. And some of the guys I used to hang with…well, I see them sometimes.'

'Do you give them anything?'

He gave me a modest smile. 'Yeah. Food, mostly. They hardly eat anything. And sometimes I'll give them money, but not enough for them to score. Five bucks gives you a feed at Maccas, but you can't buy anything else with that.'

This was news to me, but I was delighted to hear it. This was Paying It Forward on steroids. Because I had helped him, he was helping his junkie friends.

'All right, Jason, that's very good of you. Really it is. But I'm going to ask you something very import–'

He cut me off immediately, clever boy that he is. He already knew what I was going to ask, and shook his head with maximum prejudice. 'No, Corinna. I've *never* let them into Insula. Because you can't do that. They don't want to screw you over, but they will if they see a chance to score. Cap'n, I know, 'cos I've been there. If I cook for them, I bring the food to them out on the street.'

Did I believe him? Yes. He is utterly transparent. And if I couldn't trust my midshipman to tell me the truth, what chance did any of us have? He'd never lied to me. Not even when he stole a bottle of grog and got pissed. Even then he had confessed, repented, and never slipped again.

'Okay, Jason, I believe you. So what do you know about Kilmarnock? You do know a lot of people, don't you? Have you heard something on the streets about it?'

He shook his head. 'I dunno why they're coming here, but that's not good. They're bad men out there.'

'Does Azerbaijan mean anything to you?'

'Dunno, Cap'n. Never heard of him.'

'Never mind. What sort of bad men?'

He clasped his hands on the table. 'Corinna, they're gangsters. Real gangsters. They deal. And they shoot people. If they really don't like you, they'll blow up your house. Everyone's scared of 'em.'

'They sound like bad men all right,' I agreed. 'Do you know if there's more than one gang?'

He thought about this, closing his eyes and wrinkling his forehead.

'Could be. 'Cos if there was only one gang they wouldn't need to shoot people so much, would they?'

'Jason, how much shooting are we talking about? How much blowing up of houses?

He sat forward in his chair, his nostrils twitching. The sounds and smells of frying emanating from my kitchen were speaking volumes to his animal instincts. He inhaled deeply and shook his head, wrenching his attention back to the matter at hand. 'At least one house. Early this year. You might have seen it on the news.'

I remembered it now. Police baffled; no one talking to anybody. But I expect the police knew more about it than they let on.

'Go on. So just the one house?'

'That's one too many in my book. Shootings? At least three this year. I know they shot one of their own guys because he tried to go solo and they didn't like it.'

'I bet they didn't.' And that seemed to be that. Even if Jason had any more to tell me, it would have to wait, because Daniel appeared with enough food piled on a dinner platter to feed six people and the family dog. It was the same big breakfast Daniel had eaten, but with added hash browns. Jason fell on it ravenously and did not pause until the plate was swept clean down to the last crust of sourdough. I was impressed enough to venture a small handclap. He grinned. It was like the sun coming out from behind clouds.

'Yeah, well, Corinna, I've got a lot of catching up to do.' He looked at me expectantly. 'Anything else I can help you with?'

'Unless you can remember any snippets of conversation, no. Don't try to force your memory. Just think about anything you may have heard about these creatures. We haven't got much to go on here, and anything that sounds out of the usual run would be useful. And…' I paused, not wanting to ask but unable to help myself. 'Um, I don't think I've ever asked you this, and it's really none of my business, but I would love to know what you do on your days off. If you don't mind telling me.'

'Nah, no problem. 'Cos it's Saturday I'll be off to Anon.'

I raised my eyebrows in query and he explained, 'It's like AA, only for drugs. We meet once a week and tell each other how we're going.'

'Jason, that's wonderful. I never knew you were still going.'

He nodded. 'Yeah, well. I went there first up, but then I drifted away. I thought I could stay clean without help. Then one of me mates got off the stuff by going to Anon and he reminded me how helpful it was. And since then I've never even been tempted.' He looked me straight in the eye. 'I started going again when I nicked that bottle of grog from you, Cap'n. 'Cos I realised how much worse that coulda been. When you fall off, it's a lot harder to get back on the bus.'

I could see it now. *Hi, my name is Jason and I'm here to tell you about the wonders of bread, and how it changed my life.* Bread of heaven indeed. 'You intrigue me,' I said. 'That's brilliant. And what do you do after that? What does Saturday night have in store for you?'

'I stay in, Cap'n.'

What a great deal I was learning about Jason!

'I stay in 'cos Mrs Dawson got me a subscription to Stan. So I stay in with a big bottle of Coke and some snacks and I catch up on all of the movies I missed when I was too busy trying to score every night. I'm not putting meself in harm's way. City's not safe after midnight. But that's all right 'cos I'm asleep by then.'

'Jason, you are a wonderful man,' I told him with perfect conviction. 'So you're still happy living this life?'

He blinked at me in what looked like honest surprise. 'Sure, Cap'n. I'm thinking about getting a cat. Or maybe a rabbit. Still tryin' to decide which.'

News to me, but okay.

He gave me a shy look. 'I never belonged anyplace before. I never knew who my dad was. He's nothing to me. And all Mum cared about was getting the money she got for me until I turned sixteen and there wasn't gonna be any more. But I've got a family now. My first.'

I did not know what to say, so I smiled encouragingly. Then Daniel came in to clear away the crockery and cutlery, and Jason rose to his feet.

'Thanks, Cap'n. See you first thing Monday.'

And with that he was no longer with us.

Daniel took my hand and kissed me. 'Well, now. Who would have thought it?'

I kissed him back. 'Come back to bed and kiss me some more?'

He took my hand and led me back to my room.

Philomela: Today I am going to open my mouth and I really am going to speak. No doubt about it.

Chapter Fourteen

I do begin to have bloody thoughts.
—William Shakespeare, *The Tempest*, Act 4, Scene 1

I woke later, barely aware of Daniel kissing me again and letting himself out to go on his travels. My alarm clock told me it was eleven forty-eight a.m. I felt exalted. I always did after a night (and indeed a morning as well) of my beautiful Daniel. My toes tingled. I stretched them luxuriously. I felt as though I was swimming on clouds, effortlessly, like a dolphin. I admire dolphins, even though I can't swim as well as they do. And a glow of delight had settled over me. I found Horatio lying next to me with his paws in the air, sleeping like a satisfied bunny. Whatever sensual delights I was currently exuding from my body were clearly pleasing my cat as well. His whiskers twitched. I found myself crinkling my nose in sympathy. So whither now for my day off? My phone informed me it was thirty degrees outside, expected maximum thirty-six. I dressed casually, in a light cotton caftan and sandals, and the hell with anyone who would be shocked by the sight of me in semi-undress. I examined myself in the mirror. My face was grinning uncontrollably. The white fabric hinted rather than revealed. The hand-embroidered flowers, trees and parrots (supplied by

Therese Webb, whom I had employed to do this) looked wonderfully brazen. For brazen was what I felt, as who would not?

I examined my emails. A quick note from Mistress Dread,
enjoying the comparative cool of Hobart. After a number of
late-night BDSM sessions she had pronounced herself officially
Fed Up with the heat and her clientele, and she had left her shop
in the custody of a thin, colourless girl with magenta hair and
a permanent expression of hand-crafted artisanal ennui. I had
wandered in the day before (in my copious spare time) just to
pass the time of day, but the girl appeared to have no interests. She
reluctantly conceded that her name was Scarlett, but beyond that
I could find no common ground with her at all. She wouldn't even
talk about her extensive tattooing, which must mean that in her
hierarchy of social credit I ranked rather below micro-organisms
growing under toenails. This seemed rather a pity since, as inked
bodies go, hers was potentially intriguing. Faux-manga black-eyed
girls seemed to be wrapped around oddly tentacular creatures
that frollicked and gambolled in and out of her underwear. I suspect the graphic designer responsible suffered from migraine,
if not schizophrenia. I reasoned that in midsummer (after the
Christmas/New Year madness had dissipated) Mistress D would
not be missing out on much trade. Scarlett may have had the
interpersonal skills of activated mildew, but bondage and discipline is a fashion statement better suited to the cooler months.

Jon and Kepler seemed to be in Laos. I received a couple of
emails studded liberally with photos of smiling villagers and
impressively militant grannies. One ancient woman looked as
though she might well have led the charge against the colonialist
powers in person, probably wielding a battle-axe in one hand and
an AK-47 in the other. There was also a picture of an elaborate
banquet held in an impressive-looking grass hut. It seemed to be
in Jon's honour. I wasn't surprised. He was, I already knew, a global
food relief guru. It seemed that he spoke all the major languages
of South-East Asia fluently, and many other languages besides.

I had once heard him berate a drunken St Patrick's Day reveller in Irish Gaelic so scorching that the man had been beaten to his knees in ancestral shame. It seemed that Jon was now a sort of liaison officer for Western volunteers. One paragraph in his latest email rather stood out.

> Despite our best endeavours to discourage this sort of thing, some of them still appear to think that the locals should fall about and rejoice that a white person has come to save them. Strangely enough, this is not going to happen. Generally speaking, the locals only need one specific thing, and for the rest: they're doing very nicely thank you and you can all go away now. The Lao don't even like their neighbours very much, and they're suspicious of Westerners. This is where I'm helping out at the moment.

Judging by the banquet scene, it would appear that Jon and Kepler were very welcome indeed. He also sent me a Skype address, and the offer of a teleconference any time, should I wish it. I have never really Skyped. Ever since my moonbeam parents had discovered it I had avoided that little blue-and-white logo down at the bottom of my monitor screen. But it was pleasing to know that Jon would be a sane, calming virtual presence should I have need of it.

Correspondence sorted, my mind turned towards higher things. Cafe Delicious, I thought, would be an ideal place for lunch. Del Pandamus had taken to opening his shop on Saturdays. People flocked into the city even on non-working days now, and since most of his competition closed their doors on Friday afternoon, he hoped he would be able to tempt some of them. I hadn't seen him since his distressing encounter with cyber-bandits, and I thought I should show the flag. Accordingly, I let myself out of my apartment, leaving my cat to his virtuous slumbers.

'*Geiá sou,* Corinna!' Del was terribly pleased to see me. I looked around his cafe. A couple of customers were tucking into Greek salads, dolmades, and souvlakia, but business seemed slowish. 'What can I get you today?'

'An open souvlaki and a cafe hellenico, please. And some *glyki* to follow?'

'*Entaxi!*' He rubbed his hands together and shook his bald head. I do not know why this is, but Greek men and pattern baldness go together like eggs and bacon. 'You like it *metriou,* yes?' He smiled and waved his brown, gold-ringed hand towards my favourite table.

I sat down, and was immediately joined by Gully, who appeared from the back of the cafe and sat down opposite me. His lank black hair hung limply over his pallid features. He looked even less healthy than usual, as if he had spent all night in a coin-operated laundromat staring at the spin dryers.

'Hello, Gully. How are things?' I enquired.

'Good. Del says I can eat here for free today, so I've been doing that.' He patted his stomach complacently.

His unexpected appearance was a stroke of luck for me, and I had no intention of wasting it. 'Gully, that's great. But I need some intel. Can you help me out?'

He grinned. My goddess, his teeth were bad. He was going to have to do something about them one of these days. They reminded me of one of those down-at-heel cemeteries where the cracked gravestones lean together drunkenly for support.

'Sure, Corinna. What do you want to know?'

'Tell me about the malware here, which I gather you've cleaned up. Did it tell you anything?'

Anastasia Pandamus brought him a big glass of Coke, smiled down at him as if he were a favourite doggie, and patted his arm. 'You're a good boy!' she said, and departed without further comment.

He took a medium sip and set the glass down. 'I'm not sure. The images were just variations on goatse, but—'

'Goatse?' I broke in.

'If you've never seen it, you're lucky.' The corners of his mouth twisted downwards. He seemed to be attempting a moustache now, I noticed. It was losing the battle with his acne, but a few sprouts had managed to break through the surface. 'It's a really graphic gay porn image. Once you've seen it, you'll never get it out of your head. But that's been around like forever. It came from 4chan...' His bleary eyes looked at me hopefully, noted my incomprehension and blinked. 'It's like a troll usergroup. You know Anonymous?'

'I've heard of them. Didn't they bring down a government once?'

'Yeah, somewhere in North Africa. Anonymous was like a breakaway group from 4chan. Guys who wanted to change the world.' He sniffed. Clearly he didn't feel this was worth bothering about. 'Anyway, goatse came from 4chan, which is a network of nerds who spend their time trolling each other. But you want to know about the code, don't you?'

'Yes, I do. Have you seen it before?'

'Yeah. It looked Russian. Somewhere out that way anyway.' He waved his skinny arms in the general direction of Box Hill. 'There's been a bit of that around. But it wasn't that flash, as malware goes. I tracked their IP address, obviously...'

Well, obviously. I composed my features into what I hoped was an expression of Oh please, do go on. I might even hear something I could understand any day now.

He continued, with added emphasis. 'As you'd expect, it was a VPN based in America. But that doesn't mean anything.'

'Gully, you'll have to tell me what a VPN is, I'm afraid.'

'Virtual private network. We all have them, because sometimes you want to get cheaper stuff if it's available overseas. Also, you can hide from spooks and government surveillance. But VPNs aren't just for dark web guys who want to look at—' He broke off. He was blushing! Who knew that Nerds Inc. could be embarrassed by anything? It was time to help him out, so I did.

'So what you're telling me is that these VPNs are used by all sorts of people, and not just people who want to look at Bad Stuff on the internet. And you can pretend you're anywhere in the world and no one really knows where you are?'

'Yeah, that's right. But the code I read from their ransomware looked very familiar. They could have bought it off the dark web. You can buy anything there.' He broke off again. I guessed he had found some very unsavoury things there. 'But what I'm sayin' is that it wasn't very good ransomware. I could do better in my sleep if I wanted to. It's just that…'

He looked around nervously—for fear of being overheard, it seemed—then he leant forward as though preparing to impart secrets of state. 'Corinna, you know what he had on his computer?'

I shrugged and widened my eyes in encouragement.

He shook his head quickly, as if unable to believe it himself. Dramatic pause, snare-drum percussion…'McAfee!'

As usually happened when talking to a member of Nerds Inc., I was possessed by the feeling of not being on the same page, or even in the same universe. 'And this would be bad?'

He snorted, like a horse being offered an inferior brand of oats. 'Corinna, McAfee comes free with Adobe updates. Every time there's a new update, you have to remember to unclick the McAfee box or it downloads automatically. Anyway, McAfee is better than nothing at all, but trying to stop a malware attack with that is like—' he waved his arms expansively '—it's like trying to stop a bullet with a box of tissues. When we set up Del's system way back, we put proper antivirus software on it. So when that met McAfee, which had downloaded along with an update, the two programs spent all their time fighting each other and the malware got through. So I deleted them both and put Kaspersky on instead.'

'And that's better?' I enquired. Memory presented me with an unwelcome calling card. I vaguely recalled seeing the McAfee logo on my own computer. Had I unclicked the box when last

Adobe had presented me with yet another unsought upgrade? I feared I had not. So would my software be fighting McAfee and letting down my cybernetic defences too? I would need to check this later. In the meantime, we were meandering off-topic. 'Gully, does Azerbaijan mean anything to you?'

He shook his head. 'Never heard of him. Sorry.'

'All right. What about Kilmarnock? Can you tell me anything about that?'

It was as if his eyes had clouded over. Amazingly, he reached out his grimy hand and grabbed my forearm. 'Corinna, you don't want anything to do with those guys. Get away, and stay away. They're evil.'

'Well, yes, I gathered as much. Gully, are you aware that our apartment building has been repeatedly broken into? We've had far too many burglaries for one lifetime already, and that was just this week.'

He picked up his Coke, imbibed a goodly gulp thereof, and shook his head. 'Really? Sorry, I've been busy. I must have missed that. You okay?'

'We seem to have got the better of them so far,' I assured him. 'But I'm wondering if the bad guys of Kilmarnock might be responsible.'

He thought about this while draining the rest of his Coke. 'Jeez, I hope not, Corinna. But I don't think it's likely.'

'Why not?'

''Cos you got nothing they're interested in. They want guns and drugs. You haven't got those, have you?'

'No. Well, thanks, Gully. You've been very helpful.'

He grinned again, rose, and wandered out of the cafe. My coffee arrived, courtesy of Anastasia, and I inhaled the bitter scent of concentrated Greek insomnia. This is totally different from Turkish coffee, according to the Pandamus family, and I would have to take their word for it. If you couldn't stand a spoon up in it, it wasn't real coffee. I had heard that Athens was powered by this stuff. My loathsome ex-husband James had gone to Athens once to stitch up one of his repellent business deals. Or so he thought. When he arrived home, a broken shell of a man, he described in faltering tones a nightmare of ouzo, super-strength coffee, appallingly late dinners, and loud parties. 'Corinna, they never sleep!' he had whimpered to me afterwards. 'It was awful!'

I wished I had been there. It sounded like fun, and when I looked over the deal that my idiot husband had signed it was surprisingly merciful. It was clear what had happened. They had worn down his resistance over six frenetic days of partying, and when he was so demoralised he would have signed his own execution warrant, they had let him off with absurd leniency. Presumably because he was Australian. Greeks really do like us. I am grateful for this, as always. The hardy folks of Athens might like it industrial-strength, but I like my coffee medium. Drunk at midday, you could reasonably expect to get to sleep after another ten hours or so. And I needed to be alert. I was enjoying what I hoped would be an andante weekend, after the allegro prestissimo of the week from hell I had just endured, but I needed answers.

What a lot I hadn't been learning about the internet today. I mentally revised this. Actually, I had, now I came to review my talk with Gully. As far as he knew, the ransomware culprits had probably been Russians, though he couldn't be sure. And whoever had put it on Del's system wasn't particularly good at cyberwarfare. This could well fit with my slowly coalescing image of a dangerous criminal gang from Azerbaijan, living in Kilmarnock and terrorising people. I still had no idea what they wanted with me, but that was a question for the future.

My present now included a wonderful open sandwich, supplied by Kyria Anastasia. There was proper grilled lamb (the Pandamus family will not have gyros on the premises) done to a turn, with lemon, olive oil, tomato, lettuce, yoghurt, cucumber, pepper, and the inevitable oregano. It was magnificent. I had already had a big breakfast, but somehow my stomach had forgotten it under the influence of this masterpiece of culinary art. I ate at my leisure, and wondered if anyone else from Insula would join me. I was doing well so far.

As if in response to my mental stage-managing, the door swung open and the actors all trooped in. To my surprise, Kylie and Gossamer were with them. I waved, and they waved back, but they went to sit at the big table up the back of the cafe. No problem there. If they didn't want to talk to me I could easily overhear them. And they were actors, so I would probably learn less about them if we spoke face to face. If they had the slightest doubt about me and my motives, they could adopt any persona they liked and leave me none the wiser. So I left them to their gossip, and for quite a while I pretended that I had no interest in their talk. Snippets did arrive my way, however. The actors were fascinated to learn that Kylie and Goss had actually been on TV, and were duly sympathetic (without excessive shows of emotion) that their TV careers had not taken off subsequently. And at one moment I heard one of the girls (Gossamer, I thought, though not with any conviction) exclaiming, 'It *looks* like English, but it's *really* hard!' Luke agreed that this was indeed the case. I hoped he wasn't teasing her.

When I had finished my souvlaki, I accepted a small bowl of yoghurt and honey from Anastasia. Not because I was hungry. On the contrary, I was stuffed. But I really wanted to continue to listen to the actors unobserved. And the snippets I heard were about Prospero and Caliban and their motivations.

'Yes, I know the plot's ridiculous. It's all about the language. It's like opera. How many opera plots make any sense? You just have to run with it.'

'There's more to it than that. It's about colonialism, white superiority, and ruthless exploitation of people classed as natives.'

'Well, yes. But Caliban is so eager to enslave himself because he's been accustomed to it, so he plays up to cultural stereotyping.

Luke carried on, getting more animated. 'And what about

Ariel? Is Ariel following the same trajectory as Caliban all along? Ariel has White Superiority but isn't any better than Caliban.'

'Yes, but Ariel doesn't get pissed. Anyway, it's just another usurpation play, like *Hamlet* or *Richard II,* where the paradigm gets subverted at every turn. Prospero was probably a rotten duke anyway. I'm not surprised he found himself with a one-way ticket into exile. He's only better than a modern dictator because he took his magic books instead of a helicopter filled with gold bullion.'

I had heard enough. They were young, they were innocent, and I was ready to scratch them from my list of suspects. I was just about to go, when there was a commotion at the door. There was barking, followed by a soothing female voice. 'Just stay there, Biscuit! Allegro? Sit down! I won't be long.'

I looked out through the glass front door and saw one of the girls from Heard It Before and the two nervous spoodles. The music girls were also new to the neighbourhood, I realised, though Daniel and I had neglected to add them to our list. I would join the young woman outside, I decided. Luck really was running my way today...

Philomela: I have had an idea. And this really is going to work. It had better. I'm getting tired of this. I miss my life.

Chapter Fifteen

How camest thou in this pickle?
—William Shakespeare, *The Tempest,* Act 5, Scene 1

I let myself out into the hot summer air. It was a pleasant day for those who like hot weather, of which I am not one. I could cope, though. The tearing hot northerlies which turn Australia into the interior of a giant pizza oven had decided not to pay us a visit. It was hot, still, but relatively painless.

I looked at the girl. She wore a pretty summer dress in black with pink spots. She was dark-haired, curvaceous, beautiful, and a little foreign. I had seen many girls like her in Paris. I rummaged in my databanks until the name Marie popped into my head. Though it might be Kate. I decided to take a chance on my first instinct.

'Hello! Marie, isn't it?' I ventured.

She looked up and smiled. Her smile could have powered a medium-sized village. She blinked behind her black-rimmed glasses and said, 'Corinna? It's good to see you.'

Allegro and Biscuit did not agree. The two dogs eyed me with suspicion, and Marie bent over them. 'Stop that!'

They gave me that Look again. Yes, we remember you, they

were saying. You're the human with the two ferocious cats. And where, they wanted to know, are your attack cats now? They sniffed the air, and Marie whispered sweet nothings in their ears. As in all fashionable pavement cafes there was a big aluminium bowl of water attached by a small chain to one of the outdoor tables. Urged on by their mistress, the two spoodles took turns to lap from the bowl. 'That's better. Sit down, you two!' They obeyed, and she flashed me an embarrassed smile. 'Sorry about that.'

'It's okay.' I gestured to one of the chairs. 'Have you got time for a coffee?'

She took out her phone to check. 'Yeah, I guess. It's just gone half the hour. Kate sent me out for a takeaway souvlaki. They're really good here.'

'They really are. Attic heaven on a plate.'

At that moment Del appeared.

Marie grinned at him. '*Geiá sou! Éna souvláki gia na páei kai éna kafé ellinikó parakaló?*'

'*Entaxi, Despina,*' Del pronounced, and disappeared within.

I gaped at Marie.

'I went to Greece for a holiday straight after school,' she explained. 'Well, Corinna, you've been having adventures lately, I hear? Did you walk into a door? It looks painful.'

'Far too many adventures for my liking. But lately it's been getting better. I've gone a whole day now without being burgled.'

She laughed. 'Let's hope it stays that way.'

'Marie, I'm fascinated by this business of yours. Would you mind telling me how it works?'

'Come see for yourself, please. I know music shops are supposed to be so twentieth century, but what we do is something different. When you have mass-market competitors like Amazon, you have to offer something special. So we do. We find music people have vaguely heard somewhere but they don't know either the track or the composer. And we remix songs for people, or we take their old vinyls and turn them into digital collections. But our main business is birthday and Christmas presents. We'll make a gift-wrapped CD or thumb drive with someone's favourite music on it—even if they don't even know it's their favourite music.' She dimpled. 'They will when they get it.'

'It sounds brilliant. Do you play your own music as well?'

'Yes, we both play. Keyboards, strings. I'm soprano, Kate's alto. We're both music majors. Tell me what you like and I'll make you a song in that style.'

'What a wonderful idea! I hope your business thrives. But...'

She laughed again. It was like listening to a magpie's morning song. 'There's always a but. I know. The thing is, we live above the shop. We'd have to pay rent anyway, and we think this might catch on.'

At that moment Del arrived with a small cup of industrial-strength caffeine and placed it reverently in front of her.

'Souvlaki, maybe five minutes, miss,' he announced. She nodded. Some more Greek passed to and fro, but I missed it completely. I don't really do Hellenic. Del disappeared, and Marie clasped the cup and sipped. A gold ring adorned her fourth finger. She caught my eye and blushed, ever so slightly.

'Engagement ring. Now that we can get married at last. All that time we weren't allowed to here, it was a bit awful. We could have gone overseas to some civilised country to marry, but we decided we were fucked if we were going to. So we waited, and finally the plebiscite happened and we're free at last. Anyway, we both love music and we think we can make a go of this. And I've paid the rent on the shop and apartment for the next two years. We'll know by then if we're on to something or not.'

She paused to sip again from the cup of wakefulness. 'When Grandpa died, everyone else in the family decided to move into a huge palace in the northern suburbs. I didn't want anything to do with it. They're more or less okay about me and Kate, but I don't want that sort of life. And some of my cousins and relatives...well.

I don't want anything to do with them. They're scary people. So with my share of the estate I've put a deposit on a block of land in Narre Warren for the two of us, and there's just enough capital left over to keep us going. We can always teach music later on if this doesn't work.'

Northern suburbs, hmm? I decided to go for broke. 'I think you've made good choices. Following your dreams is important. Can I ask where your family went?'

'Kilmarnock. It sounds a bit dire. And the house? It's like a fortress.'

'It probably needs to be. I hear strange things about Kilmarnock.'

'Me too. Young gay couple surrounded by bogans and war-lords? There's drugs and guns and warlords having fights and Dad's in the middle of a gang war with people trying to kill each other all the time. No thanks! The really weird thing is that Dad's worried about *me*. "Bad things happen in the city!" he's always telling me. As if. There's cops everywhere, CCTV cameras cov-ering every square metre and nothing bad's happened to us.' Her face clouded over. 'Oh, I'm sorry. I forgot about the break-ins in your building. But it isn't like this normally, surely?'

'Until this last week, no. I would have said this part of the city was really safe, unless you're out after two in the morning. Apparently that's when it gets a bit lively, though I wouldn't know. I keep bakers' hours.' Something occurred to me. 'Can I ask who told you about my break-ins?'

She gestured towards the interior of the shop. 'I think it was one of the actors in there. Kate and I have done some drama ourselves, and we got talking to them yesterday. They said they're living in your apartment block.'

'Can you remember which one it was specifically who told you?'

She frowned, thinking. 'The Grammar boy. Stephen I think his name is.'

At that moment Del Pandamus re-appeared with Marie's

takeaway souvlaki, and both dogs gave voice to pleadings and urgings. 'It's all right,' I said. 'They can have some of mine.' I ducked back inside, brought out the remains of my souvlaki and my bowl of *yiaourti me meli* and looked at Marie. 'Is it all right if I feed them some scraps?'

Marie looked down at Allegro and Biscuit, who gave her the most beseeching looks I had ever seen from anybody ever. 'All right, you two. Sit down, and the nice lady will give you something.' She flashed her deep eyes at me. 'A piece of meat each, and a bit of the pita bread will do them.' I wrapped up two pieces of meat in scraps of bread and watched them. They were straining at their leashes and whining softly, but doing their very best to be Good Dogs. I could not resist their entreaties, and handed over my offerings.

These proved acceptable, and Marie rose. 'I'll settle up, and then I'll have to go. Good to see you, and don't forget to drop in to Heard It Before.'

As Marie paid her bill, I stroked the two dogs. They looked with envious eyes at the paper-wrapped souvlaki sitting in the middle of the table, but they made no improper attempts at piracy. These were undoubtedly the best behaved dogs I had ever met. Not that I was a Dog Person. Some people are ambidextrous in their love of cats and dogs, but I had never attempted to diversify into canine companionship. What Horatio would say if I brought home a dog was more than I dared imagine.

Presently Marie appeared, took the leashes in her left hand and waved with her right. 'See ya!'

I nodded, thinking hard. No, I decided, nothing sinister should be read into the actors' gossip about the break-ins. They had not told Marie anything they shouldn't. But I was still possessed by the feeling that there was something missing. Some vital piece of information that would make sense of all this weirdness to which we had been subjected. But before long my reverie was interrupted again.

'Corinna! May we join you?'

The whole world was coming to sit at my feet today, it would appear. Detective Senior Constable Letitia White sat down beside me at the table, crossed her legs and gave me a searching look. Constable Helen sat opposite, smiling encouragement to Assist the Police with Their Enquiries.

'Sure, Letty. What's on your mind?'

She grinned at me. It was such a copper grin. The answer to that question, she was saying silently, was: more than you could possibly imagine.

'I was wondering if you'd managed to get through a night without being burgled again.'

'Strange though it may be to hear, yes, I did. I could even get used to this.'

Del Pandamus hovered beside my table, and Letty gave him a look. 'G'day,' she said. 'Can you get us two flat whites?'

As Del retreated to his Italian coffee machine (he does have one, for people like Letty and others unacquainted with the mysteries of Greek coffee) she leant back and sighed. 'I have to say that your burglaries don't look like the same person. The MO is all different. I don't see our friend Jordan breaking into your apartment in a mask, and anyway, apparently he was in Ma'ani's custody at the time. I'm just wondering why we have two different burglars.' She eyeballed me long and hard. 'Especially because Ninja Guy was looking for something in your apartment. I'm inclined to accept our friend Jordan at face value. I mean, yes, he's looking for heresy in Dion Monk's apartment. It's way too weird to be a fairy tale.' She paused. 'Speaking of fairy tales, I'm beginning to think that there were a few subtitles in Professor Monk's thumb drive and notebook dog-and-pony show. I think somebody might have pulled a fast one with some evidence there. Anything you'd like to tell me about?'

I returned her eyeballing and raised her an eyebrow. 'It is possible, of course. All things are possible.'

She nodded. 'Thought so. You know what? I don't give a stuff about his researches into lost Gospels. And the reason I don't give a stuff about them is that weirdo Bible stories don't give rise to Police Matters. As you know, Corinna, there are things which are Police Matters, and things which aren't. Unless you've got a kangaroo loose in the top paddock, like Jordan King, I don't think that the Mystic Scrolls of Destiny cut it as Police Matters. If Jordan ever gets away from Sister Mary's mountainous bodyguard, we'll haul his arse into the Magistrates Court, and if he promises to be a very good boy in future he can get a good behaviour bond and go away forever. Assuming, of course, that you and the Professor are amenable to this?'

I nodded, and she accepted a steaming flat white from Del Pandamus. Constable Helen continued to smile winningly at me, and did not say a word. She didn't need to. Her Look was manifest. You listen up good to what Letty says, okay?

We sipped quietly until the three of us were alone again, and Letty raked me with another piercing gaze. 'Yeah. But Ninja Guy worries me. Either you people are hiding something from me— and in that case you can colour me a very unhappy police officer indeed—or else this is something which they think you have, and you really haven't got it. I'm ruling out a rival bread consortium wanting to steal your sourdough.' She gave me a look of studied innocence. 'Daniel not with you today?'

'He was this morning,' I informed her.

Her appraising look gathered in my caftan, and my aroma of effulgent wellbeing.

'Yeah, I bet. Now the problem I have with private detectives is that they have—as it were—an Agenda of Their Own. I don't have a problem with Mr Cohen, considered as a Private Dick. He's a lot more sensible than many others I could name, and I reckon he can handle himself in a crisis. And, of course, he has Friends.'

'Friends?' I responded, with maximum studied innocence.

'Don't mess me about, Corinna. He has access to…let's say "sources of information" which a mere humble detective can only dream about. And what I want to say is this: if you and Daniel come into possession of any pertinent intel, I need you to tell me about it. Really I do. I've got a bad feeling about this.'

I wasn't going to commit Daniel to anything at all in absentia, so I merely said, 'Thanks for the warning.'

She rose to her full one-sixty-five-centimetre height then sat down again. 'Oh yes, I meant to tell you about the mask. I called in some favours and had an express DNA job done on it.'

'Sorry, but how do you get DNA off a mask?'

'It was in contact with his face, and that's all they need. Normally this takes weeks. But as I said, I'm worried about this case. There may be, as we say, ramifications.'

'Any matches with known criminals?'

'Enquiries are continuing.'

Helen went inside to pay, while Letty continued to give me the Constabulary Once-Over. 'Don't forget what I said, Corinna. I suspect even Daniel might think twice before venturing out of his depth. This one's got silly buggers written all over it. But not in a good way. Cheers.'

She left at a quick march, and I finished my yoghurt and honey at my leisure.

Philomela: I borrowed Anwyn's laptop today. At first I couldn't even remember how to do it, but it started to come back to me. After some practice by myself, I decided that this will work after all. I cannot even begin to tell you how horrible it has all been.

Chapter Sixteen

Adversity's sweetest milk, philosophy.
—William Shakespeare, *Romeo and Juliet*, Act 3, Scene 3

On my way back to Insula, I was rather astonished to see Marie again, sans dogs. She ran towards me, looking like someone who had just remembered that she'd left the gas on.

'Marie? Forgotten something?'

She patted my arm and looked mortally embarrassed. 'I did forget something. I don't suppose you have any bread left, do you? I really need some sourdough. It was the one thing I forgot. Half a loaf will do.'

'I might have. We're closed now, but I usually keep some leftover bread for myself. Care to come and have a look?'

I unlocked the front door and looked behind the counter. Sure enough, I had a loaf and a half left. I held up the half. 'It's yesterday's. Is that OK? And are you sure that's enough?'

'That would be awesome.' A huge grin broke across her flawless features. 'Thanks. How much?'

'Oh please! Don't bother. I've locked the till, and the day's finances are concluded with maximum prejudice.' I tucked the half-loaf into a brown paper bag and handed it over.

Her gaze then fell upon my Bosch print. 'That's *The Garden of Earthly Delights*,' she commented. 'Bosch was a bit out there, wasn't he?'

'I think he was so far out there he'd gone through a doorway into Narnia.' I noticed her fingers tracing around a figure in the third part of the triptych, which depicts a musical hell. God knows what Hieronymus was snacking on. Magic mushrooms, at a guess. There was a hapless man with a rather nice bum halfway into a terrible fate. And, yes, there was music inked on his buttocks. She began to sing—without words—what sounded to my untutored ear like something sweetly medieval.

'Of course, you can read music. That sounds pretty.' A sudden inspiration struck me. 'Marie, if I hum you a tune, can you tell me where it comes from?'

She turned to me with a puzzled air, but nodded. 'Sure. I can try.'

I did my best to recapture the hum I had overheard from my burglar. At first, Marie could make nothing of it. Suddenly her eyes lit up, and she blushed fire-engine red.

'Corinna, it wasn't this, by any chance?' She began to sing in a language I had never heard before: repeated descending phrases, each one starting a little lower than the one before. She looked at me, half defiant and half enchanted.

'I really think it may have been that. What is it?'

She laughed. 'It's called "Beautiful Mountain Girl". It's a traditional song from Armenia, where my family comes from. I learnt it when I was little. The first boy who wanted to marry me used to serenade me with it. Then Kate learnt it and sang it to me, accompanied by a duduk she'd borrowed. That's when I knew she was my true love.' She fluttered her eyelashes playfully. 'Where did you hear it?'

I considered telling her that it had been hummed by a man who was burgling my house at the time, but my mouth closed like a mousetrap. Of all the things to share with this wondrous girl, this wasn't in the top thousand. 'Oh, just somewhere around. But it's been haunting me ever since.'

She laughed again. 'Music's like that. Gotta run now. Thank you so much. Kate really wanted some sourdough. I think we may be having garlic bread tonight.'

I let her out, and returned to Insula in a thoughtful mood. The sun was still shining down from an eggshell-blue sky, and while we'd probably hit our expected top of thirty-three it wasn't unpleasant for those who didn't have to walk far. But the atrium was blessedly cool, and I ran my fingers through the waters of the impluvium. The fountain gurgled away melodiously to itself. No wonder the Romans had liked this sort of thing. Italian summers aren't as fierce as Australian ones, but days like this are common enough there.

I let myself back into my apartment and took out my phone. *Ave, Corinna, we're in Ceres. Care to join us?* Only Professor Monk would send me a Latin greeting, though he had refrained from putting the whole message in the tongue of Cicero out of deference to my linguistic deficiencies. He had come fashionably late to the world of mobile phones, but appreciated the convenience. And I appreciated the invitation. I wondered what other mysteries might be elucidated today.

As I waited for the lift, I went over my earlier lunchtime meetings. The actors? Probably not involved, as I had suspected. Letty White? Good news about the mask, anyway. For the rest, she knew that I knew more than I was letting on, and wasn't happy (in that peculiar constabulary Not Happy fashion) that I was holding out on her. Too bad. There's no fun being a private investigator without a certain interplay of mutual distrust with the law. But I would try to keep her in the loop, as much as I thought appropriate. Marie? What a girl! Her beloved was a lucky woman. But how bizarre that all roads seemed to lead to Kilmarnock. I really would have to visit this mythical land someday soon. But not without my Daniel.

At the summit of Insula the lift doors opened, and I beheld a charming sight. Sitting on garden chairs around the large, white-painted wooden table amid the greenery were Therese Webb, Anwyn, and Philomela in her wheelchair. All three were stitching away at a large piece of calico, with Anwyn holding up the middle and the other two at either end. Professor Monk sat opposite them, holding a book which I perceived to be his favourite recreational reading (Lucretius's *De Rerum Natura*). On the ground, facing off with mutual mistrust and agonised apprehension, were a small chocolate point Siamese cat and Therese Webb's King Charles spaniel Carolus.

There was a certain frisson in the air. The dog was attempting to burrow backwards into Therese's trouser leg, all the while looking with brown-eyed incredulity at the cat. The cat was hunched down next to Anwyn's skirt, looking balefully and fearlessly at the dog. Eventually Carolus retreated behind his mistress's shoes and averted his gaze, and the cat settled down on delicate paws and relaxed. I squatted down and held out my hand. At once the cat strolled over to say hello, and allowed me to caress its silky head. Which I did until Anwyn looked up. 'Bellamy? Where are you? Oh, hello, Corinna.'

The cat immediately leapt up onto the table and sprawled out on the centrepiece of the tapestry, which seemed to feature a number of men in early homespun armour and some viridian grasslands.

'Corinna, my dear,' said the Professor, laying down his book. 'You're just in time for some formation cat worship.'

The other two laid down their needles and thread and leant back in their respective chairs while Bellamy (for I presumed it was he) displayed his spotless cream-coloured coat under Anwyn's caressing hands.

'Bellamy is the reason I'm visiting Melbourne,' Anwyn explained. 'He appears to have hitched a ride from my house and turned up in the northern suburbs. I picked him up on the first morning.'

'You have a feline hitchhiker? I have to say that's…unusual,' I observed.

'It is rather. But he's a very unusual cat. Carolus is so far unimpressed, though.'

Therese Webb laughed. 'Well, yes, to an extent. I'm surprised it's taking him so long to get used to him. He gets on fine with all our local cats here, but something about Bellamy seems to have him worried.'

Anwyn leant forward and continued to caress Bellamy's head. His paws stretched out horizontally and his citrine eyes closed. Loud purrs filled the fragrant garden. 'I think the reason Carolus is put out is because back home Bellamy has two dogs called Nutmeg and Digby who are his most devoted servants. I only got Bellamy because the dogs were heartbroken when their cat Onslow died from renal cancer. Onslow bossed the dogs around and they loved it, and him. So they needed a new cat and Bellamy fitted in immediately.'

'The dogs love him, so he expects all dogs to do the same?' I suggested.

'Oh yes. And while Carolus is a polite and friendly dog, he's not ready to commit to that sort of relationship.'

Dion Monk administered some cat caresses of his own, and cooed appreciatively. 'Well, you'll just have to content yourselves with human admirers today.'

Bellamy looked as though he was absolutely fine with that and went on purring.

The Professor gave Anwyn a sidelong glance. 'Did he really hitchhike from Adelaide? Did he stand on the side of the highway holding up a sign in his paws reading *Melbourne or bust?*'

Anwyn grinned. 'Possibly. He was found in someone's backpack. He's always climbing into my shopping bags and I think he must have stowed away and gone to sleep there. The people who found him in their car in Northcote had just driven from Adelaide, and they checked his microchip and rang me. The mystery is how he came to be in the backpack in the first place. They'd been in Bedford Park, which is where I live, but they swear they hadn't been near my house. Just one of those little mysteries.'

The Professor nodded sagely. 'Siamese are notoriously inscrutable. So you drove here yourself to pick him up, of course?'

'Of course. And I thought I may as well make it a proper visit, since we've got this tapestry to work on.'

'And where did you find this paragon of cats?' I wanted to know.

'My friend Celsa occasionally breeds Siamese kittens. So I bought him for one hundred and fifty dollars and a knitted cap. She lives in Ballarat, but she's one of us.'

I looked at her in incomprehension.

'We're medieval role-players. And this is my latest project, ably assisted by my hearth-companions.' She inclined her head at Therese and Philomela, both of whom smiled: Therese with some pride, and Philomela like a mouse menaced by a cat. Anwyn lifted Bellamy up into her arms. 'Come on, dear. Mummy wants to show off our handiwork.'

Bellamy protested, but allowed himself to be laid across her lap. He subsided into immediate slumber. Anwyn stroked him with loving hands. 'He really could be an Olympic sleeper. Well, Corinna, what do you think?'

I couldn't make much out of it, and turned enquiringly to Professor Monk.

He scanned it approvingly. 'No Normans here, I see. Vikings and Saxons, I think. And the writing looks like Old English, which I don't speak, unfortunately. But that is a fine piece of work. Please, Anwyn, do expound, if you would be so good.'

She beamed at him. 'Very good! The Bayeux embroidery was made by English women; the Normans didn't have the skills. And yes, the text is Old English.'

I scanned the writing at the top. Ða ðær Byrtnoð ongan beornas trymian meant nothing to me. The stitching I thought I recognised. 'Brick-stitch for the heavy work, and couching for colour contrast?' I ventured.

Anwyn grinned. 'Well done, Corinna! Recognise anything else?'

There was a huge (presumably English) warrior in chain mail waving a sword, and water in front of him labelled *flod*. There were other men in armour with evil-looking expressions. Several scenes had been blocked out, including what looked like the death of a giant. There were also borders top and bottom filled with serpents, houses and other decorations. It was like a Dark Age cartoon, or graphic novel. I scanned to the end. It didn't look good.

'Those guys look like Vikings,' I suggested, pointing at the attackers.

'They are. The quote is from the Battle of Maldon, in 991.' Anwyn's face took on a faraway expression. 'It was a tragic defeat for the English, because their idiot commander Byrhtnoth allowed the Vikings to cross the river to make a fair fight of it. He and all his men fell where they stood.'

Now she closed her eyes and began to chant. '*Hyge sceal ðe heardra, heorte ðe cenre; mod sceal ðe mare ðe ure maegen lytlað.*'

She opened her eyes again. 'That was put into the mouth of one of his warriors. "Mind must be harder, heart the keener; spirit burn the brighter as our strength lessens." One of the others also said: "I shall not stir a foot's pace from here, now that my dear lord lies dead." He was an idiot, and his men died for it. But they killed and wounded so many of the Vikings that the latter all went home to East Anglia afterwards.'

'So it was all for nothing?' I asked.

She shook her head. 'I wouldn't say that. The East Anglian Vikings were pretty quiet for the next few years, but Alfred the Great wouldn't have put up with commanders who gave up strategic advantages out of a misguided zeal for glory. He saved Anglo-Saxon England from the Vikings when everyone else had given up.'

'This is nearly a hundred years after Alfred's death, of course.' Professor Monk looked up at the sky for a moment. 'Did you say Byrhtnoth?'

Anwyn nodded.

'I believe I have paid my respects to him. He's buried in Ely Cathedral. Bishop West's chapel, from memory. Right next to someone called Archbishop Wulfstan. I remember asking the vergers who he was, and they didn't seem to know. Wasn't he a giant of some sort?'

'Six feet nine inches tall. So much for the theory that everyone was tiny in the Dark Ages. But he really was that height; they measured his bones in the eighteenth century.'

I thought about this. 'Anwyn, weren't the Welsh and the Saxons hereditary enemies? Yet here you are, commemorating a heroic Saxon defeat. It just strikes me as rather odd that you would do so.'

'Yes, they were our enemies, though after they turned to Christianity they improved. Do you know, they blamed us afterwards for not converting them?'

'Really? That's unexpected.'

'Yes. They were converted by the Scots, who were converted by the Irish, and then they turned to us and said, "Well you might have told us before about all this!" I found them quite different from what I imagined. Did you know the West Saxon Royal House was descended from a son of Noah born on the Ark?'

Professor Monk's jaw dropped. 'That's disturbing. Shem, Ham, and Japhet didn't fit in to their genealogical wishes, so they invented a new one? I would have thought the god Woden might have been a better fit for them.'

'Him too. The Old Testament and saints' lives were their TV. Most of their surviving poetry is about that. Beowulf is a bit of an outlier.'

Professor Monk grinned, his eyes sparkling. 'Only four dragon-scorched manuscripts made it to the modern age, as far as I've heard.'

Fascinating though this scholarly symposium undoubtedly

was, I felt that now might be a good time to interrupt, before the Remembrances of Things Past slipped into overdrive. This was my day off and there were still things I needed to find out. But I didn't want to tackle Philomela directly. She still looked scared and on edge. If she had something to tell me, it had better be approached in a roundabout fashion.

'Dion, I was wondering if you'd given any further thought to our little mysteries?'

At once his eyes focused on me, and his white-bearded chin nodded almost imperceptibly in approval. 'Well, yes and no. I am yet to solve the mystery of what abominable heresy I am supposed to be harbouring. Although, thanks to your quick wits, Corinna, I have managed to get a little further in my researches. It would appear that Jesus and Mary Magdalene really were married, and seem to have had at least one child if not more. However, all this has been common coin for many years now, and not just through our friend Dan Brown. So we have not really advanced on that front, although…'

He paused, and gave me a sidelong look. 'There is a rather exciting development in the travels of Mr and Mrs Jesus and family. I'd prefer not to say more about it until I'm more certain of my studies, but there may be something altogether new which we have not seen before. Perhaps this may be what our friend Jordan has been overexciting himself about. But unless Burglar Secundus was after my Gospel as well—which seems to me quite improbable—I am beginning to believe that somebody else thinks I have something in my flat which is an artefact worthy of active pursuit.'

I looked at his aged face. He was glowing, like an old warhorse roused by the sound of bugles. In the bright sunlight his short, clipped beard shone and his bright blue eyes could have held all the warships of Agamemnon. There was something different about him of late. I wondered whether it was the burglary that had so galvanised him, or the obvious attentions of Mrs Dawson.

'Letitia White and Helen think so too. I just saw them at Cafe Delicious. But you haven't such an artefact, have you?'

'On my life, Corinna, I really haven't. I am the temporary guardian of some biblical-era scholarship. I have some Greek pots, but nothing valuable on the black market. I will continue to give my mind to the problem, but I have nothing to add for now. I wish I did.'

Therese Webb spoke for the first time. She slipped her needle into the calico embroidery and smiled. 'We have made significant progress in another area. Philomela has been practising on Anwyn's laptop. She can't speak yet, but she can manage a little typing. Ask your questions, and she can answer you.'

I tried not to get too excited, but my heart did a few cartwheels. Anwyn picked up her laptop from the table and handed it to Philomela, who opened the lid and fumbled with her finger and thumb at the pad until she had produced a blank Word page. Her terrified eyes locked on mine for a long moment, then she bowed her head.

'Can you remember what happened to you?' I asked softly.

She tapped a few keys and turned the screen towards me.

YES.

'Did someone hurt you?'

YES.

'Was it someone you know?'

NO.

'Where did this happen?'

AT HOME.

'Philomela, where is home?'

It took her a long time to spell it out, and she made a few mistakes before she was satisfied. She turned the laptop again, and without too much surprise I read *KILMARNOCK*.

'And what happened?' I held my breath, because this was the big one.

Again she struggled hard, her brow creased with effort. Then she sighed, closed her eyes, and turned her screen to face me.

I gasped.

THEY KILLED MY SISTER.

Philomela: Finally! Now it will be easier. And maybe some-day I shall be able to speak with my mouth again, rather than relying on a laptop with a faulty caps lock key. It looks like I'm shouting. Then again, why should I not shout? I feel like shouting. I want them hounded to their graves and beyond. My sister's blood cries for vengeance.

Chapter Seventeen

Villain and he be many miles asunder.
—William Shakespeare, *Romeo and Juliet*, Act 3, Scene 5

For the moment I leant back in my chair, because things were happening quickly and I did not want to add to the melee. Professor Monk, like me, was staying out of it. The other two women had risen, and their arms met around Philomela's shoulders. Philomela's eyes had closed, and she was resting her head on Therese Webb's bosom. Endearments and sympathies were being uttered. But these were drowned out, because in the general confusion someone had trodden on Carolus and he was letting the world know all about it. Bellamy, instantly awake, had fled in a cream-coloured streak of outrage into the undergrowth.

Feeling that I might be better employed as a cat-rescuer, I followed the trail into the parsley forest. 'Bellamy?' I called, but could neither see nor hear anything. Then I looked back, in time to see the following.

Carolus had launched himself straight into Philomela's lap. Instinctively her small, scarred hands had wrapped around the little dog and begun to caress him. He stopped barking immediately and whined a sad, thoughtful little whine and lay still. The others fell silent, and Philomela's mouth opened. She crooned the words '*Agape mou!*' and everyone froze.

In the pool of silence, Dion Monk looked at her. '*Taxeis Ellenika?*' he asked softly.

'*Ne.*'

'*Kai mileis Ellenika?*'

She opened her mouth to speak again, but nothing came out. The Professor's hand made soothing gestures. 'It's perfectly all right, my dear. We know that you can speak, but you're not ready just yet. But it will come. Some time when no one's expecting it. Don't try to force yourself to talk. Just wait for it to happen. You will get there in good time. But what we need for you to do is tell the story, if you can, on Anwyn's laptop. I'm sure she will let you borrow it for as long as you need.'

Anwyn's arm was still around the younger woman's shoulders. 'Yes, of course. And once you've written it all down, it will be like a crushing weight has been lifted from your shoulders.'

Philomela nodded, and Carolus wagged his tail hopefully. He was still in Philomela's lap and wasn't going anywhere. Philomela pulled the laptop towards her, tapped a little more, frowned, and shook her head in frustration. Finally she typed:

ASK ME.

Professor Monk waved me over to the table and I sat down next to Philomela. The computer was open in front of us. I pressed the caps lock button and the little green light faded. Then I stared at the screen. It was very hard to think up appropriately precise questions. It would have been so much easier if she had been able to type it all herself, but the trauma had gone deeper than the merely physical.

I began: 'So this happened at home? Were you in the house, or outside?'

Outside.

'And you were there with your sister when it happened?'

Yes.

'Did you see them?'

Yes.

'How many of them were there?'

???

'More than one?'

???

'So you didn't really see them?'

No.

I had a long think about this. Clearly I wasn't asking the right questions yet. I looked at Dion Monk and the others, but they merely shrugged. I presume the idea was that it would be better with only one person asking. What was I missing? She'd seen them, only not really.

'Did they shoot her?'

No.

'Was it a knife?'

No.

'Did they kill her from far away?'

No.

'Up close then?'

Yes.

'But you didn't see them properly? Were you out the front of your house, or out the back?'

Front.

What could have happened? I risked a quick look at her. She was very pale, and her thin lips were trembling. Perspiration beaded on her face. 'Do you want to stop now?'

No.

No, she really didn't. Her deep brown eyes shone with absolute determination to see this through. So. We needed a murder weapon that killed up close, yet didn't let you see the assailants properly. What could do that? Then illumination dawned.

'Was it a car?'

Yes!!!

At last. Now it would be easier. 'Were you in the driveway?'

Yes.

'Do you have a garage that locks with a sliding door?'

Yes.

'And they rammed into you both against the garage door?'

Yes.

'And your sister died immediately?'

Yes.

I was expecting tears, but her delicate oval face had now set in a frozen mask. 'And you were badly hurt. Was anyone else home?'

Yes.

'Did they see the car?'

Drove away.

'Is there any chance you could describe it?'

Yes.

'A big car?'

Yes.

'What colour?'

Black.

Out of the corner of my eye I noticed Professor Monk was writing busily. I was glad he was taking notes. We would need them for Letty White. While I was not abdicating my rights to independent action, we would have to let her know about this.

'A big, black car. Tinted windows?'

Yes.

'Have you seen it before?'

Yes.

'Is it local? You've seen it parked in your neighbourhood?'

Yes.

'An SUV?'

Yes.

'Do you know the people whose car it is?'

No.

'You think this was a case of mistaken identity?'

Yes.

It seemed only too likely. Gangsters being in most respects utter morons, their victims are frequently innocent bystanders. 'They may have dumped the car by now. Then again, they may not have. Would you know it again?'

Yes.

I wondered how to proceed now. I didn't want to have to take Philomela with us, but we had to be certain of the address if we were going to stake them out. I now suspected that Philomela's assailants were mixed up in at least one of our mysteries. Maybe more? It was too early to tell; but perhaps our cases might not be as separate as they seemed. We needed to go and see for ourselves, preferably without taking a traumatised and wheelchair-bound victim to revisit the scene of her sister's death. I wasn't sure of myself, but I now suspected that her sister's killers and the dognappers might be the same people. Or maybe the ninja burglars instead. Why? I didn't have anything concrete yet. But my best guess was that they were also the dognappers. Maybe it was all about drugs and they thought Geordie could smell them out. Philomela and her sister were the victims of mistaken identity. Melbourne's criminal classes had developed a cavalier disregard for innocent bystanders in recent years. But there was more here than coincidence. There had to be.

'Can you write down your address?'

A vestige of a smile touched the corners of her lips. She reached into a small handbag then handed me her driver's licence. From this I learnt that Philomela Venizelos lived at 34 Anzac Drive, Kilmarnock. I hadn't even considered the idea that she might have a driver's licence. I handed it to Dion Monk, who wrote down the address and handed it back to her.

'Would you prefer not to go there? Because, thanks to you, we've got a lead now.'

Not yet.

'You can stay here for a while. You're not going anywhere if you don't want to.'

Thank you.

'Is there anything else you can tell us?'

Yes.

'About who it might be? Do you think they might be gangsters?'

Yes.

'You say you've seen the car. Was it outside a big house?'

Yes.

'Did it look fortified? Like a motorbike gang clubhouse?' I was thinking of some TV footage I had seen, with iron gates, barbed wire and sentry towers during a police raid on one notorious gang. I had been struck at the time how much the fortress looked like a prison, which, in essentials, it was.

No. Normal big house. Rich people.

I paused. This was the biggie, and I really didn't want to ask it. But I had to. Even though Letty White would be asking it herself in due course, anyway, she wouldn't necessarily let me know the answer. 'All right, Philomela, I know you said you think this was a case of mistaken identity, but are you sure? While you and your sister mightn't have done anything wrong, it's possible someone else in your house has got mixed up in bad company.'

She shook her head, frowned, and began to type again. She had several tries at it, but eventually came up with the following:

No. Mum housewife. Dad teaches school. Brother George is good boy. Works hard at school. No trouble ever.

I mused. Mistaken identity it was, then. 'Philomela, is there another house that looks like yours where criminals might live?'

Yes. Four, five houses away. Other side of road. Bad people go there late at night. We stay away from them.

'Have you heard them speaking?

Yes. Only once.

'Was it a language you knew?'

No.

'Did it sound like Russian?'

No. More like Turkish, but not.

I had no means of knowing what her guess was worth. I must find out about Azeri and what it sounded like. But...I remembered that the dognappers couldn't be Muslims. Did we have two rival gangs of different ethnicities? It looked like it.

'All right, Philomela, is there anything else you can tell us? This has been very traumatic for you, I know—you can stop now if you like.'

She shook her head, smiled weakly, and handed the laptop back to Anwyn, who gave me a steady look. 'I'd better take her back inside, I think.' She turned to Philomela. 'Would you like that?' she asked.

Philomela nodded.

'Now, where is that cat of mine?'

I suddenly remembered an episode of *The Goodies*—that vintage British comedy show–which was a send-up of *Watership Down*. I made my way under the foliage and began to call out. 'Bellamy! Where's Bellamy?'

Anwyn came to join in, grinning.

'I named him after that show,' she confessed. 'Bellamy! Where's Bellamy?'

Out from the parsley forest came a small cream-coloured cannonball, launching itself straight into Anwyn's arms. At once Bellamy was folded into a loving embrace, and I followed them back to the long table. Bellamy was carefully lowered into Philomela's lap. He glared briefly at Carolus, who had carefully alighted on the ground, then closed his eyes. Anwyn pushed the wheelchair back towards the lift, accompanied by Therese, with Carolus padding behind like a small, flop-eared footman.

I glanced at Dion Monk, who gestured to me to sit down. It appeared that he might have more to contribute to the elucidation of our mysteries.

Philomela: So tired now.

Chapter Eighteen

The rarer action is in virtue than in vengeance.
—William Shakespeare, *The Tempest*, Act 5, Scene 1

Soon the Professor and I had the rooftop garden to ourselves. The bright sunlight made his white beard and tonsure shine. He looked as if he might have stepped straight out of the Book of Kells.

'Well now, Corinna, that was something of a surprise, was it not?' he offered.

I lay back in my chair with my back to the sun and stretched. 'Indeed it was. That wasn't anything like what I had expected. It would appear that our mysteries are connected after all.'

One cautious eyebrow rose. I realised that he wasn't up to speed with our investigations, and filled him in accordingly. 'And so,' I concluded, 'aside from our Catholic soldier of Christ, it appears that we may only have one mystery—or one set of mysteries—after all. We have at least one, and probably two different criminal gangs, one or possibly both resident in the mysteriously threatening land of Kilmarnock. And they have erupted into our little urban village because somebody wanted Alasdair's dog, for whatever reason; because some of them crippled our unfortunate guest and killed her sister; and—' I gave the Professor what I hoped was a penetrating look '—because somebody thinks one of us has something which will give them an advantage in their turf war. Whether it's a thing I'm supposed to have, or you, or Mrs Pemberthy for that matter—I have no idea. But they're looking for something. This hasn't been random break-ins. They want a specific thing. Maybe a mystic artefact? Are you sure you don't have anything like that?'

He shook his head. 'My dear, unless organised crime syndicates have begun to take an interest in biblical scholarship, I have not the faintest idea. The trouble with criminals is that we tend to invest them with demonic subtlety, when most of the time…' He raised one aged hand and waved it dismissively

'They are merely stupid beyond belief,' I finished. 'Indeed. There's one thing I may not have told you. Alasdair thinks he overheard the dognappers say something in a foreign language.' He looked at me expectantly while I tried to disinter the indigestible fragment from a memory overfilled with recipes and constant crisis. 'Ah yes. Something like *vorteh nizaky*. Does that ring any bells?'

He pursed his lips and picked up his notebook and biro. 'If you would be so good as to say it again?'

I did so, and he scribbled something down. '*Vorteh nizaky?* I've got that down in standard phonetic script, so it doesn't wander. It really doesn't ring any bells. Hmm.' He thought for a moment, then shook his head. 'So, Corinna, what are your plans for the evening?'

'A sleep first, I think. And then I'd like to join Sister Mary on the Soup Run.'

'Is this a hunch?'

'Indeed it is a hunch. I was going to see if I could get anything more out of Jordan King. But—who knows? I'm mostly looking out for news of Geordie, though anything else about our gangland wars—who knows? Maybe someone might let something slip about that too. I mean, yes, Daniel is the pro and I'm just the amateur, and he's already been out and about asking questions. But...'

'You feel that some of the downtrodden masses might be more inclined to open their hearts to a baker than a private investigator? I think so too. Sorry, who is Geordie? Remind me.'

'Geordie is Alasdair's missing dog.'

He nodded. 'In that case, you might want to take Alasdair with you, if he's up to it.'

I reached for my phone, texting Daniel as follows:

> If you think it advisable, why not send me A?
> Am doing Soup Run. He may want to join in?

There was no answer. I don't ring Daniel when he's on duty. He could be tailing someone in conditions of secrecy, or up to his armpits in venomous snakes. His phone would be on silent. Until he answered my text I would await developments.

Dion Monk nodded his approval. 'It is possible that the Soup Run may provide further clues. I gather some of the dispossessed can be helpful, if they decide they want to be.' He patted my hand. 'You have coped magnificently thus far with this impenetrable series of mysteries and irruptions, Corinna. Well, I shall not take up any more of your valuable time. Do let me know how it all turns out.'

He rose and departed, and I stared into the depths of the parsley forest, trying to get my head around it all. What was I hoping for exactly? That the answer to one or more of our problems would leap out at me. It seemed a remote possibility. Then again, doing something positive was better than staying in my apartment trying to reason and theorise from insufficient data. Then my phone buzzed.

> Excellent idea. I'll bring him round at 8.

Whatever my Daniel was doing was clearly undercover of some sort. I wished I had him under the covers of my doona, but that could wait. I was already looking forward to my afternoon nap, but there was one thing I wanted to do first. Still dressed agreeably *en boudoir,* I made my way downstairs and out to Heard It Before.

The shop occupied a small sliver of Calico Alley which had hitherto been an op shop. Unsurprisingly, it had not prospered. I could not even remember who had been optimistic enough to open an op shop for second-hand clothes and oddments in the central business district. I opened the glass door and there behind her counter was Kate, surrounded by concert programs, amplifiers, turntables, MP3 players and CDs in cases. I believe I caught a glimpse of vinyl LPs, lurking in stacks under a bookcase. I pondered for a moment the improbable resurgence of vinyl records. Would cassette tapes be the next instalment of retro chic? I thought this wildly improbable. She grinned at me, her brown eyes flashing with welcome.

'Corinna! Great to see you! Marie told me you might drop by.' What I could see of her was encased in a neat white T-shirt bearing a strange musical staff in black letters over her breasts. I must have looked longer than was polite, because she grinned again. 'Haven't you ever seen an alto clef before?'

'Is that what it is? It looks confusing. Is that middle C on the third stave?'

'Well done! Yes, it is.'

'I hope the souvlaki measured up?'

'It was magnificent. We're going there again.' She waved her hand around the shop. 'Can I interest you in something?'

'Please. I want something for my beloved. Maybe a mix of something Irish?'

'Are they Irish?'

I must have blinked, because Kate rushed to explain. 'If they're Irish, they may not want their own ancestral music, because it was probably hammered into them growing up and they might be all Celted out. Otherwise, sure.'

I blinked again, realising that the use of the third-person plural was intended to cover all possible genders for my aforementioned beloved. The idea that people could choose their own personal pronouns was still a little new to me, but I appreciated the general inclusiveness of the thought. 'He's Israeli. But he likes Clannad and the Corrs.'

'Okay then. Is there a particular album he wants, do you think, or just something in that style?'

'Something in that style would be lovely. Gift-wrapped?'

'Of course. Is seventy-five dollars too much? We can give you a CD and a thumb drive, with a gift card and list of tracks.'

'Are you going to write something specially for him? If so, that's way too cheap.'

'Well, not really. What's his name?'

'Daniel.'

'What we'll do with this is make Daniel a mix tape. We've done some multitrack Irish already, from traditional and completely non-copyright sources, so he can have them. We've also done some more-or-less Clannad/Corrs improvisations, and we'll put them on too. And we'll do one track especially for Daniel. What's he like?'

I paused, momentarily at a loss. What could I tell these girls about my wonderful man?

She tilted her head. 'Tall, short, funny, serious?'

'Tall, dark and handsome. And dangerous, but only to bad guys.'

She thought about this. 'Okay, that should be enough. When would you like it?'

'Is Monday possible?'

'Sure. We don't have a party on tonight, so we'll write something and record it after dinner.'

'How wonderful. Thank you!' I reached into my purse and disinterred a fifty, a twenty, and a five. 'And you must let me pay you in advance.'

Her small, perfect white teeth flashed for a moment. For a commission like this, she would always ask. 'Tell all your friends.'

'I will.' I grasped the receipt and she smiled again.

I left the shop, intending to go home to sleep, but standing outside her shop was Meroe. She beckoned, looking rather like a prophet attempting to sell the Sibylline books to the King of the Romans, and I followed her into her shop. It smelt, as ever, of perfumes, incense, herbal teas and watchfulness. I stood for a long moment to admire the crystals (amethysts still seemed to be very popular), the dreamcatchers, the inspirational CDs and all the rest. I saw many boxed sets of tarot cards, which seemed to be making a comeback. Above them I noticed a placard inscribed in a sans-serif font which stated:

PLEASE DO NOT ASK FOR ALEISTER CROWLEY'S TAROT CARDS
AS A CURSE OFTEN OFFENDS.

I inhaled the odours of sandalwood and patchouli, and Meroe waited. She has a genius for it. She seems to live in a small, gently rippling pool of silence. Today she wore her usual black dress with a pale green shawl. She closed the door behind me and I waited. Then she laid her slender hand on my arm and sat me down in one of her antique wooden chairs. There was no one else in the shop.

'Corinna, you are walking into peril, aren't you?' she said, her voice like small stones tumbling into a pond.

'I fear that this may indeed be the case,' I agreed.

She rummaged under the counter and brought out a tiny wooden suitcase with a brass handle on it, about the size of the palm of my hand. 'I think you should have this,' she stated in her quiet, matter-of-fact voice. I noted a small label on it saying forty dollars.

Meroe never tells me things like this without good reason, so I paid up at once, and opened it. Inside was fine straw, and buried within was the most beautiful ring I had ever seen: wooden, with a glorious blue stone with what looked to be a petrified forest within.

'This is the Ring of Otherworlds,' she stated. 'It will help you see when all the lights go out. Wear it until the danger is passed.' She walked to the front door again and turned over the sign saying OPEN so it faced inwards. 'I'm not expecting any more customers today. I want to read for you, if you're agreeable?'

I nodded, and she brought out a small wooden table and put it in front of me, sat herself down in a chair opposite, and produced a small silk bundle. Unwrapped, this showed itself to be a deck of cards with blue-and-white-checked backs and intriguing designs on the obverse. 'Have you ever had a reading before?' she asked, putting her head on one side and shuffling the deck.

'Once, as a student. I don't think he was very good at it.'

She handed me the pack and I shuffled it too.

'Cut the deck,' she instructed, and I did so. The lower half she turned around the other way and resumed shuffling.

We did this three times each, then she fanned the cards, face down, across the wooden table. 'I use the Rider deck. It is hallowed by tradition, and is also completely safe. In my hands, anyway. Unlike some decks, which aren't.' I glanced at the sign and she managed a thin-lipped smile. 'Especially not that one. I had three enquiries for it this week. Crowley was a complete pervert. I will go a long way for my customers, but I won't stock that. Now you need to pick a card. Take your time, and remember which way up it is. Upright or reversed are quite different.'

I probably imagined it, but one of the cards seemed to be saying: *Pick me!* I handed it to her and she placed it face down on the table.

'The Star. Very well. You feel that you are at the mercy of forces far too cosmic for you, and it's all too outré. Correct?'

'That is an excellent summary of my life of late.'

She began to deal from the top of the pack until we had a double cross laid out. It certainly looked colourful enough. She touched the card at the extreme left. It showed eight staves slanting diagonally across a green and pleasant landscape.

'The Eight of Wands. This is your immediate past. Same as the Star, really. Life is strange and out of control, and you have been doing your best to cope.'

I nodded. Then she touched the card in the centre of the cross, which showed an angel holding a lion's mouth shut. It looked promising. Even the lion didn't look too unhappy about it.

'Strength means pretty much what you think, except that it's spiritual strength rather than something that comes out of a jar of protein supplements and far too much pumping iron. You have powerful allies looking after you. Crossing you is the Seven of Wands. I like sevens. And these two are related.'

I looked as a man on top of a hill with a big staff was beating off six other staves.

'You are in a struggle, and outnumbered. But you have the higher ground, and a stalwart protector.'

Next came a card with more coins on it than a Bollywood wedding. 'It would appear that the next thing you attempt will be successful.'

Well, that sounded good.

Then the corners of her mouth turned down. 'But these...' She touched four cards, all of which showed people holding swords. 'Three of these are bad. The Ten is what it looks like. This is peril of death, and I mean actual physical death.'

I stared at the prone figure. Ten swords protruded from his body. That looked about as unequivocal as anything I'd ever seen.

Meroe gave a slight cough and resumed. 'The Page down here? I'm not sure. It may be you. But having swords above and below means there's no way around this. You have to face what is coming. And what you will face is this here...' She touched a card with a blindfolded woman holding two swords. 'The Two reversed is unnatural passion. Are you in trouble with criminals?'

'We've been broken into a lot, as you may have heard.'

Meroe leant forward, ran her hands down her front and frowned. 'Yes, but there's something worse here than just a break-in. It's hidden, for the moment. The good news is this one: the Seven.'

I stared at it. Next to a fairground pavilion, a stealthy character had picked up a bundle of swords and appeared to be making off with them.

'Someone is going to help you, unexpectedly. But covertly.'

'I should expect surreptitiousness?'

'Indeed you should.'

I liked the fact that the last card showed what looked like the Holy Grail. She nodded. 'The ruling card here is the Three of Cups. This means you need to keep your emotional balance. The Ace down here reinforces that.'

She smiled again, closed her eyes and was silent for a long time. I looked at my watch. Three-thirty-eight! My afternoon nap was slipping away.

Suddenly she stared straight at me, her deep brown eyes narrowed. 'Corinna, you're going on a journey soon. For some reason I see a dog. Make sure you carry some doggie treats. And...do you have an amber bracelet?'

'Yes, I have one. Should I wear that too?'

'Yes, you should.' She gripped the arms of her chair and muttered, 'Do you know, these four cards here usually represent occurrences in the distant future. But there's such an air of haste about all this that I don't think so. Are you going out tonight?'

'Yes, I'm going on the Soup Run. Is the danger there? I can always put it off.'

She shook her head. 'Yes, that should be all right. Be bold, but careful. And do not go alone.'

'I won't. Anything else?'

She rose, and took my hand. 'No. If you don't seek it, it will come for you anyway. Be prepared.'

And so, with the Boy Scouts' motto still ringing in my ears, I returned to my apartment and went to bed.

Philomela: I smell vengeance brewing. It has the sweetest of scents. I managed to play Jenny Plucks Pears on the recorder today. I still can't speak, but I can play. My fingers remember!

Chapter Nineteen

'Tis not so deep as a well, nor so wide as a church door;
but 'tis enough, 'twill serve.
—William Shakespeare, *Romeo and Juliet,* Act 3, Scene 1

Sleep is indeed a wondrous thing. I woke again in the late afternoon to find Horatio stretched out next to me on the bed. His eyes opened briefly and closed again. He stretched out his front paws, spreading out his vestigial fingers in an ecstasy of sybaritic comfort. I did the same. Life had been running far too fast for me to catch up, but my mutual catnap with Mr Horatio had been just what I needed.

As I prepared myself a light Caesar salad I reviewed what I had learnt. Our multiple mysteries were certainly beginning to crystallise. And while Meroe's tarot reading had scared me, I was oddly comforted by her insistence that this crisis could not be dodged. As I already knew, the forces of the ungodly would come to me whether I wanted it or not. It was all very well for Wonder Woman to barge into the midst of foes and make everything right. This is the prerogative of goddesses, not humans. Sensible people don't go looking for trouble. But if trouble were coming anyway, stepping out forewarned and forearmed to meet it didn't seem so bad.

I was now convinced I knew where Geordie was. And we were going to rescue him. Why had the Kilmarnock crime gang taken him? I didn't know that. And I didn't much care. He had to be there. Because if he wasn't, then he must surely be dead and I wasn't prepared to countenance that. I was also convinced that our three break-ins were committed by two people. Jordan we knew about. But my ninja and the Professor's Second Burglar had to be the same people. And they probably were the dognappers as well. Once I had reluctantly accepted Jordan King as a coincidence, the rest seemed to be connected. Was this reason, or intuition? A mixture of both. But there was nothing especially sinister about Jordan. He was a farcical footnote to a series of menacing crime scenes. The rest seemed to be all of a piece.

I sprinkled some munchies into Horatio's dinner dish in case he felt peckish, and set one of my best metal bowls on the kitchen table. I laid out a circular wheel of cos lettuce in the bottom, sliced two hard-boiled eggs, sprinkled some leftover cooked bacon, added a few croutons, a liberal serving of mayonnaise and some ground salt and black pepper. And anchovies! I swear by them. Alas, some can only swear at them, it seems. Professor Monk says he loves the idea of furry fish, but the actuality is too much: a bit like trying to swallow an aquarium. A half-glass of chilled sauv blanc was duly poured, and I browsed my way through my dinner in contentment. Through a small gap beneath my heavy-duty sunshades golden sunlight peeped nervously. According to my resolutely analogue wall clock, it was a little after seven o'clock when I finished dinner. I washed up, dressed myself in comfortable summer trousers, a loose blouse and sensible flat shoes. My doorbell sounded and I pressed the intercom button. 'Corinna? We're early. I hope that's all right.'

That was Daniel's chocolate-smooth voice, gloriously welcome as always. I let him in, reflecting that even though he has his own key to my apartment he usually rings anyway. Just to make the point.

I opened my door and ushered them into the sitting room. 'Drink?' I offered.

'A sauv blanc for me,' Daniel responded. 'Alasdair?'

The bereft squaddie shook his head. 'No thanks,' he murmured.

I waved Daniel towards the bottle and took a close look at Alasdair. He looked weary beyond words, but some colour had returned to his features. His eyes had stopped darting left and right, and he no longer gave the impression of a violin wound too tight for comfort. He looked calmer than I remembered. That would not be difficult. He was comfortably dressed in black jeans with holes in the knees (an old pair of Daniel's, I noted) and a plain black T-shirt. Only his boots, and the air of hidden menace steaming gently off his stringy, muscular biceps and forearms spoke anything of the military. He looked up at me with something vaguely approaching hope in his pale sapphire eyes. He lifted his shoulders and sighed.

'Daniel tells me you've been seein' some action,' he ventured.

I laughed. 'I think that's putting it mildly. But yes, I have. And I think we have only one plotline after all. We have a promising lead. And while I don't know for sure, I think we know where Geordie might be. I think he's being held captive, and I believe I know where.'

'Aye, somewhere in Kilmarnock.' He shook his head. His hair was growing out, I noticed, from its soldierly close-crop. 'It seems a wee bit strange, though. I've been tae Kilmarnock in Scotland. I'm guessin' this one's a wee bit different.'

'A lot more sunshine, for one thing.'

He thought about this. 'And mebbe they grand hooses with big garridges?'

'I think that would definitely be the case.' I looked at Daniel. 'Are you coming with us?' I asked.

He laughed. 'You'll be safe with Alasdair, I'm thinking. Meanwhile, I badly need a rest. Is it all right if I stay here?'

Music to any woman's ears—this particular tune like an

effervescent Mozart piano concerto. I sternly suppressed my libido, telling it that work must come first. It almost listened to me. 'I hope you haven't been doing anything too dangerous?'

'I've been casing the joint. Several joints, in fact.' His mild, dark eyes seemed alert with mischief. Seeing the blatant concern in my expression, he took my hand and clasped it firmly. 'I have visited a few Armenian warlords, or so I believe. And that I was not expecting. I knew about the Azeris, but these people look uncommonly armoured up, and dangerous. But don't worry. I was sufficiently disguised, or so I hope.' He handed me a card on which was a logo for El Dorado Real Estate, with the name Gordon MacTavish proudly in the centre and a mobile phone number beneath it. At the bottom, in small print, was a web address: www.eldoradorealty.org.au.

'Armenian?!' I exclaimed. 'That's a coincidence.'

'Oh yes?'

And I told him about the hummed tune, and how Marie had identified it as an Armenian love song.

'So,' I concluded, 'it is only too likely that our Second Burglar—the one who wasn't the ineffable Jordan—is in fact Armenian.'

'Hmm. That seems quite likely, under the circumstances—which I'll come to in a moment.'

I noticed that Alasdair had subsided unobtrusively onto a chair in one corner of the room. Soldier instincts, no doubt. A clear field of fire and no possibility of unexpected ambush.

Daniel sat down in the chair next to mine and took my hand again. 'Gordon MacTavish?' I asked him. 'Really?'

'A patently fake Scots name, such as might have been adopted by Glaswegian Jews a few generations back to avoid suspicion.'

'And you impersonated a real estate agent because nobody thinks of them as anything other than a mildly annoying nuisance. Daniel, that's brilliant! What did you find out?'

'Several things. I spoke to many Armenians. We have a kindred interest, both being holocaust survivors, so by and large we get on. I tried one house, where I got a reception around the temperature of liquid nitrogen, but I think they were Caucasian Muslims, and they may just have been responding to my self-evidently Hebraic appearance. But the Armenians worried me. One house in particular is a proper fortress, and nobody came to the door. I gave them my spiel through the intercom, and their dismissal was…brusque. I need to talk to Uncle Solly again.' He leant back in his chair and poured himself another glass of my sauv blanc. I noticed he was a little paler than usual. Despite his offhand manner, I guessed that his enquiries had been stressful in the extreme. I wanted to embrace him and bury his head against my breasts, but not in front of an audience. Even one so unobtrusive as Alasdair.

'Did you meet any Greeks?'

'Yes, I did. Why?'

I explained about Philomela and her sister. When I mentioned Anzac Drive his face split into a grimace.

'They looked at me as though I were an inferior brand of gastropod. It probably was number thirty-four, as you say. But they didn't look anything like gangsters, so I left quickly.'

'I'm glad.' I turned to our tame squaddie. 'Are you sure you wouldn't like a drink, Alasdair?'

He shook his head slowly and smiled. 'No thanks. Shall we go and do this Soup Run thing?'

I looked at my clock. Seven-thirty. It was still light, but why not? In summer the Soup Run began in daylight.

I kissed Daniel goodbye and bade him make himself well and truly at home. Taking the lift down with Alasdair was a strange feeling. I trusted him. The British Army does not make mistakes with their psychological profiling. Yet this man had been tried beyond endurance, I guessed, and was still on the road to recovery. We exchanged glances as the lift descended, and he smiled. 'Ye've nothing to fear, Corinna. I just wanted to gae oot. Daniel explained the Soup Run to me. It sounds grand.'

The doors slid open, and we emerged in time to see Mrs

Pemberthy and her dreadful little dog Traddles, who sniffed once at Alasdair's ankles then disappeared behind his mistress with the merest of whimpers. Mrs Pemberthy glared at me and shook her head with the air of someone who has just discovered five-eighths of a caterpillar in her salad sandwich. She pushed past us into the lift, Traddles padding next to her high heels in demure silence. As the doors closed upon her, she emitted a snort like a dyspeptic locomotive.

Alasdair looked quizzically at me. 'So whae's the auld biddy?'

'One of our tenants. She, and her dog Traddles, perform an essential role in our little community.'

'Neighbourhood Witch?'

'Actually, we do have one of them. You remember Meroe? '

'Aye, she give me the sleep charm. So what's her story? '

'Mrs P is someone no one else can get on with, so she impels us together like little magnets. I doubt we'd manage half as well without her.'

'Aye, my grandma wis the same. She swung a mean umbrelly back in Paisley.' His eyes swept across Calico Lane and his chin jerked downwards. 'Whaur now?'

I led the way towards the cathedral, where the Soup Run began its nightly ministry under the benign aegis of the Anglican church. Alasdair stared in wonder. As did I. Since I had last seen the van, it had grown. There was Sister Mary, tiny and indomitable in her grey habit and blue wimple. Inside the van, wearing an apron and stirring a large pot of soup, was none other than Jordan King. His eyes caught mine for a millisecond, then with a toss of his dark fringe his head bent once more over the pot. Beside him was a sweet-looking girl assembling sandwiches. But next to the van were two new erections. Within a small marquee barbers were plying their trade at two chairs, barbering, shaving and generally prodding. And next to that was a busy laundromat, in which two pairs of windows showed forth the gladsome sight of soapy laundering and tumble-drying.

Sister Mary appeared beside me and stretched out her wrinkled hand with pride. 'Corinna, it's good to see you. Are you coming out tonight? Oh, and Alasdair! Splendid to see you looking so well. You're coming too?'

Alasdair bowed his head stiffly. 'Sister,' he muttered, with the tiniest bob of his head. No Catholic this squaddie, obviously. I recalled now that Strathclyde had long been a hotbed of sectarian strife. But he would be on his best behaviour. Of that I was certain. She beamed up into his face and took his hand. He flinched, ever so slightly, but relaxed. Doubtless the love of God was flowing freely into him and calming him down.

'Sister Mary,' she announced brightly. 'Glad to have you, Alasdair. We have Ma'ani tonight, but he might need some backup. Saturdays are always a bit fraught, especially on these hot summer nights.'

He grinned weakly, and she let go his hand at last.

'Corinna, isn't this wonderful? We have our own laundrette now, and it's made such a difference to our poor lost souls.'

'And the hairdressing salon?'

She laughed like a peal of small silver bells. 'That's down to Kelvin.' She pointed her determined chin towards a young man with a full bushranger beard busily snipping away at a dishevelled street kid. 'He was a long-term patron of our operation until he got back on his feet at long last. He quit the grog, got a job as a hairdresser and next thing we knew he had his own thriving business. So he comes here on Saturday nights, sets up his tent and ministers to them all. She exchanged glances with Kelvin, who nodded briskly and returned to his craft. 'That's his girlfriend Stephanie next to him, doing the women.'

I lowered my voice. 'And Jordan?'

She patted my arm. 'He's getting along fine here. As long as he keeps doing what he's told, I'll put in a good word for him when his case comes up.'

'And he's quite penitent?'

'Quite. But I doubt he'll want to talk to you. The poor dear's a bit embarrassed, to say the least.'

'All right. I'll keep clear of him. But...' I left my sentence hanging, and she shook her head with emphasis.

'I have my suspicions, dear. Something absurdly doctrinal, I believe. If the poor lad spent less time bothering his head about matters best left to the clergy, it would be a fine thing. But let it go. I hear you have matters of more moment on your plate at present?' She looked down at my new ring, gave me a penetrating look from her gimlet eyes, and smiled. 'The Lord will protect you too, dear. Now, it's time for the sandwiches, I think. Would you like to help with that? After all, it's your bread we're using.'

I did so. Tonight's lawyer, I noticed, was rather more kempt than I remembered them being. This one wore about five-eighths of a business suit, but without the tie of bondage that would have sent too much of a Corporate Guy signal. He conversed with our clients in a soft voice. It may only have been my imagination, but our down-and-outs seemed less hapless than usual. Perhaps it was the laundry and haircuts. But there was more to it than that. Those who sleep rough used to be angrier. These seemed humbler, and more willing to give the Normal World a go. And unless I was quite mistaken there were fewer junkies. I tried my best not to stare at their faces and arms, but I couldn't help noticing. These unfortunates were mostly clean, or I was out of my reckoning altogether.

'You've noticed it too?' Sister Mary was suddenly at my side. I looked at her all-forgiving features and shrugged. 'I thought you might. Some are the lost souls you remember. But every night there are more and more ordinary folks who suddenly find themselves on the streets and are still wondering how it happened.'

'Greedy landlords?' I suggested.

She shook her wimple. 'Not necessarily. Now that Missing Link has abandoned all pretence of looking after the poor, all sorts of people are having their benefits cut off, for any or no reason. You remember the Robot Letters?'

I did. For reasons that entirely escape me, The Missing Link Corporation (the agency that was supposed to dispense charity to the poor) had embarked on what was the postal equivalent of a drive-by shooting spree. They had a computer program, apparently. This explained everything, though it was cold comfort to those who received letters out of thin air telling them that they suddenly owed the government ten thousand dollars, three goats and an aardvark. Middle-class folks accustomed to fighting for their rights were able to prove that they owed no such thing. The poor and meek were not so fortunate. There were suicides, which was probably just fine as far as the government was concerned. End of problem! I could almost hear them chuckle, and crack open a jeroboam of bubbly in celebration.

Sister Mary went into a short conclave with tonight's nurse, who was dressed in jeans and a white T-shirt, issued a few orders and came back to me. 'They're mostly a lot quieter than they used to be. They're cowed. This worries me.'

It worried me too.

Just then there appeared to be a disturbance up ahead of us. It was beyond the cathedral precinct, heading towards the Russell Street corner. Something was undoubtedly up. People were running towards us. Alasdair moved into the shadows of the church, but he was looking intently straight ahead, ready to spring into action. And out of the soup kitchen rose the vast, imperturbable figure of Ma'ani. He caught Alasdair's glance and made a flicking motion with his jaw. 'It's all right, mate. I've got this.'

Alasdair fell in next to me, almost humming with suppressed tension. I was pleased to see that he accepted Ma'ani as his superior officer for the night. But he planted himself directly in front of me, feet braced slightly apart and hands hanging loose at his sides. Towards us came a running man: tall, shaggy with facial growth, and the eyes of a crazed tiger. I saw he was brandishing a machete, and he was coming straight towards me.

Chapter Twenty

O! so light a foot will ne'er wear out the everlasting flint.
—William Shakespeare, *Romeo and Juliet*, Act 2, Scene 6

Ma'ani took two quick steps along the footpath, grasped the man and lifted him high into the air. He held him aloft, high above his head, with one hand. With the other gigantic fist he knocked the machete to the footpath, where it landed with a clatter. At once Alasdair whipped out a handkerchief and swept it up. He looked around to see a uniformed constable running towards him. Alasdair placed the machete on the footpath, still wrapped in his hanky, and raised both arms. The cop slowed down, looked at the tableau before him, and inclined a granite face.

The entire episode had lasted maybe five seconds. We all stopped to catch our breaths, except the cop, who was now speaking urgently into his radio. The discussion ceased, and we all stared at Exhibit A. He struggled frantically in Ma'ani's grasp, and the gallant officer walked over towards him. 'What's your name, son?'

'Fuck off, cunt!' came out more or less as a bellow: the sort made by a Mallee bull with its hoof caught in a cattle grid.

'So which one of those is your first name?' the cop enquired, as if asking a child what sort of ice-cream he wanted. The offender groaned. Some of the fight had gone out of him, unquestionably. His face was still brick-red, and his eyes a window into a pit on which I had no wish to speculate. Inarticulate noises escaped from the half-open mouth, but nothing resembling articulate speech. And there he still dangled, waving his legs ineffectually and attempting to kick at the man-mountain who continued to hold him aloft without apparent effort. The total effect was as if a Dalek had been interrupted in its quest for world domination by an unexpected staircase. Ma'ani grinned at the dapper police uniform. 'You want 'im?'

The cop smiled a wintry smile. 'Not till my backup arrives.' He gazed, fascinated, at the feebly kicking captive then raised an eyebrow at Ma'ani. 'You okay until then, mate?'

Ma'ani grinned proudly. He was wearing a yellow singlet which inadequately covered his bulging chest, mighty biceps and gargantuan shoulders. Even his muscles had muscles. It was as though he had at least three other men inside him, and they were all taking turns at this citizen's arrest. 'Yeah, bro, I'm fine. Reckon this one's on ice?'

The cop's expression turned reflective for a long moment before arriving at a decision. 'Well, we won't know that until later on,' he conceded, 'but he's had quite a night of it already, by the sounds of it. We've had reports of disturbances all along Flinders Street. Can you give us a hand with him until we get him back to the station?'

The cop turned to look at Alasdair, who was still standing alert, obedient, and reserved. 'I'd like you to give me that machete, please. It's evidence, and we'll need it later.' He produced a ziplock bag and stowed the weapon, carefully holding it by the handkerchief. The officer sealed the bag and his eyes raked Alasdair again, noting the quick, neat movements and military bearing. 'What's your name, soldier?'

'Alasdair Sinclair.'

That was intriguing. No rank, no serial number, no further

information. Alasdair was not handing out anything more than was absolutely necessary.

'Are you his backup for tonight?'

'That's right.'

The policeman nodded. 'Well, that's handy, seeing as I'll be borrowing your friend here.' He gestured to our Maori enforcer.

The offender had subsided for the moment into inertia. But I knew enough about ice and related substances to know that uncontrollable rage might return at any moment. He didn't look human right now. More like an animated zombie. Or a vampire suffering from an overdose of garlic. I saw that his mouth was bleeding. I guessed he had bitten himself, and felt a momentary pity for the poor man. Another urban casualty of wasted youth. Just then, a police car ground to a squealing halt at the kerb, and more policepersons erupted out of it. Handcuffs were produced. One of the newcomers caught a flying boot in the chest, and Ma'ani grasped both the man's wrists and forced him down to the footpath.

'Listen, bro,' he rasped. 'These blokes are goin' to take you away for a nice rest. If you don't start playing nice you're going to get hurt a lot more.' Ma'ani pulled both hands behind the man's back, and one of the cops clicked the handcuffs shut. 'You want they should put leg-irons on you?'

The captive went as limp as a dejected celery stalk. I was keeping well clear of any of this, but from my safe distance I saw a semblance of sanity return to his features. He was quite young: Caucasian, probably mid-twenties. Torn T-shirt, gym-enhanced muscles, two days' growth on his unhealthy-looking chin. He blinked. 'Have I been bad?' he enquired in a child-like voice.

Cop Number One laughed. 'Mate, I think that's putting it mildly. Now you're going in the back of this divvy van, and your new friend Ma'ani here has very kindly volunteered to accompany you. Now do as he says, play nice, and nobody else gets hurt. Deal?'

A silent nod, hunched shoulders, and a general air of complete resignation. The rear door was flung open, and Ma'ani stepped into the back with one of his arms around the offender. The police car pulled away from the kerb sedately, and I turned to the soup van. We had a number of fascinated observers, but at the front, arms stretched out protectively, was Sister Mary. Beside her, also with outspread arms, was Jordan King. He was still avoiding my eye, but doing his very best impression of Good Catholic Boy. I nodded to Sister Mary, and she dropped her arms. I grinned weakly at her. 'The Iceman Goeth?' I suggested.

She smiled tolerantly. 'I think that must have been the reaction of the Philistines when Samson dropped in on them.'

'If Ma'ani is that strong with his number-one haircut, imagine if he grew his hair long.'

'I think he's quite strong enough as it is. But the poor lost creature! He looked far gone. I shall pray for him.' Sister Mary lifted her determined chin.

'And so will I,' Jordan intoned. He met my eyes, blinked, then wandered back into the kitchen area to make more sandwiches.

And that was that, for the time being. The rest of the Soup Run was uneventful. Ma'ani returned after an hour or so, with the news that the offender was safely under lock and key in the watch house. The van chugged around the city blocks, aid and comfort was duly administered, and nobody tried anything on with Alasdair. He was quietly omnipresent: patrolling the perimeter and occasionally asking questions of a few of our clients. I served soup, collected sandwiches from Jordan without comment, and watched the sky fade to black above the glaring lights of central Melbourne. By midnight I was done, and Alasdair walked me back to Calico Alley. Twice I noticed people move towards me, but they caught Alasdair's eye and melted away into the shadows again. I wasn't worried. The city can get rough later on; but, as a rule, before midnight nobody is drunk enough to do anything spectacularly stupid.

'Did you find out anything?' I enquired, with a sidelong look at his pale features.

He shook his head. 'Ah'm no' certain. But I did have one strange encounter. One of the blokes I spoke to was better educated than most. He gave me a look and asked me if I had a smoke. I said I didn't, but the lawyer offered him two. He put one away in his shirt pocket, lit the other one, and looked straight at me. "You're the bloke who's looking for a dog, right?" I said I was. 'You want to look sharp, Mister. 'Cos I hear the Petrosians are looking for you."' Alasdair blinked, and ran his hands down his shirt. He was so tense I almost expected to hear his muscles creaking. 'He wouldn't say more. I've no idea what that means.'

'Are you sure about the name?'

'I think so. Maybe Daniel has heard of them.'

I hoped so. It might be another lead. Or another red herring, of which I probably had enough for a medium-sized sushi bar by now. I kept Alasdair talking as long as I could. I didn't want to touch on the war, but I asked him if he'd met anyone like Ma'ani before. He laughed, for the first time since I had known him.

'Aye, we met some of his folk over there.' He flicked his head vaguely northwards. 'They're totally fearless. The locals are terrified of them. They think they're cannibals. I think the Maori love that.'

'It would certainly be helpful.'

'I mind once they did a haka fae the locals. About twelve or fifteen o' them, under the desert sun. It was terrifying, wi' they tattoos and the glaring eyes and pokin' tongues. So then we had a bit of a ceilidh with the pipes, and that scared them even more. Our village was extremely quiet after that.'

I stole a careful look at my companion, and crossed my fingers. We had to find his dog.

When we arrived at the door to Insula, Alasdair took his leave. 'Daniel's given me a key to his place. I won't disturb you.'

I watched him walk away smartly into the night and my heart leapt down. I was no closer to finding his dog, and he had all but given up hope. It was also probable that he had not wanted to intrude on Daniel and me, which was thoughtful of him. Not that I was in the mood for passion now. But a calming embrace from my beloved would be very welcome.

I met no one in the vestibule or the lift. Most of Insula's denizens had long since gone to bed, and those who hadn't wouldn't be expected back for some time yet. As always on Saturday nights I uttered a small prayer for the safety of Kylie and Gossamer. They loved their Saturday nights and would not return home to their possibly virtuous beds until the small hours. I hoped they were out with the actors. They would presumably look after my girls and return them with their virtue, such as it was, unscathed. And Jason would be ensconced in his bedroom doing Jason things, like watching old movies or reading. Reading! I was still getting my head around this. I would have expected that he would disdain such things; but he said no, because he'd never learnt to read at school and this was getting back a little more of the childhood he had never had. I have heard it's never too late for a happy childhood. I was more than a little awed to think that I was providing the means for him to have it.

I let myself into my apartment. All the lights were off, and I turned on the living room one with its dimmer function on. I could not hear any sound beyond the soft thrum of my bedroom air conditioner, but Daniel was almost certainly asleep in my bed. Horatio padded across the carpet and rubbed his cheek against mine. I fed him some munchies and he curled his tail neatly around his paws and addressed himself to his bowl. Soft crunching noises filled the silence. I heard stealthy movements beyond the bedroom door. My pulse roared into overdrive. I wanted his strong arms around me, and his hard, muscular body pressed close to me. The door opened, and he emerged, looking adorable and dressed in a blue bathrobe. He would not be wearing anything underneath it. I had not been thinking of anything other than hugs tonight, but I was prepared to change my plans. He reached over, picked me up in his strong arms and carried me into the bedroom. His mouth closed on mine, and my limbs dissolved into liquid fire.

Philomela: Upon the house of them that have afflicted me, may doom cast its awful shadow. I wish upon them the boils of Job, the leprosy of Namaan, and the nine plagues of Egypt. May they be consumed in fire.

Chapter Twenty-One

…a word and a blow.
—William Shakespeare, *Romeo and Juliet,* Act 3, Scene 1

Sunday morning! I stretched out my toes in slow, sensuous luxury and nestled against Daniel's strong, lean muscular back. He was fast asleep, as well he might be. Normally I would now subside gratefully into the arms of slumber. But I didn't, because for no good reason I could think of, the hairs on the back of my neck were standing out like porcupine quills.

Apparently I wasn't alone in thinking something was amiss. There was a small disturbance beside the bed, then a scuttling of paws, and a familiar furry shape burrowed straight under the doona and hid down by my feet. I lay there in complete silence, thinking hard. Horatio sometimes did this, sure. He was frightened by thunderstorms, and would generally go to ground next to my feet when they paid us a state visit. He had also been known to seek refuge from cold in the depths of winter. But it was summer, and there wasn't a cloud in the sky so far as I knew. What the hell was going on here?

My skin crawled. Just on the very edge of hearing, furtive noises of formation stealth were performing a small toccata and fugue up and down my spine. The bedroom door was ajar. (Horatio must have opened it. He had learnt that by standing up on his hind paws and flicking the door handle with his front paw—it was a bar rather than a ball—he could rectify my inexplicable omission in locking him out.) And intermittent flashes of muted light seemed to be happening in my living room.

I lay quietly, alert and patient. Because I wasn't frightened anymore. I was furiously, murderously angry. Whoever this was would pay for it. Little by little, I felt the hot blaze of a righteous wrath flood through my body. No need to hurry this. Meanwhile, my mind was racing, but taking the corners calmly and expertly. Just outside the bedroom door was a light switch. And beneath it, I recalled, there was a skillet standing on the carpet. It was an old skillet, and I had decided to retire it, with grateful thanks for many a fine feat of bakery. I now resolved to rescind this order.

Far down by my ankles, Horatio began to purr. Whether this was a purr of fear or a semi-mute vote of confidence I didn't care.

As I grasped the edge of the doona, I realised that I was naked. Under the delightful circumstances of the previous evening, this was not surprising. Could I be bothered getting dressed for the benefit of my unwelcome guest? Nope. I remembered my friend Jane the criminal lawyer telling me that by statute and common law, you had to take your victim as you find him. My guest would have to put up with me as I was. I threw back the doona and jumped to my feet. Despite being large, I possess fast reflexes and the ability to move in utter silence. I slipped to the door, took three small, tight breaths, then leapt into action.

The results were gratifying in the extreme. My dancing feet propelled me past the light switch, which I flicked on. I executed a pas d'une in seizing the skillet, and with an impressive grand jeté across the floor I swung my weapon up and down onto the repellent, ninja-hooded creature rummaging through my book-shelves. I got him right on the top of his insectoid skull, and he collapsed with an agonised groan and dropped his torch. What did I have to secure burglars with? There was a packet of black cable ties in the bathroom: a relic of some DIY plumbing I had attempted. These would be perfect. I tore the packet open and bound his hands and feet together, his dark eyes gazing at me with unspeakable horror all the while.

When (and only when) I judged my victim to be rendered harmless and recumbent, I gave vent to my feelings and expressed myself accordingly. 'This is my house, not yours, you microcephalic moron! I am *not* running a hotel, or a guesthouse, or a drop-in centre for the terminally bewildered! Whatever it is you're looking for, *I haven't got it.* What do I have to do to convince you that you're wasting your time? And who the hell do you think you are, anyway? Toshiro Mifune?' I leant over him and ripped away the ninja face covering.

I felt a furry presence next to my calf, and there was Horatio standing next to me, with his fur standing on end. Like me, he was glaring at the intruder in furious affront. Who, he wanted to know, is this creature, and what is it doing in my house? He flicked his tail angrily and hissed. A distressing ammoniac scent, as of incontinent tomcats, began to waft towards me. From my carpet, and the lower sections of my trussed-up burglar. Oh, good.

I looked at the misbegotten burglar before me, trussed up like a Christmas turkey. The face I had revealed told me nothing except indescribable terror. Now perhaps we might get some answers. Just then, an adored voice spoke behind me. I turned to see Daniel, dressed only in a white towel. His dark eyes raked the room and his mouth twisted in a smile.

'You seem to have coped, *ketschele.* How very clever of you.'

With barely a backward look, I seized Daniel and kissed his mouth. Partly, I had to admit to myself, to ram home to our burglar the idea that I was the most fearsome apparition he had ever encountered. It wasn't loathing or disgust I had noted on our little friend's face. The impression I got was that he had been confronted with the Venus of Willendorf. I had a sudden, momentary vision of his shivering, cave-dwelling ancestors confronted by a buxom, curvaceous naked goddess, holding the promise of warmth and fertility in a freezing, cheerless world. *I am Woman!* I exulted inwardly. *Look upon my arms, breasts, thighs, and belly. I am strong and beautiful!* In a flash I seemed to divine that this gibbering creature was possessed of a primeval terror of Woman. I was going to play up to it for all it was worth.

At the same time, I was aware of my impressive twin black eyes, now of a hue resembling European smallgoods. I have no doubt this added to his general Shock and Awe. And now, for the first time in this maddening case, we might have a chance to get some information. But if the man on the carpet really did belong to a crime gang, then we needed to be even scarier than his godfathers to get him to talk. My choice of attire for the citizen's arrest was looking better and better by the moment. Because he was taking it all in. As Daniel waltzed me around in a half-circle I peered over his bare shoulder and looked steadily at our captive.

With the face mask removed, he looked a suddenly pitiable figure. His skin had formerly been golden biscuit-coloured. Now he had acquired a veneer of dirty ecru. His eyes looked as though he had plugged himself into the national grid and received fifty thousand volts to his spinal column. The aroma from my carpet was mutating into a full-sized miasma. But there was something else. My memory was tapping me insistently on the shoulder. Had I seen him before? I wondered. Somehow I was convinced I had indeed met this sorry specimen, some other place and time. Where and when? I couldn't track it down. I'd have to wait for inspiration to strike.

My beloved Daniel was playing his part tremendously. Yes, we would at some point have to call the police and let them take him away. But I thought Letty White would forgive me for not calling her at this hour. And we might never get this opportunity again. I relapsed into Daniel's embrace for another round of passionate kisses.

Our eyes met, and we reached a silent decision. He would be the Good Cop, and I would go and put on a nightgown. I thought my point—that I was Woman Incarnate and could reduce him to bowel-knotting terror any time I felt like it—had been well and truly made by now, and Daniel might get more out of him if I took my time. I chose a light, translucent cotton gown—ideal for hinting that there was always more Extremely Bad Cop available if we wanted it—and I walked into the kitchen to make some coffee. On a whim, I called to my beloved, 'Ask him if he wants any coffee.'

Daniel cast a glance at the prisoner, who nodded.

'All right. He's getting it black.' I inhaled the delicious scent of Arabica beans—so much nicer than the distressing odour of *essence du burglar* which had now permeated my entire apartment—and took my time. They were still talking softly. I have heard that once these villains crack, they go all the way and spill every bean they have and then some. When I had poured out three mugs of coffee, Daniel came to join me.

'Well done!' he whispered into my ear. 'But our little friend is so terrified that I think he'll clam up on us if you come near him again. I'll manage to get some coffee into him.'

'As long as you don't loosen his cable ties.'

'I won't. I notice you haven't asked about his head wound?' He grinned.

'No, because I don't care about his head wound,' I hissed, louder than necessary. I wanted him to overhear me. 'Since, thanks to his unreliable bladder, I'm going to be steam-cleaning this carpet anyway, it is a matter of complete indifference to me if he bleeds to death all over my carpet.'

Daniel held me tight, and kissed me again. 'Excellent!' he breathed into my ear. 'He won't, by the way. He's stopped bleeding now and it doesn't look too bad. I'll take it from here.'

And with that I went back to my bedroom with my coffee. Horatio accompanied me, after a small browse at his munchies bowl. I sipped my coffee and smoothed down my affronted cat.

He permitted me to caress his fur, with many an angry lick and a stretching of paws, and gazed into my eyes with silent reproach. What are you going to do about these constant intrusions? he wanted to know. When, he continued, is Normal Service going to be resumed? Having registered his formal protest, he extended his chin and permitted me to stroke his cheeks and under his chin. After quite a deal of this, he subsided into relaxation and went back to sleep. I looked up to see Daniel entering my room. He was still in his towel, I noted. Perhaps I had instituted a new horizon in interrogation techniques.

'So?'

'I think I have everything we need. I'll tell you later. I think it's time to call the police now.'

'Just one more thing.' I returned to the kitchen and picked up my biggest kitchen knife. Standing behind the benchtop, I waved it at our captive and smiled my most beatific smile. 'Hey there!' I called.

He was sitting up now, still with his hands and feet bound.

'If we don't get the dog back safe and sound, I will come looking for you, wherever you happen to be. Please don't imagine that I'm joking.'

His grimy pallor faded still further to the colour of old tile grouting. I nodded. 'Okay, Daniel, summon the police.'

Our captive muttered something in a foreign language. Then he looked beseechingly at Daniel. 'Protective custard?' he implored. 'You promise!'

Daniel knelt down next to him. 'Yes, I know. But I'm not the police, Narek. I believe they will look after you. They are very interested in you, and they will keep you safe—as long as you continue to cooperate. If you're really good, you might even get a new identity and a fresh start in Queensland. That's if you're telling me the truth, of course, and that the car-ramming incident that left one girl dead and another one crippled really wasn't down to you. If it turns out it *was* you and your friends, then you're in more trouble than the early settlers. But that's up to the police. If you tell them everything you've told me, I think you'll be fine. They won't let Uncle Tigran anywhere near you. Now just sit tight and we'll call a divvy van.'

We did so, since I wanted to allow Letty White her sleep, but she came anyway, accompanied by Constable Helen and two taciturn, economy-sized cops who did not say a single word. Nor did they smile. They merely nodded, and left the floor to DSC White while they led our little friend Narek away into what I really hoped would be protective custard. Preferably with stewed fruit. Even though he had broken into my home twice now, I no longer felt much animosity towards him. Unless it had been he who had killed Philomela's sister. But I didn't think so. Narek had been wetting himself with fear. I pictured him as small fry: probably only useful for burgling houses and odd jobs. The most he owed me was the cost of a steam-clean. Daniel and I sat in the kitchen, waiting for the kettle to boil. Helen Black sat down in one of my kitchen chairs, and immediately Horatio sauntered out from the bedroom, considered her for a moment, then launched himself lightly into her lap. She looked pleased, and began to caress his cheeks and rub her hands all over my kitty's head.

Letty White looked anything but pleased, and addressed us as follows: 'Yes, Corinna, I get that you didn't call me personally because you didn't want to break in upon my virtuous slumbers. But, as you doubtless have guessed by now, anything connected with these home invasions—and Related Matters—have a tag on the system that says I am to be contacted immediately, at any hour of the day or night. I am very happy to have caught our little friend. I suppose it's too much to ask that you refrained from questioning the prisoner?'

I looked at Daniel, who returned my cool glance with one even more temperate. 'I may have asked him a few things. After all, this is Corinna's apartment. I think she is entitled to know what he was looking for at least, if only so that we can attempt to persuade him, and the people he works for, that we haven't got it and that they're wasting their time.'

Letty glared at me and ran her hands through her close-cropped hair. 'Jesus wept!' she grated through clenched teeth. 'Yes, under normal circumstances, Daniel, perhaps! But do you think these are anything like normal circumstances? Do you?' She spun around on her police-issue flat heel and impaled me with an acetylene glare. I shook my head silently, unwilling to say anything more in case of self-incrimination. The kettle announced itself, and she inclined her chin downwards. 'Earl Grey, if you've got it. Milk, one sugar, please.'

I leapt to my feet, only too anxious to Assist the Police with tea-making. I made four mugs and we sipped them quietly, Letty and Helen joining us at the table. Finally she set down her mug and gave us both a long, forbidding look. 'Corinna. Daniel. These are not nice people to know. You do not mess with these folks. If I have your promise that you won't go anywhere near them, or their friends and neighbours, or anyone they've ever met since they left primary school, then I will be a far happier person than I currently am. Do I have your word?'

I smiled winningly at her. 'Actually, Letty, I do have another job on tomorrow, so I'll be far too busy with that to go after home invaders.'

'Really? And what job would that be?'

'I'm looking for a lost dog.'

Daniel's eyes sparkled for a moment, and the merest echo of a smile twitched the corners of his adorably kissable mouth. My mind raced. Had we told Letty anything at all about Alasdair and Geordie? I couldn't remember doing so.

Letty's hypnotic eyes held ours for long, dragging moments. We radiated innocent helpfulness.

'I see,' she said, her tone laced liberally with scepticism. 'A lost dog.'

'Yes.' Daniel drained his cup and put it on the table. 'There's a bloke staying with me who's lost his dog and we've been looking for him.'

'That's why I went on the Soup Run last night,' I put in. 'To see if anyone had heard anything.'

She frowned horribly. 'To see if anyone had heard anything. Right. Fine. Now, before I leave, Daniel, I would like to know what you can tell us about your unauthorised interrogation.'

'Sure. Let's see. His name's Narek; he works for a group of scary people whom he won't name—at least to me—but I rather suspect that we are looking at Petrosian and Associates, that well-known firm of pharmaceutical suppliers.' He glanced at the detective to see if this produced any reaction.

She merely nodded. 'Go on, Daniel. I'm sure you found out more than that.'

'Why he keeps breaking in here is still unclear. He wouldn't tell me outright, but I'm sure he's visited twice: once here and once at Professor Monk's. All he said was: "We're looking for the Holy Thing." And I'm afraid none of us has any idea what it is.'

'Could it be Professor Monk's Dead Sea Scroll, or whatever it is?'

'Maybe. But I really don't know.'

'And do any of you here have any other Holy Things you're not telling me about?'

'No, we really don't,' I assured her. 'We don't do Holy Things here. At least, not things that would interest Armenian crime gangs. So, if it isn't the Professor's scroll, then I have absolutely no idea at all what they're after.'

'So you're going to look for a lost dog instead. Fine. Just don't get in my way tomorrow. Or any other day.' She stood up. 'One day you are going to go too far. Don't say I didn't warn you. No, I'll let myself out.'

And with that she was gone.

Daniel lifted his hand, took mine, and led me decorously back to bed.

Philomela: Vengeance is mine, saith the Lord? Maybe.
Or not.

Chapter Twenty-Two

Virtue itself turns vice, being misapplied,
and vice sometimes by action dignified.
—William Shakespeare, *Romeo and Juliet,* Act 2, Scene 3

I awoke, blinking sleepily and fashionably late, and inhaled the unexpected scent of Jamaica lime and—something else. Blood orange? I believe I had one of these new allegedly green planet cleaners in my cupboard. It appeared that all the chemistry nerds of Australia had banded together to devise new organic cleaners and sell them to supermarkets under the proud heading of *100% Australian Owned and Sourced.* I was only too happy to give them custom. I guessed Daniel had been up before me, and was overlaying the distressing odours of *essence du burglar* with something less obnoxious. It certainly was an improvement. I also detected sounds and smells of plunger coffee, poached eggs and fried zebra. I stretched my toes in sensual luxury and opened my eyes fully, to see Horatio stretched out in lordly splendour across my queen-sized bed. I stroked his cheeks and flanks. He was purring in noisy ecstasy, but did not bother to open his eyes.

I emerged to see Daniel already dressed for the day's work in dark blue jeans and a short-sleeved shirt in a fetching shade of light grey. He grinned at me and waved me to my chair. A tall glass of freshly squeezed orange juice, with ice, and a plate of large-yolked eggs from contented hens with two gleaming rashers of fried zebra, two Cumberland sausages and half a tomato, all laid over my very own toasted bread (from Friday). I leant over the brimming table and kissed him.

We ate in companionable silence until Horatio emerged, sleepy-eyed and enquiring. I placed munchies in his bowl and he curled his tail around his front paws, crouched down and addressed his attention to the amenities of the moment. My beloved finished his own plate, placed it in the sink and resumed his seat.

I looked at him. 'Well, my beloved, what is the plan for today? Is it D-day?' I wanted to know. 'Are we going in?'

He grinned.

'And do please note my restraint in failing to cross-examine you last night,' I added. 'I hope you made notes.'

He took my hand and kissed it. 'Yes, today is the day. My reconnaissance as an unreal estate agent was very useful, and so was my chat with Narek—who, it transpires, was one of the dognappers. I know, or believe I know, where Geordie is. Though I am going to visit Uncle Solly one last time before we go in—I want to ask him about the Petrosians.'

'Have they got Geordie?' I stared at Daniel, bewildered. 'But why? I could understand wanting a dog to sniff out drugs, but why would *they* need him for that? They're dealers! They know where the drugs are, surely?' I shook my head in frustration. 'Nothing about this case makes any sense!'

Daniel leant back in his chair, clasped his hands behind his head and sighed. 'I was quite wrong about that. They didn't want him for sniffing out drugs at all.'

'Well? Were they going to enter him in a dog show? Don't keep me in suspense!'

He shook his head. 'Explosives. They knew Geordie was an

army dog, and they think a rival gang intends to blow up their headquarters. They've done it before.'

I exhaled. 'Well, that does make some sort of sense. Would it work?'

'I don't know. Army dogs don't freelance, and the Petrosians won't know any of the correct commands. If Geordie did detect explosives, he might let them know. Or he might not. Narek thinks they're safe from being blown up. But they may not be.'

'Oh, good. So we're trying to burgle a house which may blow up. And did the Petrosians kill Philomela's sister, or was that the opposition?' Outrage was causing my voice to tremble.

He squeezed my hand briefly. 'Narek says not, but I don't know for sure. They may have. If they did, Narek wasn't involved. He is just a small tropical fish in a think-tank of sharks. His uncle Tigran is the mastermind.'

'All right.' My wrath subsided, without disappearing. 'So what time do you think? Late at night? Not too late, please, I have to bake in the morning.'

He patted my arm. 'No. They'll be more alert at night. Today's going to be hot. I'd say mid-afternoon would be best.'

'And what, if I may ask, is the plan? We drop in to a heavily guarded fortress, knock on the door, and ask if we can have our doggie back?'

'Well, no. But I did pay attention on my visits. These palatial dwellings all look very impressive from the street…'

'More front than Myers?'

'Oh yes. And if it's the house I think it is, it's a fortress all right. Iron bars, high walls, twin surveillance cameras, probably overlapping fields of fire. There's an intercom grille set into the brick pillar there, and I suspect entry is by password only. Around the back, however…'

'You were able to see around the back?'

'I managed to sneak around and get a decent look. They have a double block, and the trouble with that, of course, is that there's another street entrance leading to their back door.'

'Which isn't so extensively fortified?'

'Well, no. If there are cameras, I couldn't see them. There's a steel door with a combination lock and a three-metre brick wall. We could conceivably climb the wall, but I don't think we'll need to do that. I'm not joking, Corinna. The headquarters of most of these crime lords is bristling with security at the front, but that's mainly for show. So we're going to lurk in the bushes nearby and wait for someone to come out the back for a smoke or to accept a delivery. And if that doesn't work, I do have other plans. But first I'm going to double-check with Uncle Solly, who will warn me against doing what I intend to do, but there it is. The one thing we don't need is mistaken identity.'

'Because mistaken identity has already killed one girl and crippled another.'

'Quite. I'll pick you up at three o'clock this afternoon. Come dressed for sudden flight if necessary.'

'Are you sure I won't be in the way?'

'No, I want you there.' He leant closer and kissed me again. 'The problem is that we don't have any means of knowing what we will find there. What if there's a woman guarding the dog? In that event, you will have to talk to her. She is likely to be alarmed by a strange man and cry for help, whereas she might be disarmed by another woman.'

I kissed him back, and resumed my seat as he strode purposefully from my apartment. My clock announced that it was just after eleven am. And I resolved, on a whim, to talk to Jon in distant Laos. Since we were definitely dealing with Armenians, Jon might know something. He had had an Armenian boyfriend once, I seemed to recall. Laos was three hours behind Melbourne, so he might be having breakfast still.

I sat down at my computer, stared at the white letter S in a pale blue cloud, and clicked on it. Ah, but what password had I chosen? I tried *bakery, insula* and *corinna*, none of which appeared to be satisfactory. Inspiration struck. I typed in BosworthJumbles.

Success! Three messages from my parents, none of any consequence. In case there might be persons with cultural sensibilities
watching me, I picked up a plain black scarf and tied it around my
hair. You never knew. I clicked on Jon's icon. Nothing happened
for a little while, and suddenly there he was. I broadened the
screen and he grinned at me.

'Good morning, Corinna. What a pleasant surprise. I was just
finishing breakfast.'

'Are you free for a little chat? And are you okay? You keep
freezing on me.'

He laughed. 'Unlikely in this weather. Though it's not really
hot yet. And yes, I can spare all the time you need.' His eyes narrowed. 'I hope the other guy is more injured than you are? That's
a serious pair of black eyes.'

'Oh yes. He has been chastised.'

'Good. Now, when you say freezing, do you mean my image
stops and starts?'

'Yes. It's a bit disconcerting. Am I doing the same for you?'

'Nothing to worry about. It's just your third-world internet.
Whereas here in Laos we can get proper first-world speeds.'
We grinned at each other. In his case it was stop-motion. I half
expected to see Wallace and Gromit waving from behind him.
Don't start me about our botched National Broadband Network.
His white shirt was spotted with perspiration already. His power-
ful chest and shoulders looked formidable, and his biceps bulged
impressively. Yet that wasn't really what struck you about Jon.
It was more the calm self-assurance of a man who knew exactly
what he wanted to do, and did it.

'So what's been happening in your life, Corinna?'

I told him all. It took some time. Usually he had a superb dead-
pan, but my story really did make his jaw drop. When I reached
the end of my peroration, I watched him thinking hard. Finally,
he clasped his hands on the table in front of him.

'I'm a bit apprehensive about this, Corinna. Yes, I've heard of the Petrosians. They have a branch office just down the road from here.'

I gaped. 'Really? What's there for them? It isn't opium country, is it?'

'There're a few plantations further up in the hills. But the Petrosians deal more in ice and what they would like their clients to believe is ecstasy but is actually industrial solvents cut with rat poison.'

'Charming.'

'Well, yes. They have an established network. And some of their neighbours would like to muscle in on the racket.'

I looked carefully at him. 'Are these the Azeris?'

His eyes widened. 'Yes. I'm surprised you know about them. They're the new kids on the block. And they fight dirty.'

'Dirtier than rat poison?'

He laughed and shook his head, again in stop-motion. 'Oh yes. The Armenians are like the Salvation Army compared with the Azeris. But…' He paused. 'Corinna, this looks a bit outré, even by the exotic standards of Insula. You said there was a phrase you couldn't identify? Can you remember what it was? It's been a long time since I spoke any Armenian, but try me.'

'Don't forget I didn't hear it myself; I've only got what Alasdair said. But he said it sounded like *vorteh nizaky*. Does that mean anything to you?'

'Could it have been: *Vortegh nizaky?*'

'I suppose so. What does that mean?'

'It means: "Where is the spear?"'

I sat back in my chair. Crestfallen doesn't even begin to cover it. My crest was so far down it was rolling in the gutter. 'Jon, that makes no sense.'

He stared at the ceiling for a while. Kepler brought him a cup of something hot, and they had a short conversation. I sat where I was. At this point I was waiting for a miracle. I watched him take a sip of something pale in an earthenware cup, then place the cup carefully on the wooden table. He folded his hands and leant forward. 'Corinna, when did this fragmentary conversation happen?'

'When Geordie was being dognapped.'

'And you're certain that the dognappers are the same people who've been burgling Insula so indefatigably?'

'As sure as we can be. The burglar was so terrified he soiled my apartment. I think he was telling us the truth.'

'And it was Dion Monk's apartment they burgled first?'

'Yes. But he doesn't have any spears. Jon, why would they be looking for a spear?'

His lips curved, showing his shiny, regular teeth. 'What if they thought he had the Lance of Longinus? I think that would be worth looking for.' Jon began to recite, from memory. His eyes seemed to be looking at vast distances of time. I had no idea he could recite the Bible from memory but then, he's full of surprises.

'St John's Gospel, chapter nineteen. *But one of the soldiers with a spear pierced His side, and forthwith came there out blood and water. And he that saw it bare record, and his record is true: and he knoweth that he saith true, that ye might believe. For these things were done, that the scripture should be fulfilled, a bone of him shall not be broken.*'

I suppose my mouth must have fallen open. I closed it tightly. I was remembering the book I had been reading in Cafe Delicious. *The Spear of Destiny.* And with a vast sense of astonishment I remembered my fugitive sensation of having met Narek before.

Jon was watching me carefully. 'Corinna? What is it? You look as though you're having a light-globe moment.'

'I really am. And now I finally understand something which has been bothering me all along: why on earth our little friend should have chosen my apartment to burgle after he'd drawn a blank at Dion Monk's.'

'I was wondering that myself. Why you indeed?'

'When we caught him and I finally saw his face, I had the strangest feeling I'd met him before. And I think I have. I was sitting in Cafe Delicious, reading a book. Ever since Dion Monk started doing his biblical research, I thought I'd do some background reading myself—just so I could understand what he was talking about, more than anything. So I was reading a book called *The Spear of Destiny* in the cafe, and I had the sense that somebody was staring at me. I had a glimpse of him as he was leaving, but I didn't make the connection with the ninja in my apartment. I mean, why would I? But it was Narek. I'm certain of it now. He saw me reading the book, so he thought I must have it if Dion Monk didn't.'

'That would make sense.'

'But why does he think either of us would have it?'

'There you have me, unless–' He paused, and looked at the sky for a moment. 'The Spear is in Vienna. Hitler stole it during his rise to power, because he thought he was the reincarnation of Klingsor, from the medieval German epic poem *Parzival,* later commemorated in one of Wagner's little pantomimes. The spear is supposed to bring victory to whoever holds it.'

I face-palmed myself. 'Yes, all right. And the Armenians are technically Christians, even though they're also an organised crime gang.'

'Though hardly in Hitler's class,' Jon interposed.

'And they think that, like Geordie, it would be a useful addition to their arsenal in this turf war with their neighbours. But that doesn't get me any closer to understanding why on earth they should think we've got it here.'

Jon clasped his hands in front of him and stretched. There was something catlike about him, I realised. A large, friendly cat, with perilous claws. 'Corinna, what you need to recall about the Armenians is that they've been Christians a lot longer than we have. They see themselves as the Real Thing, along with the Copts and the Antiochians. As far as they're concerned, the rest of us are people who hopped on board for the ride when the Byzantines instituted a hostile takeover and made the Christian Church into

Salvation Incorporated, which was the brainchild of the Emperor Constantine. And one of the artefacts Constantine borrowed in order to consolidate his reign as emperor of the Romans was the spear of Longinus. Ever since then, everyone who was anyone wanted it. And whoever had it prospered.'

'Except Hitler?'

'He had a pretty good run with it. Now whether the spear in the Hofburg in Vienna is the same one is another question. But that doesn't really matter for our purposes. All that matters is that the Armenians could quite easily believe in it. And that would account for the multiple burglaries of Insula.'

'It would?' I said doubtfully, as Horatio leapt onto the table and sniffed at my laptop. Jon leant close and held out his hand. Horatio gave a little mew of recognition, and touched his nose to Jon's hand on the screen. 'I can't think offhand of anyone less likely to be holding a sacred relic.'

'They may think Dion Monk took it from the Third Reich in the last days of Hitler.'

'WHAT?!'

Horatio disappeared, at speed, with a mad scuttle of claws on the floor. I stared, utterly stupefied, at the smiling face on the screen.

Chapter Twenty-Three

They'll take suggestion as a cat laps milk.
—William Shakespeare, *The Tempest*, Act 2, Scene 2

Gobsmacked doesn't even begin to cover what I was feeling. It was as though he had calmly announced that we were going to be invaded any day now by battalions of flying beetroot. Steady breathing, Corinna. I seemed to hear Meroe's voice telling me to be centred and calm.

'All right, Jon,' I managed. 'I am assuming you haven't gone troppo. After all, why should you? You're used to the tropics. So you are telling me this on the level. Not that I assume Dion Monk actually has this Heavenly Spear of Destiny or whatever it is.'

'I don't think so either. I think we would all be living far more resplendent lives if he had it. At the very least we should have taken over Southbank by now and be looking speculatively down St Kilda Road.'

'Jon, how could our very own Dion Monk—whom we love dearly—even be a slightly credible suspect for this? I imagine criminals are ridiculously superstitious, sure. But why him? Oh, hang on.' I paused, thinking hard. 'One thing I forgot to mention about our dear Professor is that he's been working on a new Dead

Sea Scroll, or something like that. Is there any conceivable way the Armenians might know about that?'

Horatio sat down, still with ruffled fur, next to my feet. I reached down and stroked his head behind his ears. He began to purr, clearly feeling that the loud noise I had emitted might have been only a regrettable and never-to-be-repeated obtrusion.

Jon nodded. 'I think it highly possible. Who knows what they think is important? They might even be trafficking in holy relics.'

And that was true enough. 'But I don't see how he could have any connection with these people. How would they even know about him?'

Jon's eyes twinkled. 'What about his former students? Can't you imagine some quiet, studious little Armenian sitting up the back of the lecture theatre busily taking notes?'

I considered this. 'He must have taught thousands of students. Tens of thousands. Most of them he won't even remember, unless they spoke up in class. And one day he makes a casual remark about this spear, someone leaps to a conclusion, and ten years later…'

'Our bright little guy or girl tells the Godfather that this retired professor has the Spear of Destiny.'

We stared at each other. It was possible. 'No, wait. You were saying it's in Vienna?'

'That's right. I think it spent most of the war in Nuremberg. Near the end, in 1945, it was supposed to be removed to a safer place, but Allied bombers destroyed the underground bunker. The Allies discovered it and brought it back to Vienna, where it is today—so far as we know.'

'Meaning there's still a possibility it was stolen in transit and a fake was handed back to the Austrians. But I still don't see how Dion Monk fits in to any of this. It's ancient history now, surely?'

Jon leant back and sipped his tea. 'He certainly knows Vienna well; he and I have swapped travellers' tales about Austria. He was born in Wales, he went to Cambridge University, he made his way out to Australia, became an academic…and in one of his lectures he says something quite innocent which conveys the impression that he has seen this spear. Someone does the maths and works out he came to Australia to live after the war, and…'

'But he can't have been in Vienna in 1945,' I objected. 'That would make him nearly a hundred.'

'Well, yes, it would. And he isn't. He looks a fit sixty. I believe he's quite a bit older than that, but he isn't a hundred. Yet…'

I thought I caught his drift. 'Yet if he really had the Spear of Destiny he could be any age?'

'Not exactly. As far as we know, the spear doesn't grant eternal life. But do they know that? Criminals are the most superstitious people on earth. They probably think it has all sorts of mystical properties. If you ask me, I'd say your little friend was indeed one of his former students; one of the quiet ones who sit up the back of the lecture theatre, up to no good and constantly making notes. This burglary was probably his idea. I doubt that the Godfather is that interested in holy relics. It would be a great coup for an unimportant member of a crime family to come up with the actual spear. There'd have to be a promotion in it.'

'"Job description: Senior Assistant Standover Man. Key selection criteria: The applicant must be ruthless, appropriately villainous and able to bully, maim and kill. Highly desirable: The applicant should have experience in acquiring holy relics"?'

He laughed. 'You would be amazed to know how accurate that might be.'

'All right, Jon. Thank you. I really mustn't take up any more of your time. Should I ask Professor Monk about this?'

'I wouldn't. You don't want to alarm him any more than he is already, do you? Are you really going to burgle the Petrosians today? Please be careful. They are, as I have already noted, not nice people at all.'

'We just want the dog.'

'And then you're getting out of there as fast as possible?'

'Promise. The cops can have them after that. Thanks, Jon. Have a splendid day.'

He grinned. 'It'll be less eventful than yours is likely to be, I hope. I'll pray for you.' He bowed, with his hand on his heart, and the screen went blank.

I looked at the kitchen clock. By now it was eleven-forty, and I fancied a cup of herbal tea and a lie-down before I did anything else.

A cup of steaming rose-hip tea later, I stretched out on my bed and gave renewed thanks for my air conditioning. How anyone had managed to do anything constructive in Australia before the invention of Winter Boxes was more than I could imagine. Our settler forebears did some daft things, sure. Not for the first time, I wondered how I would have gone on a farm in the scorching heat of an outback summer. I sipped in comfort, while a light sensation of Settling In at the end of the bed announced the arrival of Horatio to keep me company. He lay on his side, with his belly exposed to the air-con outlet vents, and closed his eyes. And I reviewed my case anew.

Some historians don't believe in causation. Stuff just happens, they exclaim. All your attempts to impose a narrative structure on the course of events are the merest post-hoc rationalisation. I had heard this view expounded (usually by philosophers in resolutely unfashionable clothes) and I didn't care for it. The whole civilisation project depends on cause and effect at least shaking hands occasionally. The repeated and cordially detested incursions into our home by zealots and gangsters could not be a random series of happenings. There had to be some urgent reason for it. Had Jon uncovered it? The more I thought about it, the more convinced I grew that he was right. It was a crazy theory, yes. But violent criminals generally are crazy. If they had any sober talent for cerebral crime they would be manipulating the stock market and defrauding the gullible. And while it was crazy, there was a berserk logic to it. Except possibly for Jordan King.

There I had no ideas at all. Who knew that freelance Inquisitors still walked the earth?

I closed my eyes, and rested my head on my down pillow. I had not seen Professor Monk since yesterday, when we had had our rooftop meeting with Philomela. I wondered if he was still staying with Mrs Dawson. The police had surely finished with his apartment by now. But Mrs D had seemed very insistent that he share her quarters. I looked at my cat, who returned my look.

'Horatio? I believe that Mrs Dawson and the Professor's feelings for each other may have ripened into something more than mere friendship. What do you think?'

Horatio arched his back luxuriously and subsided, closing his eyes. Human relations were no concern of his. And I wasn't going to intrude on their privacy. They had been the Couple Most Likely for some time now. It appeared that she had chosen her moment well with the burglary. It would be just like him not to wish to obtrude himself upon others, and perhaps she felt that matters required a Certain Expedition. I wished them joy of each other. And I remembered I had another call to make before we commenced our harebrained schemes. I had asked for my present to be ready on Monday, but they might have it ready now. I rose, put on my summer shirt and slacks and wandered out into Calico Alley to visit Marie and Kate. I doubted the girls would open their shop early, but a lot of Sunday traders opened at noon.

Heard It Before was open. A resolutely bearded hipster was searching grimly through an enormous cardboard box of vinyl LPs. Without haste, but seeking…something. I exchanged glances with Marie. She and Kate were holding hands behind the counter. 'Hi, Corinna.' Kate handed me a beautifully gift-wrapped package about the size of the palm of my hand. 'It's a thumb drive, but you can have a CD as well if you want.'

I accepted it gratefully. 'That's okay.' I didn't think Daniel even had a CD drive on his computers anymore. 'Thanks so much.' I looked longingly at the rainbow ribbons. Someone had spent time on this. It looked like a paper orchid. Marie's perfect face dimpled.

'If you want to listen to it yourself, you can have the disc, if you like?' I nodded, and she handed me a black plastic CD cover. I drew in a breath. Entwined in the midst of a tropical floral arrangement was the name Daniel in a script I had never seen before. Marie's finger pointed to the bottom. 'There's his name in Hebrew.'

'That is amazing!' I was impressed, as who would not be? I was a little bit at a loss as to how to express proper thanks. They had gone to so much trouble over this, and all for seventy-five dollars. At this moment, the hipster covered my embarrassment by erupting in quiet, bearded exultation.

'Brilliant!' he announced, grasping a record cover and rushing to the counter with it. 'Dad will be rapt.'

'Birthday present?' Marie took it from him then paused, holding it up. 'You do realise this hasn't got Stevie Nicks on it, don't you?'

'That's why he wants it. Some guy called Peter Green. And this has "Albatross" on it.'

I admired the cover art. A nun appeared to be holding an enormous seabird in a stone quarry. It could be an albatross, I supposed. What they were doing there was anyone's guess.

'Gift-wrapped?' Marie wanted to know. Her hands were poised in mid-air, and I saw for the first time a treble clef inked into the underside of her wrist.

Mr Hipster shook his head and handed over his credit card, accepted his package in a brown paper carry bag and strode out happily into Calico Alley.

I raised my eyebrows. 'Who knew?'

Their lips curved in matching grins. I gained a distinct impression that these two were Sharing a Moment, so I left them to it and ambled back towards my apartment. It was half past noon, and already the sun was getting its eye in. There was a light breeze helping out somewhat, but it must have been thirty-something degrees already. I sat down on a seat outside Cafe Delicious. Del did not usually open on Sunday, and this was no exception. But he had left a small wooden bench outside, purely for weary passers-by. A heavy padlocked chain held it in place. Kindness to strangers was one thing, but he wasn't taking any chances.

To my surprise, a very old lady in a demure red summer dress walked straight up to me and nodded. Her hair was perfectly white, and her eyes were the colour of black olives. She sat on the bench next to me and stared straight ahead for a long moment. I looked at her sidelong. She was aged beyond guessing. When she finally spoke, her voice was cracked, yet musical, like an ancient magpie.

'You know, dear, when you're as old as I am, you don't bother with formality anymore.' She turned abruptly to face me. 'You're in trouble, I know. But I think you'll be all right.'

I gaped at her. 'Hi. I'm Corinna. You?'

Her face crinkled in a toothy smile. 'Justine Rood. As in the cross. Somehow that seems appropriate right now, though I can't think why.' She extended a slender, wrinkled hand towards me. I shook it with care, as though greeting a newborn kitten. She nodded again. 'Well, good luck, Corinna. You'll need it.'

And with that, she stood up and disappeared around the corner. I clutched the Ring of Otherworlds Meroe had given me tightly in my fist for a long while. The hot summer wind buffeted my hair, and I rose, looking around for any more accidental sibyls. No one else was about.

I let myself back into the cool darkness of my apartment, took the CD from its case and loaded into my Big Box. Then I lay down on my bed and let the Celtic twilight wash over me. Except it wasn't. There were cool, sweet airs, and some measured dances, and some catchy tunes in a style quite different from what I expected. As I drifted away to sleep I heard Marie's and Kate's blending voices singing about love and contentment. But my dreams were anything but content...

I was walking on stony earth in bare feet, and my feet hurt. Thunder and lightning sounded all around me. I smelt the acrid scent of wet earth, and voices were crying on the wind. On a hill-top above me I saw three crosses, and from each hung a man in a loincloth. I stared at the central figure, hoping for a sign, but his head was lolling and his eyes closed. Rain fell on him and marked his brown body with streaks of reddish-brown mud. Roman soldiers stood by the crosses. They looked bored. Two were playing with knucklebones: holding them on the backs of their hands, tossing them up and catching them again. I looked to the right, and three women in black stood with their arms outstretched.

I saw their cowled faces, and knew them. There was Meroe, and Kate and Marie. Tears streamed down their cheeks to further moisten the wet earth. I saw one of the soldiers shake his red-plumed head in frustration. I heard him say, 'This is tedious.' He was leaning against a long spear with a pointed iron head. It was as tall as he was, and he gripped it in both hands. His biceps bulged and gleamed in the rain. He looked at the other soldiers, and they shrugged. He raised his weapon and pushed the spearhead into the side of the man in the middle. A stream of blood, mingled with water, flowed out onto the ground. I heard the three women scream, and I screamed with them. The spearman staggered back, and a flash of lightning illuminated his face. His dark eyes flared open in shock, and terror, and awe. His mouth opened wide. I saw blackened teeth, and his tongue lolled. His right hand still clutched the spear, but his left hand opened, and he pressed it to his brow. Then he crossed his arms over his breast, bowed his head, and thunder rolled, and lightning flashed; and I shut my eyes in pain and anguish. Someone was singing. I thought it was Meroe, but it was in a tongue I did not know.

I opened my eyes again and saw the women taking him from the cross, which was now lying on the ground. The sky was darkening, but away in the distance I saw the soldier still carrying his spear in his right hand, and three long bloodstained nails in his left. As I watched, he took off his red-plumed helmet and flung it away. I looked back at the women struggling with the cross, and suddenly I saw Jon, wearing a plain white tunic with blood splashed all over it. He embraced Meroe, Marie, and Kate in turn, and leant over the dead man, wrapped him in a long white cloth, picked him up, and carried him away in his arms. High on a distant hill I saw Philomela against a blood-red sunset, no longer in her wheelchair but standing, dressed in a Greek chiton. She was cursing. I could not hear what she was saying, but her words rang in my ears like blows from a hammer. I looked back at Jon, and saw he was still carrying the bleeding figure of Jesus. Then I saw a small ship sailing away into the distance. I stood on the seashore and waved sadly. Meroe was on the ship, and she put her finger to her lips. Then she opened her mouth, and her voice echoed like a small bell in my head. 'All shall be well!'

'Corinna?' I woke to find Daniel leaning over me. '*Ketschele*, what's wrong?'

I grabbed his hand and held it tight. Horatio had his claws fixed into my side, and had drawn blood, I noticed. 'Nothing. Is it time to go?'

'Yes. But take your time. Alasdair's got the kettle on.'

I arched my back, removed my cat from my flank, and prepared to go into battle.

Chapter Twenty-Four

Now does my object gather to a head.
—William Shakespeare, *The Tempest*, Act 5, Scene 1

We began by sitting around my kitchen table and exchanging glances. I looked at Alasdair. The haunted look was back in his light blue eyes, I noticed. But there was something else: a steely determination to complete his mission. I had changed into loose blue cotton trousers and a pale grey shirt, and had my Modesty Scarf tied around my hair. I also wore boots with thick woollen socks. If we had to run, I wanted proper footwear. Just in case. Alasdair was wearing a black tracksuit. I looked questioningly at his clothes, and he grinned.

'Corinna, back in Afghanistan, this would be a mild spring day. On the sun-baked plains it gets well over forty degrees in midsummer.' He raised his hands in dismissal. 'And of course in midwinter it's twenty below. I think we may need to run. I'm dressed for it.' He indicated a pair of runners under the table.

Then I looked at Daniel, resplendent in well-worn jeans and grubby white T-shirt. Anything less like the resplendent figure he would have cut as the representative of El Dorado, that well-known and respected firm of real estate agents, would be difficult to imagine. He too was wearing runners. Old ones, with broken shoelaces retied in knots. Daniel followed my gaze and grinned, his adorable agate eyes flashing at me in that way that makes me go weak at the knees.

'Yes, I'm expecting to run as well. Are you up for that?'

'In these boots, yes. The heels have a built-in roll and I can raise quite a respectable sprint in them. Not to mention kicking the crap out of anyone who gets in my way,' I added vindictively.

Alasdair laughed softly. I thought I caught a flavour of heather-clad hillsides in the sound. 'Now, just so you know before we set out, I'm no' armed, Corinna. I don't know if you're thinkin' mebbe I'm goin' tae gae in wi' guns blazing like a Spaghetti Western. I want Geordie back, sure. But ah've no commission tae carry firearms here. And I won't. Just because.'

'But I have,' said Daniel. 'And I am armed with both a gun and a licence to carry it. But I will only use my weapon if the alternative is one of us dying.'

'All right. And we really are going to drive to their back gate and see if we can burgle the joint?' Somehow this didn't seem like such a cunning plan, now we had come to it.

'That's pretty much the idea. We aren't even going to drive past the front of the house. I don't want any warning of our advent at all. Narek tells me that Geordie is chained up outside the back door. They bought him a doghouse from Bunnings, apparently.'

'That's very thoughtful,' Alasdair commented. 'Now I do have one more question, Daniel. Are you certain we're going tae the right house? We don't want any Gallipoli landings here.'

'Narek swears it is, and I believe him. And just to be sure, I've been to see Uncle Solly and his team. They have excellent TV footage of the back of the house. There's a combination lock and that's it, as far as we can see. They've seen the gate opening and shutting, and men going out the back for a smoke. Apparently Uncle Tigran gave up smoking last year and he takes a dim view of his employees indulging in a habit he has renounced.'

'Do they keep tabs on all of our organised crime figures?' I wondered aloud.

Daniel laughed, took my hand and squeezed it.

'No. Only those whose doings may impact upon our people. We're not sure about the Azeris. None of the other Muslim gangs are game to take us on. They fear the Sword of the Lord and of Gideon.' He grinned. His teeth, I swear, shone. 'But these Armenians are very new in town. We aren't sure what they want, and what they're intending to do. This is a new feud. And we won't do anything until we know more.' Daniel stood up. 'All right. Ready?'

Alasdair and I exchanged glances. 'As ready as we'll ever be.'

We slunk out of Insula with as much surreptitiousness as we could manage. I hadn't even asked Daniel how we were going to get to Kilmarnock, despite the fact he has no car and doesn't drive. I thought I had a pretty good idea.

We walked west along Flinders Lane and waited at Market Street. The sun was getting its eye in, blazing down between the skyscrapers. And the wind was stirring: a pollen-infested northerly smelling of drought and heartbreak. I leant against the lone plane tree that gamely clung onto the corner and looked at Daniel. 'Are we waiting for Timbo?'

He took out his phone and scanned it. 'Yes, he'll be here in about thirty seconds. I'm not sure if we're being watched, but I thought a little walk might be a good start. Just to stretch our legs and make things harder for any putative spies.' I took his arm and inhaled the scent of Daniel. I hadn't felt this keyed up for a long time. Deep breaths, Corinna. You can do this.

A light blue sedan of some sort drew up next to us. I watched it move, but it was as silent as a wraith. I gave Daniel a questioning glance. 'I've got us a Prius today. It seemed like a good idea.'

I agreed with him, and climbed into the back seat with Daniel. Alasdair joined Timbo in the front seat and we slipped away northwards. I heard the petrol motor kick in softly. My clever

Daniel! Approaching the back gate of a gang HQ in a silent car sounded like a brilliant idea to me.

'So you like the Prius, Timbo?' my beloved enquired.

Timbo turned his head for a moment and gave us a beatific smile before returning to the matter in hand. As ever with Timbo, discarded food wrappers draped themselves around the dashboard. He seemed to be eating Cheezels at present. Smudges the colour of an unsuccessful spray-on tan adorned his thick lips. His eyes were more bovine than ever. They contrasted agreeably with his sumo wrestler's body. And he remained a man of fewer words than almost anybody I had ever met. Just what you need in a getaway car driver.

We drove through the People's Republic of Moreland in companionable silence. As we crossed Bell Street (the famous hipster-proof fence) I realised that Alasdair had begun to sing softly under his breath. I gathered he was singing 'Oliver's Army,' and I joined in. The two of us sang our way right to the end. Daniel clutched my hand tightly. I don't think Elvis Costello was on his adolescent playlist.

Alasdair turned in his seat and gave me a quick smile.

'He wrote that for us, you know,' he confided. 'All us British squaddies.'

I nodded. Oliver's Army, all of them. Young men without prospects except as members of Her Majesty's armed forces. Cannon fodder to be fed into whatever wild misadventures idiotic politicians dreamt up for them. I shook my head in anger. But at least that wasn't true anymore. It costs a lot of money to train a modern soldier. So however crazy the war, soldiers would no longer be needlessly wasted in a tactical sense. The strategy of confusing the enemy by hitting them under cover of broad daylight at their strongest point had perished in the First World War, along with several millions of luckless squaddies like Alasdair. And Daniel.

I held my breath. Because that was what we were doing right now. All except for the frontal assault. I watched the sun-struck suburbs go by through the tinted window. I wondered what life would be like there among the cream brick boxes. I was grateful I would never find out. How many Philomelas had tried to escape and fallen back into the gravity well?

Daniel whispered in my ear, 'Not long now, *ketschele.* The plan is simple. We go in, grab Geordie, and run for it. We don't care about them.' He tapped Timbo lightly on the shoulder. 'When we turn off the main road, switch over to the electric motor. It should have enough charge to get us there.'

Timbo inclined his chin and kept heading north. Then we turned west and drove through a wilderland of cream-brick mansions with gleaming fake marble porticos. Depressed dry grasses rattled mournfully on the nature strips and filled empty blocks between them. For Sale signs hung from the front fences. No wonder people wanted to build mansions in these god-forsaken plains. Playing outside was not going to be much fun for children hereabouts.

'Do you think Uncle Tigran's people killed Philomela's sister?' I whispered in his ear.

'I don't know. Maybe. We'll leave all that for the police. I'm just hoping we don't run into Letty White. If she's staking out the place she will not be a happy policeperson at all. All right, Timbo. Slow down, if you would. I want to keep an eye out for plainclothes cops.'

Our car went into stealth mode and we cruised along a quiet road. Daniel looked from side to side, looking for parked cars with passengers. 'There's one car of interest. The driver is looking at his phone. But that could be just about anybody these days. I think we'll risk it. Let us out here, Timbo. Stop a few doors down, if you would, and be ready for us.' He turned to me. 'Remember: we do this in silence. Alasdair and I will give you hand signals. That's all we'll need. There may be microphones.'

We got out of the car and it purred off down the street. There was nobody visible outside. I looked with sinking heart at the high cream brick wall of 47 Anzac Grove. It was at least three metres tall, with no footholds or handholds visible. The top was rounded off, presumably to discourage visitors not already put off by the forbidding keep. To our left was a huge garage. Daniel ran to it, tried to open it, and returned at once, shaking his head. We looked instead at a tall, narrow steel door. A combination lock was set into it. Daniel's lips pursed, and he pointed at a small plaque inlaid in the surface. A slanting diagonal line, and above it three vertical lines. My eyes widened. Was that the spear of Longinus and the three nails of Christ?

Daniel nodded to me, and looked at Alasdair with his hands upraised.

Alasdair waved us back and addressed the lock. I noticed he was wearing thin cotton gloves. He twiddled with the dial for a moment, and the door began to open. Did they teach safe-cracking in the British Army? I wondered. Then I noticed that the door was opening by itself; it was a hydraulic door.

Next to me, Daniel stiffened. He exchanged a tense look with Alasdair, who shrugged.

When the opening was wide enough, Alasdair slipped inside. Daniel followed him, and so did I. I wasn't going to be left out in the street by myself.

We found ourselves in a large yard, open to the sky except for the enormous carport. Along the left fence there were rows of enormous amphorae which might once have contained enough wine for a Roman orgy, but now contained a bright profusion of flowering shrubs. I vaguely noticed three enormous cars and some large sheds along the right-hand wall, but really I only had eyes for the back of the two-storey house. Next to a forbidding steel door was a dog kennel. And crouched inside it, with his head on the concrete, was a smallish spotted dog. There were no humans in sight.

The dog lifted his head at once, muzzle pointed.

'Geordie! *Tiugainn!*' Alasdair's voice was low-pitched, but clear. I had heard once that whispering was far more perilous than low-pitched speech.

The dog tried to move, and whined softly.

'*Isd thu!*' Alasdair turned to look at Daniel and shook his head. I understood. He was chained up, and Alasdair would have to go and untie him. Meanwhile, we could probably be seen from the back windows of the house.

My heart began to pound, and Daniel backed me around the corner of one of the sheds. He placed his finger on my lips. I realised I was shaking all over. Then I looked at the door through which we had come and gaped. It was closing, all by itself. I pointed. Daniel flung himself towards the portal and tried to hold it open, but it was powered by some motor far stronger than he was. The lock clicked shut with terrible finality.

Suddenly Alasdair was with us, carrying Geordie in his arms and murmuring Gàidhlig endearments into his fur. Geordie's tail was pounding against Alasdair's thigh, and he whimpered again. Then his body went as stiff as a board, and his nose was pointing directly at the house. 'Oh, shite,' said Alasdair. His face had gone the colour of ash. Even our serving soldier was scared. My blood turned to ice in my arteries. Alasdair produced his dog-sling from somewhere inside his clothes and slipped his faithful companion into it. Geordie nuzzled him and whimpered again.

And then came the sound of shouting from the front of the house, followed in quick succession by gunfire.

Chapter Twenty-Five

Knowing I lov'd my books, he furnished me
From mine own library with volumes that
I prize above my dukedom.
—William Shakespeare, *The Tempest,* Act 1, Scene 2

I clutched Meroe's Ring of Otherworlds tightly in my fist. The noise was deafening, and the smell like the fires of hell. Why had I never known that guns were so loud? I noted with gratitude that I was being jammed up against the aluminium shed wall, with Alasdair and Daniel between me and harm. Daniel had his gun out. It was larger than I was expecting: a jet-black handgun of some make or other. I didn't care. He was covering the narrow angle from which any attack would come. The guns kept on firing, accompanied by shouts that sounded like orders being given. I shrank still further and tried, for the first time in my life, to think slim thoughts.

The back door to the house was flung open. We couldn't see it, but we could hear it. People were running along the concrete. They would be upon us in seconds. I felt Daniel tense. Alasdair had his fists clenched, ready for combat.

And there they were. At least a dozen of them, right in front of us, for a long moment. But they were not at all what I was expecting. Mothers with children first, a couple of aged uncles, young boys, and impressively elderly grandmas. I saw Daniel's gun disappear into his holster. One of the boys was holding a cat carrier, from which outraged yowling emanated. Another boy had, I swear, a large frill-necked lizard in his arms. There were little girls in pinafores carrying teddy bears nearly as big as they were. A middle-aged mum was pulling at the arm of a small girl carrying a brown, flop-eared bunny in her arms. Car doors were yanked open, and deep-voiced engines roared into throaty life.

Last of all came what had to be the family matriarch. She paused for a moment, looked straight at us, and lifted up her black walking stick. I saw Alasdair raise both his hands, palm outwards, towards her. The woman saw Geordie, now secure in the sling around Alasdair's neck, and grinned. Her front teeth flashed golden, and her black eyes took us all in. Then she nodded, and joined the others in the vast carport, footfalls echoing in the roomy cavern.

Car doors slammed shut, and there was a grinding of hydraulic gears as the immense garage door began to open. The shooting was still going on, but there was less of it. Tyres screeched, and the cars exited the premises at speed. The grinding sound of the garage door began again. Alasdair and Geordie exchanged glances, and nodded. Daniel gripped my arm tight, and impelled me through the closing portal. Alasdair was doing something behind us, but I did not know what. I risked a quick look back and saw him fling himself onto the ground and roll under the door. I hoped Geordie wouldn't be squashed, but I assumed this was a manoeuvre long-practised on Afghanistan's plains.

The gate boomed shut and we raced towards Timbo and safety. I have not run, as such, since the humiliations of my boarding school. But I was running now. Terror seemed to have filled my limbs with liquid fire. And when we were three houses away, the world erupted in flame and thunder.

My ears rang as though I had been clubbed by a lead-filled

shillelagh. I found myself lying flat on the footpath, with Daniel lying on top of me and covering my body with his own. It felt like a tidal wave of molten lava had rolled over us. The aftershock of the explosion was still echoing, or perhaps I was just imagining it.

I slowly lifted my head off the concrete. I was afraid it might come off. Cautiously, I opened my eyes. Daniel's face was covered in soot. I touched my finger to my lips and began to dab at the black marks. He grinned and did the same to me. 'Are you all right, *ketschele?*' he enquired.

'Apart from the regiment of dwarves using my head as an anvil, yes.'

'Come on, you two!' That was Alasdair, looming above us and tugging at Daniel's arm. 'No time for that now!'

I staggered to my feet with Daniel's strong arms around my waist and under my shoulder. We flung ourselves into the Prius and sat, stunned. Police sirens were sounding, not far away. A stentorian voice with a megaphone was issuing instructions, stage left. Clearly there was still a great deal happening in whatever was left of the Petrosians' HQ. But all this was more or less at the periphery of our thoughts, because standing right in front of the car, one accusing arm stretched out with fingers spread, was Letty White.

'Give me the keys, Timbo,' she instructed through the open driver's window, and he handed them over without a word.

She stowed them away in her trouser pocket, opened the rear door and raked me with a baleful glare. 'You're not going anywhere just yet.' She shook her head in disbelief. 'What did I tell you? I said don't go anywhere near these people! I distinctly felt my lips move, and I am certain that an unambiguous instruction to stay right away from here left my vocal cords and reached your ears. We've been staking out this place for quite a while now. Obstructing the police is a serious offence. And you!' She glared at Daniel and shook her head again. 'I am, regrettably, all too familiar with tripping over Daniel Cohen, private investigator, in the course of my duties. But what possessed you to bring Corinna into a war zone?'

'She volunteered.' My beloved had his soothing voice on now: like dark honey poured over a sore throat. 'Come on, Letty. She and I are partners. You know that. And we didn't obstruct the police.'

'That's a debatable point, Daniel. I am strongly tempted to handcuff the lot of you and bring you in for questioning. But what I really want to know is: what the bloody hell are you doing here, of all places? Are you completely out of your minds?'

I gave her my most dazzling smile. 'I told you we were looking for a lost dog. That was absolutely true.'

'And here he is,' put in Alasdair from the front seat. He lifted the dog in his sling. Geordie wagged his tail weakly, blinked, and tucked his head back into the harness.

Letty abandoned Daniel and me, opened the front passenger door and looked from Alasdair to Geordie and back again. 'Who are you?'

He saluted. 'Sergeant Alasdair Sinclair, British Army, retired, ma'am. And this is Geordie.' Hearing his name spoken, Geordie's head reappeared briefly to say hello.

Letty shook her head wearily. The bullhorn was still issuing orders, flames could be heard crackling behind us, sirens still resounded through the baking plains of Kilmarnock, as far as we could tell the walls and roof were falling in, but we had eyes and ears only for her. 'Well, Sergeant Sinclair, would you care to tell me what this is all about?'

'These bastards stole ma dog from me in the city. I sustained a number of injuries defending meself and Geordie. He and I went through a lot together in Afghanistan, and I wanted him back. So I engaged Daniel to find him.'

Letty's mouth opened once or twice. 'Why on earth would they steal—no, wait. They wanted him to check for explosives, yes?'

'That's right. And Geordie knew all along there were explosives there, but he didn't tell them because they didn't know the right words. Geordie only answers to commands in the Gàidhlig.'

'Garlic? What? Oh, never mind. I don't care. So if I arrest the lot of you on a charge of police obstruction, your defence is that you were looking for a lost dog, and the fact that it happened to coincide with a bigger and more important crime was pure coincidence, is that it? All right. I've seen the dog. Get out of here.' She fished in her pocket for the keys and returned them to Timbo. 'Just make sure you drive straight ahead and clear right out of the area.'

'Soggies taken over the crime scene?' Daniel ventured.

'Yes, Daniel, they have. They've been standing by all day. Because I was expecting this to blow up today and we called them in as soon as the shooting started. Luckily for you, I don't think you precipitated the shootout, otherwise you really would be helping me with my enquiries. Off you go. Straight ahead till the T-junction, then turn right and don't come back here for any reason whatever.'

Dismissed, we slunk away towards the T-junction.

For those unfamiliar with our police force's ultimate weapon in crisis management, the Soggies, or Sons of God—their real name is the Special Operations Group—are the ones who do most of the shooting. I thoroughly approve of this, as does everyone acquainted with them. We do not want rank-and-file cops blazing away blammity-blam and shooting anything that moves. If there is to be a shooting war, it is carried out by the Soggies. They are without exception experienced marksmen and women who do not fire off ordnance out of animal high spirits. They can stake out a target for hours on end. They will shoot when instructed to, and not otherwise. They are quite happy to hold fire, should fire not be required. Because this is Australia, and we do not worship firearms or constitutional amendments.

I let out my breath slowly. We really had got away with it all. We had the dog, we had solved most of our mysteries, and we were still in one piece. I wondered about this. 'Daniel, are we all right? Please tell me we still have all our necessary bits. Please tell me that we aren't dead, and merely imagining that we've escaped.'

He took my hand and squeezed it. 'Can you feel my hand, *ketschele?*'

'I can. It feels warm, alive, and reliable. And you've still got soot on your face.'

'So have you. I think we're alive.'

'Erm, well.' Alasdair turned to face us. 'I'd say we're definitely alive, because my arm hurts. The fact that I've got Geordie back might be no more than the fulfilment of a dream, but I doubt I'd be hurtin' so much in the afterlife.'

'I notice you came out of the yard with an impressive dive under the door, Alasdair.' I looked at him. He seemed to have escaped the blanketing cloud of soot. Maybe as a soldier he had special soot-avoidance skills. 'What were you looking for, if I may ask?'

'Clearing our line of retreat. I wanted to make sure there was no one behind us.'

'And please,' I wanted to know, 'how did you find the combination? I've been wondering, but there wasn't any time to ask before.'

He gave a short bark of fox-like laughter.

'I tried 1-2-3-4. It's amazing how often that works. Where are we going, Corinna? Because this poor wee doggie is seriously underfed.' I saw him stroking Geordie through the sling. 'He's no' been eatin' much, I guess. *Ach, mo chu!*' Alasdair's voice died away into muttered Highland endearments.

'I'd like that too,' Timbo volunteered. 'I'm fresh out of supplies.'

'All right.' Daniel closed his eyes for a minute. 'There's a Nando's not far from here. Do you know it, Timbo?'

'Oh yeah!'

'Good. Let's go there. Immediately. I'm starving.'

Alasdair looked at him doubtfully. 'Will they serve Geordie as well?'

'They will if we go to that one. The owner owes me a favour.'

'A big favour?'

'Tolerably big. He was being stood over for protection by a certain family—no, not the Petrosians this time—but I persuaded them to back off and leave him alone.'

'Guid for you.'

And so it was that twenty minutes later we were seated at a sidewalk cafe. Daniel was tucking into a splendid-looking paella and Alasdair was devouring a terrifying peri-peri chicken. Perspiration streamed down his face, but he didn't even seem to notice it. I recalled that hot curries are the national dish of Scotland. I would not have approached it without fireproof gauntlets myself. I had chosen a chicken, bacon, and avocado salad. It tasted heavenly. Sometimes simple, well-cooked food is just what you want, especially after narrowly avoiding being blown up or shot.

Beside us, Geordie was tucking into a metal water bowl filled with raw chicken pieces, courtesy of our grateful host. I gazed at our rescue dog. Alasdair's left hand was stroking the fur around his head. Geordie was a medium-small, happy little fellow with a whiteish coat and a few black spots indicating that some near ancestor had been fraternising with a cast member from *One Hundred and One Dalmatians*. If dogs could purr, he would be purring.

I looked back at Alasdair. The haunted, despairing look on his face I remembered had vanished. I looked at the imperturbable Timbo, steadily working his way through a supersized plate like a front-end loader through a gravel pit. And I looked at my beloved Daniel, wielding his knife and fork with quiet pleasure. We raised our glasses of iced cola and clinked them together.

'We made it!'

'Aye, we did.' Alasdair grinned. 'I cannae tell ye how grateful I am. Thank you all.'

Chapter Twenty-Six

Said dog my heart is true
And steadfast more than you
And love binds more than words what I can do.
—David Greagg, 'Cat and Dog'

Daniel dropped me home, then went back to his apartment to superintend The Homecoming of Geordie. I was glad for him, and for Alasdair, but I had gone deep into adrenaline debt and it was presenting its bills with more than its usual insistence. Besides, Daniel didn't have to get up at four a.m. to begin baking bread like I did.

Horatio nuzzled my ankles as I ran myself a lavender bath and poured myself a stiff gin and tonic. When, he wanted to know, would his dinner be served? Clearly you are skipping dinner, he noted. Probably because of all the chicken flavours decorating your clothes and hands. Will there be chicken for a virtuous cat who has been stuck here for far too many hours all by himself without company of any kind? This is not good enough.

He sniffed my fingers experimentally and began to wash them, licking up the residue of my lunch. I sighed, and opened the fridge to see if I had any cold chicken for him. There was a sealed plastic box with some chicken pieces in it. I shook some out into his bowl, and he sat down, flicked his tail around his front paws, lowered his shoulders and set to work. I sipped at my G and T, with double ice and cold lemon slices. A refreshing waft of summer hillsides was emerging from the bathroom. Come and lie down, Corinna, it was suggesting. Bring your drink with you. And despite the manifest peril of falling asleep in the bath, dropping my G and T into the tub, and giving myself the laceration of a lifetime, I obeyed the summons.

It was but the work of a moment to doff my clothes and leave them in an untidy heap on the bathroom floor. And why not? It was my floor. I'd deal with it in the morning. Meanwhile, my entire body felt as though it had been used as a tilting ground for knights on horseback. I grabbed the steel railing firmly in my left hand, lowered myself into the water and leant back, resting my head on the bath's edge. Lavender essence drowned my senses. I wiped my face clean of dynamite residue and patted my features with moisturiser. With aching care I reached for my drink, drained it to the dregs, then set it down carefully as far from me as I could reach. Now it wouldn't even matter if I fell asleep where I was. I listened to my racing pulse slowly subside from allegretto to a stately adagio. Then I surprised myself, and greatly alarmed my cat—who had, as usual, followed me in to observe the strange ritual of the bathtub—and punched the air with my right arm.

'Yes! We did it!' I exulted.

Horatio padded out of the bathroom in disgust, but I was having none of it. I had been serially burgled and all but shot and blown up; we had been led royally up the garden path with as wild a profusion of mysteries as ever belaboured a semi-virtuous baker; and yet we had been triumphant. And with that I drew myself out of the bath, pulled out the plug, threw on a summer nightie and flung myself into bed. Just before sleep closed over me I set the alarm; and I had no dreams at all.

Four a.m. struck with less than its usual feeling of imminent doom. I stretched my limbs experimentally. Everything seemed to be more or less there. My ankles and calves were issuing pianissimo complaints, but I seemed miraculously alive and well. When had I fallen asleep? It could not have been long past six p.m., which meant almost ten hours of virtuous slumber. I wandered into the bathroom with more than my usual spring in my step. Some slattern had left a pile of clothes on the floor, but I kicked them into a corner and had a steaming hot shower. Then I threw on a light robe and sauntered into the kitchen.

I made my first cup of steaming Arabica coffee and inserted two sourdough slices from last Friday into the toaster. I watched the toaster carefully, wondering if it was going to explode or do anything else untoward, but it didn't. It popped up, its slices a creamy mid-brown, positively begging to be covered with butter and cherry jam. I bit into them with relish and relaxed.

No one was trying to break into my apartment. There was not a sound from anywhere except for the soft padding of Horatio, who draped himself around my calves and announced that he too was ready for breakfast. Kitty dins (dry) rattled agreeably into his bowl, and he settled down to give them his full attention.

I finished my early-morning repast, donned the stout overall and cap, and the stouter shoes. Down the stairs to the bakery, where the big air conditioners had already come on, along with the ovens. And there was Jason, reading a book (another Patrick O'Brian) while waiting for his first rising to mature.

'Cap'n on deck!' he said, jumping to his feet and saluting.

What I wanted was a pleasantly dull, quiet day of diurnal bakery. I hoped I would get it. If you listen to some people, they claim to crave adventures. *My life is so* normal! they will complain. *Why doesn't anything exciting happen to me?* If only they knew. The last week's adventures had offered way more excitement than I had ever wanted in my life. I returned my midshipman's snappy salute and we set to work. Today we would make normal bread and normal fruit muffins and do totally normal things.

I inspected the bakery floor. There were Heckle and Jekyll, sitting obediently by their bowls and proudly displaying the results of their night-shift exertions. Four mice and a truly enormous rat. Only slightly damaged to look at, but apparently dispatched with their customary brusqueness and lack of sympathy. I made my customary oblations and the bakery was filled with the sound of contented crunching. Then I let them outside to sit their patient vigil outside Nippon for their second breakfast of tuna oddments.

Sugar was sifted, flour beaten into shape, yeast was introduced with maximum formality, and dough hooks clicked. Coffee steamed in its pot and was cautiously imbibed. I admired Jason's muscular arms kneading with astonishing expertise. It really was extraordinary how good a baker he had become.

He caught my eye and raised an eyebrow. 'What are we making today, Cap'n?'

'Well, Midshipman? What do *you* want to make today? Your choice, as long as we're making bread and not getting burgled, shot at or blown up.'

He thought about this and scratched his cheek with a floury finger for a moment. 'You haven't been getting blown up, have you, Cap'n?'

'Yes, I have. Sorry, didn't I tell you? I expect it was all over the TV—though you don't watch TV, do you?'

'Not really. TV is for old people. But I did see something about it on my phone. Some gang got their house blown up, and there was a full-on gun battle. You weren't in on that, were you, Cap'n?'

'Yes, I was. When we get the baking properly underway I will tell you about my weekend. Filled With Incident doesn't even begin to cover it. So tell me: what are we making today?'

His eyes unfocused for a while. 'Usual sourdough, olive, cheese and herb, and—I think I'd like to try Irish soda bread. Muffins? Cheese and ham, and apple and spice.'

I nodded approvingly. 'Good choices, Jason. At this time of year people want more traditional muffins. I don't know why, but they do. Probably because they're sick of mince pies and other exotica after Christmas and New Year. All right, Midshipman. Let's to work, and I shall tell you all about it.'

I dragged out the tins for my sourdough and we began. As we rolled, kneaded, soothed, and caressed our farinaceous charges into their ovens, I expounded at length on the events of Saturday and Sunday. He did not ask any questions, but I could see he was taking it big. When I concluded my account, he grinned. 'Cap'n,' I'm really happy it's all over. So, no more cops in the building? I don't like cops. Never have. And we aren't getting broken into any more?'

'As far as I know, we should now be safe. Cross fingers, touch wood. I still don't know a few of the side details, but the survivors of the Armenian gang will be under arrest, and the Azeris as well, I expect. So both gangs will be busted.'

'They're bad people, Cap'n. We won't miss them at all.'

I thought of the women and children with their teddy bears and pets. And the matriarch who had looked us straight in the eye, realised that we were only there to rescue Geordie, and let our presence pass unremarked. 'It takes all sorts, Jason. The women and children will probably be set free. They'll have to find somewhere else to live, but I expect they have other places to go.'

'You said they looked like normal kids?'

'Absolutely normal. They probably don't even ask themselves what Daddy does for a living. And one of the kids was carrying a bunny. Which reminds me: have you got a bunny yet? You said you were thinking of it.'

A slow, adoring smile broke out over his floury visage. 'I'm getting one tomorrow, Cap'n. I was going to wait a bit longer, but I've found one I like.'

'That's wonderful! What's it like?'

He looked, for a moment, about twelve years old. Beneath his patina of flour he may have been blushing. His eyelashes flickered. 'He's grey. Small ears; not those long floppy ones. Real calm and placid. Just what I need in my life.'

'Please tell me it's a boy.'

'Yeah, Cap'n.'

I was relieved. Rabbits will increase their tribe on the slightest provocation, and I didn't want his flat looking like a casting call for *Watership Down: The Musical*.

'What are you going to call him?'

Embarrassment and fierce pride contended in his eyes. 'Bruce.'

'Bruce?'

'I had an uncle called Bruce. He gave me a Christmas present once.'

'What was it?'

'A lightsabre.'

I forbore to press him any further. I imagine that Christmas presents would have been exceedingly rare coin in what had passed for his childhood. 'Well, don't forget to introduce me to Bruce, if you've a mind to.'

He grinned proudly. 'Aye-aye, Cap'n.'

By seven a.m. we were well underway, and Jason departed for his trucker's special: the one that makes my arteries go into shock if I just think about it. Exit Jason; enter Heckle and Jekyll. They had dined to their own satisfaction. In the baking summer air that wafted in through the door the scent of fish was unmissable. Kiko and Ian had come to the party, it seemed. Both cats gave me their customary look of satisfaction now that the daybreak ceremonies had been performed, and curled up on flour sacks to sleep the morning away. As they were well entitled to do, having worked the night shift and slain the thieving rodentia on my behalf.

The door opened again and brought in Kylie and Goss in a small whirlwind of girlish enthusiasm. They had a lot on their minds, and did not hesitate to share it with me.

'Corinna! We saw you! Are you all right?' Kylie enthused. They were exuding Method Acting with every gesture. I hesitate to judge Generation Millennial, but there is something immortally wrong with selfie culture. Do young women spend their whole lives posing for Instagram, or rehearsing for it? I registered formation puzzlement and let them tell me all about it.

'Kylie, what do you mean you saw me? Please tell me you weren't there?'

Gossamer shook her head. 'Of course not, Corinna! Someone took a video. It's going viral!' She took out her phone, flicked the screen a few times and handed it to me.

Oh my. What I saw was as follows: A smoke-filled street scene, with alarums and excursions offstage. And running down the street, right across centre stage, was Daniel, self, and Alasdair with Geordie in his sling. We leapt into the Prius, slammed the doors, and there was our cameo scene with Letty White. After we had been allowed to drive away, the camera panned to the crime scene. Police were running and taking cover. The bullhorn could be heard a long way off. It sounded like it was under a few metres' worth of water. And there was one impassive-looking cop with an assault rifle. She wasn't looking at the camera, which was just as well, else the unknown auteur would undoubtedly have been Helping the Police with Their Enquiries.

I handed the phone back to Goss and took a deep breath. 'Oh good. Do you know, once upon a time, when suburban streets erupted in flame, people used to duck for cover. Now it seems everyone's first reaction is to whip out their phone. Does anything about this strike you as wrong?'

Kylie looked at me as though I had just dropped in from Planet Weird. 'Well, duh! Something like this can get you thousands of subscribers on YouTube. There's huge money in it, potentially.'

I gave up. 'Well, if you say so. And yes, we're fine, give or take being a bit bruised and scared out of our wits. As you—and apparently all the world—saw, that was Daniel and me, and of course Alasdair. We went there to rescue his dog, and we were successful. We just weren't expecting to be pitched into the Siege of Sarajevo.'

Kylie hugged me. Being hugged by someone as stick-insect-like as she is always an odd experience. I was always too terrified to hug her back in case she broke in half. 'Corinna, that's amazing! Well done you! And you haven't been broken into again?'

I laughed. I couldn't help myself. 'No, I managed to go a whole weekend without a home invasion. I don't know how I'll get used to it, but I think I'm going to enjoy it. The people whose house got blown up had kidnapped Geordie, for reasons we needn't go into right now, and we are pretty much certain that it was also they who've been breaking into Insula.'

'Do you know what they were looking for?'

I opened my mouth and shut it again. How could I even begin to explain to these adorable yet feather-brained girls the spear of Longinus, its significance, and the bizarre reasons whereby they had come to look for it here?

'Whatever it was, they didn't find it. And now they're all in prison. And the bad guys are too, I would imagine.'

'There were lots of news stories,' put in Goss. 'The cops said that a number of arrests had been made, and lots of houses raided. Kilmarnock? Is that even a place? I've never heard of it.'

'Neither had I until quite recently. I would have been completely happy to have remained in ignorance of it.'

Kylie was fiddling with her phone again, and frowning. Her face cleared. 'Here's one of the news broadcasts, Corinna. Have a look. It must have been terrible.'

I peered into her phone. There was smoke and debris and hard-faced police. What must have been the front of the house looked like it had lost an argument with a hurricane. Out the front of what remained of Maison Petrosian a Very Senior Cop gave a granite-jawed, unsmiling account of it all. Two fatalities, one more in intensive care, arrests made. Gangland violence was not being ruled out, but it was too early to be certain of anything. Simultaneous raids. Enquiries were continuing. I was about to look away when a fresh-faced female reporter pushed a microphone towards the cop, and I could feel my blood pressure going into overdrive. 'Inspector, we understand that a small group of people were seen leaving the scene of the crime directly after the explosion, and one of them was carrying a dog. Are you able to tell me if they are suspects?'

Not a muscle moved in his obsidian features. 'At this stage, it would appear that these people are not directly involved in the case.'

'They are not suspected of any involvement?'

'No, they are not of further interest at this stage. Enquiries are continuing,' he repeated, and the video mercifully wound to its inglorious conclusion. I silently thanked Letty White, many times over. Kylie gave me an overexcited look.

'That was you, wasn't it?'

'If they were carrying a dog, then yes, that was us. Oh my. All right. What did you get up to on the weekend, anyway?'

I noted that while I still appeared to have Kylie's attention, Goss was lost in her phone. I had a quick look over her shoulder at the video she was watching. It appeared to be a rehearsal of *Othello,* starring none other than our guest actors. One face kept appearing, centre stage. I exchanged a look with Kylie, who shrugged and rolled her eyes.

'We've been partying with the actors. You didn't hear us come in on Sunday morning? It must have been around dawn.'

'Dawn and I have this understanding, Kylie,' I informed her. 'We say hello every weekday morning. At weekends, we go our separate ways.' I looked again at Goss. Oh dear. Now she had freeze-framed on none other than Stephen, our public schoolboy and Trinculo impersonator. Oh dear. This looked like an outbreak of romantic love in its most virulent manifestation.

'Well, I'm glad somebody managed to stay out of trouble.'

I made shooing gestures with both arms. 'Howsoever this be, we have work to do. Jason and I bake the bread, and you two sell it. To arms, ladies. *Aux barricades, citoyens!*'

Kylie all but wrenched the phone out of Gossamer's hands, and they began hauling bread trays out into the shop.

Chapter Twenty-Seven

Well, here's my comfort. (Drinks)
—William Shakespeare, *The Tempest,* Act 2, Scene 2

Around nine a.m. the bread and muffin trays were clearing away nicely. We don't work at full capacity in January. Full service is resumed only after school holidays end, but I was relieved to find—as I was every single morning—that my customers are faithful and buy my bread all year round. By this time of the morning everyone who is going to come in on their way to work has already done so, and it's a good moment for everyone to take a short breather. This was, therefore, the ideal moment for Meroe to walk through my front door and look me over. She wore her customary straight black dress, some lightly chiming jewellery and the inevitable purple gypsy wrap and she looked—as ever—calm, composed and exalted.

'I see you're all right, Corinna,' she observed, moving closer to me. Her face crinkled in delight.

'I am, thank you. Your supernatural assistance came in handy. It was a close-run thing, but we got in and out and Alasdair has his dog back.'

'So I heard.' I did not ask if she'd seen it on TV or somebody's phone. Perhaps there's a special psychic channel out there some-where and all she has to do is tune in to the twenty-four-hour feed and pull news off the ether. It would be rude to enquire, so I didn't. She looked at the ring she had given me and smiled. 'Your courage was equal to the test.'

'It was. Though I've never experienced gunfire before. Or explosions. It was...'

'Testing?'

'Absolutely bloody terrifying. I think I would have been furiously angry afterwards—how dare these thugs start treating our town like the Fall of the Assyrian Empire? But we had the dog, and that was what we came for. And after that I was too relieved to be really cross.'

'How is Alasdair?'

'Blissfully happy. A man and his dog. It must have been love at first sight.'

'Those two have a deep psychic link. When you trust your life to another sentient being, the bond is strong. I am so glad.' She leant over, kissed me lightly on the cheek, and whispered, 'Blessed be.' And with that she melted away into the street again before I could offer her a muffin. But she so rarely seemed to want anything.

Our next visitor was Mrs Dawson, in search of bread. I looked her over with care. She was dressed in a light brown suit and appeared steadfast, but somewhat sad. While Gossamer attended to the financial aspects of the occasion, I asked her how she was.

'Tolerably well, thank you, Corinna. But, alas: it seems my guest must return to his apartment. The police have quite finished with it, and he is anxious to return to his studies. I shall miss the company.'

'You can have dinner with him every night if you want to,' I suggested.

She smiled. 'There is that. So much more satisfactory than breakfast. Only dull people are brilliant at breakfast. I shall ask him to dinner tonight. Thank you, Corinna.'

She turned on her heel and departed. I wondered about her and Dion Monk. Especially the latter. I was eager for a talk with him. Jon's revelations about our good Professor had intrigued me.

Since we had the shop to ourselves for the present, and Kylie and Goss, whom I had permitted to consult their phones, were engrossed, I mentally reviewed our cases. Most were tied up with a little pink bow around them, but there remained some annoying loose threads.

Sitting in the Solved column were Narek's break-ins, the abduction of Geordie, and the attack on Philomela. With the latter, we didn't know for sure it was the Petrosians, but it certainly looked like it. All part of a ridiculously ham-fisted gang war. Neither ensemble would be troubling the scorers for a while, I guessed.

As for Jordan King…As far as I could make out Dion Monk had committed some nameless heresy of interest only to holy warriors like him. I could see that Jesus being married with children might upset a strict Catholic, but that was old news; many writers had already posited as much. If Dion Monk had found a manuscript suggesting that Jesus had founded a society of pole-dancing tax lawyers I could understand his outrage, but I couldn't see what was exercising the young man in the Gospel of St Joseph. Perhaps he might eventually confide in Sister Mary, and she would tell me.

My other loose end was the cyberattack on Cafe Delicious. At the time, I had assumed it was the same folks who had done everything else. The more I thought about it, though, the less likely this became. Someone else had probably done it. Just a common everyday cyberattack then? Presumably so.

My train of thought was interrupted by a sudden inrush of customers, and I returned to my core business: baking bread and bready products and selling them. I decided I would stick to that.

The rest of the day passed without events of note. Kylie went to the bank to deposit the day's takings, and I returned to my apartment and had a lazy afternoon playing with my cat and making a light dinner of salade nicoise. Horatio demanded tribute from my bowl and took the tuna away to the bathroom floor to be alone with it, and I poured myself a glass of chardonnay. For years I had abominated the stuff and drunk only sauvignon blanc from New Zealand's Marlborough Sounds. My unlamented husband James had drunk chardonnay, and would pontificate endlessly on the subject unless discouraged with a cake fork. I thought it tasted like *chateau collapso* shaken up with pine bark: the stuff you smear all over gardens if you wish to discourage unauthorised plant life. But I had recently discovered some wonderful offerings from South Australia which tasted like heaven in a glass, and I had decreed that James or no James, I was going to reintroduce it to my life.

Sipping the cool, fruit-filled nectar at leisure, I switched on the TV. I might as well find out what the rest of the world was learning about our gangland wars. I really hoped there would be no repetition of the video with our inglorious flight from Petrosian HQ. Fortunately, there wasn't. Instead, the headline story carried the banner CRIME BOSS ARRESTED. A small army of detectives ranged themselves around a handcuffed man, and the camera zoomed in on his face. Deep brown eyes, cafe latte skin, small hands, very sharp black suit. He eyed the camera with impassive hostility, like an accountant with a brain tumour. Meanwhile the newsreader could barely contain her enthusiasm.

'Tural Aldjanov, alleged Azeri crime boss, was today arrested and charged with the murders of Tigran and Aram Petrosian and the attempted murders of several other people. In all, forty-nine charges have been laid against five men from the Aldjanov family. This follows from yesterday's attack on the Petrosians' home in Kilmarnock. It will be alleged that this attack formed part of an ongoing drug-trafficking turf war between rival gangs of Armenians and Azeris in Melbourne's north.'

The scene now shifted to a replay of yesterday's explosion and exchange of gunfire. Our cameo roles had been left on the cutting-room floor this time. I didn't want to think about it ever again. I hadn't had any nightmares yet about the roaring madness and the rush of heat passing over me like a tidal wave, but I expected they might be lying in wait around the corner for me. If we had been any closer our clothes would have been scorched off our backs.

The newsreel segued effortlessly into something asinine and political, and I tuned out. Nobody expects anything politicians say to make any sense. When they do it is an unexpected bonus, like challenging a parking ticket and having it withdrawn. I received a text from Daniel which said: *All very well here see you tomorrow.* I responded with *yes please* and a suitably lascivious emoticon. Then I watched something anodyne that entirely escapes my memory and put myself to bed with Horatio.

Tuesday morning began as dull and uneventful as Monday, with breakfast, baking and the Stately Minuet of the Bread Trays. I couldn't get enough of dull and uneventful. Kylie and Gossamer arrived as Jason left for his Cholesterol Surprise and all was for the best in the best of all possible worlds.

Barely had such smug thoughts occurred to me when Jason returned at double speed. 'Cap'n! You gotta come now! Del Pandamus is strangling one of the actors!'

'Kylie!' I bellowed, pointing an admonitory finger at her. 'You're in charge! I may be some time!'

I grabbed my purse and hared out into Calico Alley, with Jason at my side. The sun hadn't made it over the skyscrapers yet, but a hot wind was buffeting the passers-by, ourselves included. It plucked at my sleeve like an insistent relative, but I ignored it. I barrelled into Cafe Delicious and caught Del's eye. He had young Stephen in his grip and wasn't showing any signs of wanting to let go. Peloponnesian oaths filled the cafe. Yai-yai was standing by the kitchen door with her arms folded, looking like all three of the Erinyes at once. She was watching her son's efforts with what looked like solid approval. Several customers, including the other actors, were watching Del's performance from a safe distance. Clearly some form of intervention was required before Del did serious damage to the young man.

'Del, I wouldn't dream of interrupting your chastisement, but what's going on?'

Del did not answer at once, but tightened his grip once more. Stephen was struggling. He looked like someone who had probably played rugby or some such pastime. He came across as one of those disgustingly healthy boys with muscles on his muscles, but he was clearly no match for a man who had probably spent his boyhood chasing down goats on Mediterranean hillsides. Or tanks; I wouldn't put it past him. Stephen went limp, and Del pushed him down into a chair.

'Siddown!' he ordered, in English this time. And Stephen sat cowering in his chair, with Del's left hand still gripping his collar. 'You! You drink my coffee, you eat my baklava, and you do this to me? What you say, huh?'

Fascinating though this undoubtedly was, I wanted some subtitles immediately. I had my own business to run, and use of the fast-forward button seemed appropriate. 'Stephen,' I ordered, 'explain yourself.'

'Speak up, *listis!*' growled Del. 'You tell her!'

Stephen gave me a winning smile. Except it wasn't. He wasn't winning anything right now. 'I, er, I put the ransomware on the cafe website. Look, I didn't mean any harm. But I need the money for our production. Arts Victoria wouldn't give us a grant, and neither would the university. So I had to improvise.' His eyes willed me to understand. 'Art is important. And this production has to go ahead!'

I stared at him. 'You horrible little man,' I managed. 'You sit there with your socks full of feet and tell me you were intending to steal from this hardworking family business to finance your dramatic indulgences?' I turned to Luke, Claire and Sam. 'And you? Did you know about this?'

The trio were glaring at their erstwhile friend and colleague. 'You said you'd ask your father for money!' Sam said.

Stephen ginned weakly. 'I did. He told me to use my initiative.'

'You were going to steal from an old lady?' demanded Luke, his tone one of utter loathing. 'Dude, just no. I think we're done here?'

Two emphatic nods from the girls.

They rose, still shaking their heads, and exited the cafe without another word.

I turned to Del. 'What shall we do with this miserable worm, Del? Would you like to press charges? Do please feel free.'

Del let go of the boy's collar. '*Ochi.*' He shook his head in silent fury. 'I can't be bothered with you, boy. Just go away. You're banned from my cafe. You never show your face down my chimney again, right?'

Stephen stood up and looked around the room for support. Finding none, he slunk out the door.

Del stalked back into the kitchen, accompanied by Yai-yai. Me? I wasn't finished yet. Because I had seen Gully, lurking in the corner. I beckoned to him. He looked at me like a cat with a stolen salmon. I gestured to the door.

When I had got him outside, I poked him in the middle of his moth-eaten black T-shirt. 'Gully, there's something you're not telling me, isn't there?'

He blinked at me. Bright sunshine was hardly his metier, and he squirmed like a snail. But I didn't want him to be comfortable. 'Don't mess me around, Gully. You fixed the ransomware straight away. And—let me guess?—you knew who it was immediately, but you spun out the process so you could get a whole lot of extra free meals from Del. You did, didn't you?'

His skinny shoulders quivered. 'Not exactly like that, Corinna.'

'But almost like that, yes?'

'No. Well, okay, yes, I did. I knew it was someone in Insula straight away. I mean, the guy's a complete amateur. His VPN was pretty easy to crack. I knew it was one of the actors. I've been tracing their online footprint ever since. Which one it was I didn't find out for sure until…' He paused.

'Until when, Gully?'

'Er, Sunday? Corinna, it was a big job. I'm happy not to be paid cash. But if I'd given him an invoice it would have been a fair bit more than coffee and a meal.'

'So you delayed telling Del Pandamus until you'd got your money's worth out of him. All right, Gully. That doesn't make you as bad as that appalling little weasel. But next time you find out something, speak up immediately. You know? Like adults do?'

'Okay. Sorry.'

I relented. 'All right, you can go back and finish your meal. Your last free meal from Del, right?'

'Right.'

He went back inside, and Jason emerged, wide-eyed. As we walked back to Earthly Delights he was very quiet. Finally, he looked at me with surprisingly hot eyes. 'Cap'n, why would that actor guy do that? He's had everything easy. You can tell just by looking at him.'

'And listening to him being Lord of the Manor. You're angry, aren't you, Jason?'

He nodded. 'Yeah. Rich people shouldn't steal from the poor.'

'The poor steal from the rich because they envy them. The rich steal from the poor because they despise them.'

We had stopped in the street. I guessed Jason didn't want to have this conversation in front of an audience. But he was taking it very personally, and I realised why.

'Why did Del let him off?' he persisted. 'How come rich kids always get off? When people like me screw up, we get the works because we don't have rich parents.'

'That, Midshipman, is a good point. But if Del had pressed charges it would have been more work for him. Consider how this will pan out. Stephen's fellow actors are done with him. Unfortunately, I can't even kick the little swine out of my building because Daddy owns the apartment. But I think he's lost three friends for good today. Now, for the rest of this week, I want nothing but calm, baking, muffins, and rest. See to it, Midshipman.'

He saluted. 'Aye, aye, Cap'n.'

Chapter Twenty-Eight

Said dog my teeth bite deep
Whether I wake or sleep
No friend am I to you beware my leap
But the cat is gone from the lane
In the flying leaves and rain
And the sentry dog is back at his post again.
—David Greagg, 'Cat and Dog'

The next couple of days passed in an agreeable blur of bread, muffins and tender love-making. At long last I was able to remind myself of what I wanted my life to be like. Uneventful, save for a few carefully chosen events according to my design for living. Nobody attempted to burgle my apartment, nor anybody else's. The actors had departed on Tuesday, after some embarrassed apologies from Claire, Sam, and Luke. I forgave them immediately. After all, it wasn't their fault Stephen had not the faintest conception of right and wrong. He himself had disappeared without fanfare. I liked to think that he had slid out under the door in the dead of night. The weather remained hot until Thursday, when we had a most agreeable thunderstorm. The Garden of Ceres was thoroughly rain-swept, and after discovering that I had the place to myself I dressed myself in my thinnest nightgown and performed water-nymph dances in the rain. The plants were visibly rehydrating and were turning deeper shades of green with every moment.

No sooner had I returned to my apartment and attired myself more modestly than the doorbell rang. It was Anwyn.

'Hi, Corinna,' she said. 'I just wanted to let you know that Bellamy and I are going back to Adelaide tomorrow. But our embroidery is finished. Would you like to see it?'

'I certainly would! And I think everyone else would too. I suspect that in an hour or two the upstairs garden should have dried off. Perhaps a party is in order?'

'What an excellent idea,' she said approvingly. 'Should Therese and I issue the invitations?'

'Please do. Everyone here: even Mrs Pemberthy, of whom you have doubtless heard. Drop into the music shop and ask Marie and Kate, too.'

'Should we all bring dishes?'

'Yes, please. Everyone else here knows what to do. Some meat, some vegetarian, some fish. The usual sort of thing. Meanwhile, I'll do the setting-up.'

She departed, and I reached for my phone to invite the Pandamus family, and Daniel and Alasdair. I hoped Geordie would be able to cope with Carolus and the cats. But he was not going to be left out of the general festivities if I could help it. All those of us who had laboured in the toils of the ungodly should share in our victory feast.

The invitations issued and duly accepted, I began plotting my own culinary contribution. Apricot chicken wings, I decided, plus a dessert surprise of my own…

By six o'clock I had the trestle table set up. It had white linen tablecloths (mine). It also had transepts, because the table was not going to be big enough for such a large gathering.

Trudi had arrived first, with plates of *poffertjes* and *appeltaart*.

She left them on one of the side tables, grinned at me, and disappeared into the undergrowth, re-emerging with a large terracotta pot. She placed it next to one of the chairs and tapped the side of her nose. 'A special treat for our friends,' she explained, hardly at all. Del and his family were the next to arrive, bringing *tyropitakia*, dolmades, *horta vrast,* and baklava. Del glanced around suspiciously. 'Corinna,' he rumbled. 'That thief of an actor? He is gone, yes? He's not coming here?'

'It's all right,' I assured him. 'He has vanished without a trace. But even if he were still resident in Insula, he would not be welcome here.'

Yai-yai's ancient face creased in a toothless grimace. 'Satan take him away to Pit of Damnation. Such a bad boy!' Then she took a cheese-filled triangle and sat down, folding her black shawl around her slender body.

The lift doors opened to reveal Therese Webb, Anwyn, Carolus, and Bellamy. Therese and Anwyn were wearing gowns in light blue and light brown, eminently suitable for their roles as needlewomen of the Dark Ages. There were girdles, with brown leather purses around their midst. Therese had a large platter in each hand; one revealed itself to be a coconut cake, the other a minty beef salad. Anwyn was carrying a long roll of cloth. I guessed this must be the tapestry, which must be admired either before or after, but certainly not during dinner. Her mouth opened in a O of surprise as Bellamy took one look at Trudi's pot plant, and headed straight for it like a camel at an oasis. He lifted himself up on his back paws, sniffed, and rubbed his cheek against one of the sprays of leaves. Then he climbed right into the pot and draped himself around the bush, inhaling frequently and purring like a small, furry lawnmower.

Enlightenment belatedly dawned on me. 'Trudi, is this catnip?'

She nodded. 'I show it to Lucifer already, and he tried to knock it over so he could roll on it. I didn't bring him today. He doesn't play well with others. But he's had a good fish dinner already and he sleeps on my pillow.'

'It looks as though it will survive Bellamy, anyway.'

I looked around. The lift had returned, bringing Kate and Marie hand in hand and, to my amazement, Philomela in a plain black dress. She was walking! And more…'Hello, everybody,' she said.

I wanted to applaud. Instead, I found a spare chair and ushered her towards it.

'I have been mute, and desperate, and helpless,' she continued. 'But then I saw those who have afflicted me on television.' Her dark eyes glinting. 'It was the Armenians. The idiots must have mistaken our house for the Aldjanovs'. Every night I went to bed, praying for vengeance. Then, last night, my sister came to me in a dream. She told me to forgive them. At first I refused; my heart was hard like the Pharaoh. But she reminded me that I must trust in the Lord to deliver judgment. I realised that she was right. And suddenly I could speak, and stand up, and walk.'

Marie leant over to embrace Philomela. 'I am so sorry.' She turned to face the gathering. 'The Petrosians are my cousins,' she explained. 'Our side of the family wanted nothing to do with any of this. The drugs, the kidnapping, the murders.' She looked at Alasdair. 'Or the dog-stealing. Narek and I used to be close when we were growing up. Then he went to live with Uncle Tigran. I begged him not to—I told him this is Australia; we don't do this here—but he went anyway. From that moment on, I wanted nothing to do with him, either.' She turned back to Philomela. '*Sas échoume vlápsei kai eseís. Lypámai polý.*'

Philomela kissed Marie's cheek. 'You have nothing to apologise for. We cannot help our bad boys. Or our bad men.'

Kyria Pandamus, I noticed, was sitting nearby, and she rose to her feet. She took Philomela's hand. 'You are a good girl. And now you eat, yes? You're too thin! Look at you! Here, have some proper Greek food.'

We left them to it. Sometimes you have to back off when women are determined to come with aid and comfort.

Anwyn took the opportunity to show off the completed tapestry, and the rest of us admired it. It was magnificent.

I looked at Therese Webb. She was glowing with pride. These two and Philomela had worked wonders during the last week, while we had been battling gangsters and burglars. I felt that their work was possibly of more lasting value than mine.

While I was admiring, I found myself joined by Kylie and Goss. They were wearing matching singlets in yellow and pink with very visible black bras, their usual micro-skirts, bare legs and sandals. Had either been of a flirtatious disposition this would have counted severely against their characters, but both were at bottom entirely innocent.

'We brought salads,' Kylie said brightly. 'That's absolutely brilliant. Did you make this?'

While Anwyn and Therese were proudly showing off their work to Kylie, I gently ushered Gossamer to one side and looked her in the eye. 'Goss, are you okay?'

She looked desperately ashamed. 'I s'pose so, Corinna. Yeah, I heard about—*him*.' She could not even bring herself to say Stephen's name, and the pronoun was pronounced so as to rhyme with scum. She blinked away a few tears from her flawless features. 'I can really pick them, can't I?'

'Well, yes, Gossamer. You can pick them. Try to look under the surface next time, hmm? I don't want to be too all-knowing, but I did find his air of superiority annoying. He addressed us like we were his household servants.'

'But he's so confident! I wish I was that sure of myself.'

'He won't ever be so sure of himself again, Gossamer,' I told her.

I saw Meroe had arrived in her usual black with a grey shawl and a plate of vegetarian spring rolls (unexpected) and tropical and forest fruits on a tray (entirely expected).

'Blessed be.' She smiled at me. 'It is good to have calm in our midst again.'

'I could really get used to this,' I agreed. 'A great deal more of the same is all I ask. Do you think it likely?'

Meroe inclined her chin. 'I think it probable. But keep the ring. Just in case.'

I looked down at my hand and realised I was still wearing it. The Ring of Otherworlds seemed to have become part of my life. I took it off last thing at night, and assumed it first thing in the morning without even thinking about it.

My gaze strayed to the lift door, and it opened once more to reveal Mrs Dawson with her arm securely linked through that of Dion Monk. He carried what looked like a large ham, and they were smiling like a pair of contented lovebirds. Well, well. I had not seen either of them since Monday, but it appeared they had not wasted their time. Fragrant-smelling plates were balanced in their free hands, but they appeared sufficiently unstable to warrant immediate removal to the tables. I refrained from comment. There was not the slightest need for it. I had never seen either of them looking so blissfully content. Excited conversation filled the rooftop garden, but they were in a small, sunny world entirely their own, and glowed companionably together. Meroe looked at them with a smile of saintly benevolence, and wandered off to the tables for refreshment.

When the lift doors opened again, there was Daniel, Alasdair, and Geordie. Bellamy disappeared into the undergrowth like a small, furry missile. Carolus he had learned to treat, if not as a brother, at least as a tolerated cousin. This spotted animal was too much to cope with. Carolus, meanwhile, blinked, took a few tentative steps forward, and stopped dead. Geordie was sniffing hard. Alasdair put his hand on Geordie's head and issued some words of command in Gàidhlig. At once Geordie sat down on his paws and looked up expectantly. Carolus wagged his tail uncertainly and withdrew behind Therese Webb's chair.

Daniel meanwhile was pouring drinks and handing them around. I took one: ice-cold sauvignon blanc from the Marlborough Sounds.

I drank, and watched in alarm as Bellamy emerged slowly from the undergrowth and advanced towards the foe. He walked straight up to Geordie's nose, hissed, and batted at it with a lightning paw. Geordie flicked his nose safely out of the way and uttered a small whine of complaint. Alasdair placed his hand on Geordie's head once more and whispered more endearments.

'Bellamy! Bad cat!' Anwyn's voice rang out.

Bellamy turned towards her. Me? What do you mean Bad Cat? I'm a Good Cat! He turned his back on Geordie and returned to the potted catnip. Within a few seconds he had forgotten everything but the glorious aroma of *Nepeta,* and resumed his position wrapped around the base of the bush.

I caught Trudi's eye. She nodded in quiet triumph. The pot had been the perfect ice-breaker for this meeting.

Daniel leant over and kissed me. I returned the kiss, with interest.

Looking over the party, people were already eating and drinking freely. I realised that I was hungry.

I managed to secure some of my apricot chicken wings before they disappeared entirely, and worked my way through three *tyropitakia* and two dolmades. I noticed that Jason had appeared without fanfare and, beginning at the eastern transept, was motoring his way steadily through the bill of fare as if he hadn't eaten for weeks. I honestly do not know where he puts it all.

For a while I stood back and looked around my party and sighed with contentment. Was anything lacking? Everyone was so pleased to see each other. Except—wait a moment. The door opened, and there was Mrs Pemberthy herself, dressed in a ludicrously unseasonal twinset in brown and ochre. In her hand she carried a plate of what appeared to be rock cakes. At her feet was Traddles the Eternally Annoying. He made a beeline for Geordie, who stood up straight and examined him with a critical eye. Traddles stopped dead and retreated behind his mistress's ankles. I handed Mrs P a drink, which she accepted, pursing her thin lips.

'Thank you, Corinna,' she said grudgingly, and lowered her voice to a malevolent whisper. 'Honestly, those girls of yours are a disgrace. This is a civilised garden party, not a pornographic film set. Whatever were they thinking?' Her voice trailed off into silence, and her eyes hardened like highly suspicious concrete.

Following her gaze, I saw she was directing her basilisk eye at Dion Monk and Mrs Dawson, shamelessly basking in mutual adoration and holding hands.

'Well!' she snapped, and moved away to disapprove and sizzle in the comfort of her own society next to the wall.

I realised that I had been right to invite her. Without Mrs Pemberthy's ill wishes our party would have been too bland for words. We could survive her disapproval. Indeed, we cherished it.

I saw Cherie Holliday and her father arrive laden with two enormous picnic baskets and similarly large smiles. And I thanked the gods and goddesses who look down upon us for the joyfulness of life.

I even went to the side table and tried one of Mrs P's rock cakes. They appeared to have been baked out of plutonium. I offered a bit to Geordie, but he shook his head and wandered off to look for something more edible. I didn't blame him. But our tables contained more delights I had not noticed until then. There was some splendid fruit sorbet to take away the taste, and I spooned myself a bowl. Frozen citrus and forest fruits caressed my mouth and throat. There, there, they seemed to be whispering to me. We'll save Mrs P's rock cakes until we really are under attack and need missiles for our siege catapults.

Just then, I noticed Philomela walking towards me and smiling. Where once she had resembled a Greek goddess of vengeance and divine fury, she now looked serenely Olympian. She sat next to me and began to recite. I opened my mouth in astonishment, because I recognised the words. It was Prospero's Farewell at the very end of *The Tempest*. In a clear, accented, level tone she recited:

Now I want
Spirits to enforce, art to enchant,
And my ending is despair,
Unless I be relieved by prayer,
Which pierces so that it assaults
Mercy itself and frees all faults.
As you from crimes would pardoned be
Let your indulgence set me free.

This was the veriest of happy endings for her. And I rejoiced.

As she rose from her chair to join Therese and Anwyn, her place was taken by Alasdair. He had a plate of Greek food and was discovering it was, much to his astonishment, delicious.

'Now you've got Geordie back, what are you intending to do?' I enquired. He dropped half a spiced meatball into Geordie's mouth and smiled.

'Ah've go' a friend in a place called Hepburn Springs. He's running a bed and breakfast and he tells me he could dae wi' a hand. He's an ex-squaddie like meself. Ah've never heard of the place. What's it like?'

'I think you'll love it, Alasdair. It's quiet, hilly, and utterly beautiful. There are mineral springs there, and wineries, and lavender farms.'

'It sounds wonderful. Quiet would be juist what we both need right now.' He stroked Geordie's head in contentment.

I ate some coconut cake, sat back in my chair and inhaled deeply. Everyone was talking softly, eating, drinking, and enjoying the cool breeze. The sun would not set for ages yet, and it was glorious not to have to hurry, or stress, or fret. Though I did want to talk to Dion Monk and ask him about Vienna in 1945. If what Jon had suggested were true, he must be in his nineties at least!

Suddenly the man himself caught my eye, and waved me over. I brought a small stool to sit with him and Mrs Dawson. 'Tell me about your baked ham,' I begged. 'It is superb.'

'*Pernam ubi eam cum Caricis plurimus elixaveris,*' he quoted. 'It is from an Ancient Roman cookbook by a fellow called Apicius. Figs, honey and bay leaves lend it their particular charm.'

'Splendid,' I said. 'And…'

He lifted an interrogative eyebrow.

'What I really wanted to ask you,' I confessed, 'is if you have finished your translation.'

He inclined his head with grace and gravitas.

'Indeed I have. And the Gospel of St Joseph of Arimathea has lived up to its billing. This will indeed set tongues wagging when it is published.'

'You haven't found the Holy Grail, have you?'

'No, my dear. Though I have never understood why people seem to think it's a cup.'

'Isn't it?'

'Well, no. Wikipedia seems to think it comes from the Latin *gradalis,* and of course the medieval French leapt to the conclusion that it was a cup. I think it far more likely that it comes from *graduale,* meaning a ladder.'

'Like Jacob's Ladder?' I had not realised Daniel was with us, but he was kneeling at the Professor's feet. As indeed did we all.

'Well, yes. A stairway to heaven, if you like. But it would relate to Christ's crucifixion because it would have been the ladder from which the Deposition from the Cross was effected. However, St Joseph has remarkably little to say about that. What happened afterwards is a lot more intriguing; because, as we have long suspected, Jesus appears to have indeed married Mary Magdalene—though she is simply called Mary—and they went…well, now. Would you care to hazard a guess?'

I couldn't. Though Mrs Dawson clearly knew, because she was grinning from ear to perfectly formed ear.

'England,' he resumed, in quiet triumph. 'It is a singular fact that the Glastonbury Thorn Tree really is a Syrian thorn, and it was supposedly grown from the staff of St Joseph, where he planted it in what became the monastery grounds. The idea that Jesus visited England has long been a staple of the British Israelites. They went rather too far in suggesting that the Ten Lost Tribes of Israel had also gone to England, but nevertheless we have substantial evidence for the first time that the story really is true. Now do you see why our zealous young friend Jordan King was so anxious to impound my copy of the scroll?'

I shook my head. 'Sorry, not really. And how would he have known what was in the scroll? But you're going to tell me, aren't you?'

Mrs Dawson clasped his hand in hers and smiled. 'Oh, I think the Catholics have known about this scroll for some time. In its essentials. Word gets around in Vatican City. But they didn't want this to get out.'

'Why not?' I asked, still not getting the point.

'Because, my dear, this means that the Church of England really is the one true church after all. I have always thought so.'

I gaped, and looked at Daniel. He nodded slowly. 'That does make sense. Rome may have had St Peter and St Paul. But if England has Jesus Himself...'

I saw Kate and Marie were next to me, still hand in hand.

'Have you given him his present yet?' Kate wanted to know.

'I was saving it up for after dinner. But now seems as good a time as any. Daniel?'

Instantly he was at my side. I reached into my pocket and handed over the gift-wrapped USB. 'Any particular occasion, *ketschele?*' he asked, when he had unwrapped the parcel and was admiring the song list.

'Hanukkah?'

He kissed me. 'That was last month. But never mind. Gifts are always sweetly welcome.' He turned to the girls. 'Your work?'

'Yes.' Marie's face dimpled prettily. 'Our shop is just down Calico Alley.'

'Thank you both. And you also, Corinna. I cannot thank you enough, for everything.' He kissed me again. And why not?

But now it was time for my dessert to be unveiled. I opened a cardboard box and gestured in triumph. Daniel looked, cut himself a slice, and ate it.

'What do you think?'

'Delicious! It tastes like soda bread, but with raisins. What's it called?'

I waited until I had Alasdair's attention as well, then I announced, to general smiles: 'It's called Spotted Dog.'

Recipes

Spotted Dog

5 cups plain flour
1½ cups caster sugar
3 tablespoons baking powder
2 eggs
2 cups milk
2 cups raisins

Preheat the oven to 375°F. Grease a 12-inch cast-iron skillet. Into a large bowl, sift together the flour, sugar, and baking powder. In a separate bowl, beat the eggs with the milk. Stir the egg mixture into the flour mixture until it is moist. It must not be runny. Fold in the raisins. Spread the batter onto the skillet and bake for 1 hour or until the bread has risen and is golden brown on top.

Roman Baked Ham

3 lb 2 oz ham on the bone
9 oz chopped dried figs
3 bay leaves
3½ fl oz honey
3⅓ cups plain flour
½ cup olive oil

Bring the ham, figs, and bay leaves to boil in a large pot
of water, then simmer for 1 hour. Preheat oven to 350°F.
Wait until the ham is cold, then use your fingers to remove
the skin. Use a knife to make criss-cross incisions in the
fat and fill the incisions with honey. Make a paste with
the flour and oil, and cover the ham with it, making sure
it gets into the incisions you've made. This paste will
ensure the ham stays moist and flavoured. Bake the ham
until the paste becomes a golden-brown crust.

Apricot Chicken Wings

2 cloves garlic, crushed
1 tablespoon finely grated fresh ginger
⅔ cup apricot jam
½ cup orange juice
3 lb 5 oz chicken wings
4 potatoes cut into wedges
1 tablespoon sesame seeds
2 tablespoons vegetable oil

Preheat the oven to 400°F and line two trays with baking paper. In a bowl, stir together the garlic, ginger, jam, and most of the juice, reserving 1 tablespoon of juice. Toss the chicken wings in the sauce until they are thoroughly coated, then place them in a single layer on one of the trays. In a bowl, combine the potato, the remainder of the juice, the sesame seeds, and the vegetable oil. Spread the potatoes in a single layer on the other tray. Put both trays in the oven for 20 minutes, turning the chicken pieces and potato occasionally to brown them evenly. Serve the chicken and potatoes with a salad of your choosing.

Coconut Cake

1 cup desiccated coconut
1 cup self-raising flour
¾ cup caster sugar
¾ cup milk

Preheat the oven to 350°F. Grease a medium-sized cake tin. In a bowl, thoroughly beat the ingredients together. Pour into the tin and bake for 40 minutes or until a skewer inserted into the middle comes out clean.

Onion Pan Bread

2 large onions, cut into slices ¼ inch thick
3 tablespoons butter
2 tablespoons brown sugar
2 cups plain flour
1 tablespoon baking powder
1 teaspoon caster sugar
1 teaspoon salt
1 egg
1 cup milk
¼ cup vegetable oil

Preheat the oven to 350°F. Sauté the onion slices in 2 tablespoons of the butter for 10 minutes, stirring occasionally. Use the remaining butter to grease a round 8½-inch baking dish, pie plate, or oven-proof skillet. Sprinkle evenly with the brown sugar then spread the onion slices over the top. In a bowl, combine the flour, baking powder, caster sugar, and salt. In a separate bowl, beat together the egg, milk, and oil. Add the liquid to the dry ingredients and mix well. Evenly spread the batter over the onions and bake for 40 minutes or until a skewer inserted into the middle comes out clean. Let stand for 5 minutes before serving.

Beef Salad with Mint

1 piece (9 oz or so) tenderloin, sirloin or filet mignon
1 small red onion, peeled and sliced
1 small cucumber, peeled and sliced
¼ cup fresh mint (or basil or parsley), minced
4 cups lettuce or other greens, chopped
4 tablespoons fresh lime juice
1 tablespoon fish sauce or soy sauce
pinch cayenne pepper
½ teaspoon caster sugar

Cook beef for 10 minutes in a frying pan or wok, or on a grill. When the beef is cool, slice it into thin strips, reserving the juice. Toss together the onion, cucumber, mint, and greens. For the dressing, combine the lime juice, fish or soy sauce, cayenne pepper, and sugar, then add it to the salad, reserving 1 tablespoon. Add the remaining dressing to the meat juice, then drizzle it over the beef and serve.

Soft Fruit Sorbet

2 cups any soft, ripe fruit, washed, pitted, and dried
1 cup fine sugar
1 tablespoon fresh lemon juice

Puree the fruit in a blender with most of the sugar and some of the lemon juice. Adjust the ingredients to taste. Refrigerate until semi-frozen, then churn by hand with a mixing stick. Keep stirring until the consistency is smooth and even. We live in stirring times.

———

For more of Corinna's recipes, please visit the Earthly Delights website, earthlydelights.net.au.

If you would like to contact me, I may be found at kgreen-wood@netspace.net.au.

Bibliography

War

Anderson, Ben, *No Worse Enemy: The Inside Story of the Chaotic Struggle for Afghanistan*, Oneworld, Oxford, 2011

Kipling, Rudyard, *Barrack-Room Ballads*, Methuen, London, 1896

McNab, Andy, *Bravo Two Zero*, Corgi, London, 1993

O'Brian, Patrick, *Master and Commander*, HarperCollins, London, 1970

Scarborough, Elizabeth Ann, *The Healer's War: A Fantasy Novel of Vietnam*, Bantam-Spectra, New York, 1988

Swofford, A., *Jarhead*, Scribner, Sydney, 2003

Religion

Baigent, M. & Leigh, R., *The Dead Sea Scrolls Deception*, Cape, London, 1991

Haag, Michael, *The Quest for Mary Magdalene*, Profile Books, London, 2017

Ravenscroft, Trevor, *The Spear of Destiny*, Spearman, London, 1973

Shanks, Hershel, *The Mystery and Meaning of the Dead Sea Scrolls*, Random House, New York, 1998

Wilson, Ian, *The Turin Shroud: The Illustrated Evidence*, Penguin, London, 1978

Wilson, Ian, *The Blood and the Shroud: New Evidence that the World's Most Sacred Relic Is Real*, Orion, London, 1998

Animals

Greagg, David, *Dougal's Diary*, Clan Destine Press, Melbourne, 2010

Petraitis, Vikki, *The Dog Squad*, Penguin, Melbourne, 2015

Cuisine

Flower, B. & Rosenbaum, E., *The Roman Cookery Book: A Critical Translation of The Art of Cooking by Apicius for Use in the Study and the Kitchen*, Harrap, London, 1958

About the Author

Kerry Greenwood is the creator of the bestselling, beloved contemporary crime series featuring the talented Corinna Chapman, baker and sleuth extraordinaire. There are currently six previous novels in this series, with *The Spotted Dog* as Corinna's most recent adventure.

Kerry's much-loved 1920s crime series, featuring the marvellous Miss Phryne Fisher in twenty novels, has been developed for television and screened on ABC TV in Australia. The series also airs in the UK and U.S. The books are sold worldwide.

Kerry Greenwood is also the acclaimed author of several books for young adults, the Delphic Women series and is the editor of two collections. She has been longlisted, shortlisted, and is a winner of the Davitt and Ned Kelly Awards. Kerry is also the recipient of the Ned Kelly Lifetime Achievement Award (2003) and the Sisters in Crime Lifetime Achievement Award (2013).